The Executioner took stock of the situation

He was under no grand illusions about their effort to strike back at terrorism, in this or any other mission. The new war had shifted tactics, going preemptive in world headlines, but it was still the same never-ending battle for the Executioner.

No matter how many they took out, it was a monumental task to expect even the most skilled and determined force to rid the planet of what the Administration tagged as evildoers. There would always be more terrorists when the sun rose the following day.

It never stopped for Bolan.

Don Pendleton's **Mack**
Bolan®

Predator Paradise

A GOLD EAGLE BOOK FROM
W☉RLDWIDE®

TORONTO • NEW YORK • LONDON
AMSTERDAM • PARIS • SYDNEY • HAMBURG
STOCKHOLM • ATHENS • TOKYO • MILAN
MADRID • WARSAW • BUDAPEST • AUCKLAND

First edition September 2004

ISBN 0-373-61498-5

Special thanks and acknowledgment to
Dan Schmidt for his contribution to this work.

PREDATOR PARADISE

Printed in U.S.A.

PROLOGUE

Habir Dugula was no stranger to death. He knew there were many ways to die in his country, most of them brutal. Old age rarely claimed life in Somalia. The land itself could kill a man without water in a matter of hours.

The parched and unforgiving earth produced next to nothing to feed ten million hungry mouths. The country's famine, though, was no secret to Western relief workers, he knew, nor to the world at large for that matter, thanks to naive intrusion by CARE, UNICEF, the Red Cross and the United Nations, which seemed to take a morbid pride in denouncing his nation as a seething hotbed of outlaws, thieves and genocidal maniacs.

Starvation, so it was said, had laid waste to nearly a half-million Somalis in the past five years, another two million on the brink, if he was inclined to believe UN or Red Cross statistics. Those numbers, in his mind, were greatly exaggerated—propaganda—if only to give the West excuses to make incursions into his nation, strip him of power and return Somalia to the control of white colonial imperialists. It was true, however, that he was branded the Exterminator by the United Nations, the devils of the American media. To some extent he was responsible for the plight of the starving, at least in the area he controlled south of the city. He had his reasons, plus the blessing of God, to maintain a certain population control, and that was enough. First, they would want food, then, bellies full, education would be the next demand, minds alive and seething soon enough with what they perceived a monstrous injustice perpetrated on them by him. With the power of knowledge there was little doubt an uprising was sure to find its way to his front door.

Not if he could help it.

There would always be too many hungry mouths to feed, he knew, always the poor and the needy who would fall by the wayside, and he didn't intend to let the great unwashed, the weak and the vanquished weigh him down, hold him back from climbing the next rung up the ladder of power and glory. As long as he didn't have to look at the dying masses on his doorstep, there was no point burdening himself with guilt. Sentiment was weakness.

Then there was civil war, consuming another half-million or so lives in the past decade, what with roughly five hundred clans divided into twenty-six main factions, all of them heavily armed, shooting up one another in a running bloodbath that saw no end in sight. There was widespread disease, savaging mostly the children, but again, if he didn't have to see it…

Why bother, he decided, to attempt to search for reason when madness and the law of the gun ruled his country? How could a man show mercy to even the poor and the needy when his own survival was always in question? As leader of his clan, there was a bottom line, deemed by him every bit as important as seeing the next sunrise. If death, war, famine and pestilence appeared destined to push millions of Somalis to the edge of the abyss, the least he could do for himself— and the continued survival of his clan—was to profit from the madness somehow. Even in the hell that was his country, cash was still king.

So was the power of the gun.

Dugula had a busy day ahead. He rose from behind his desk, checking the wall map and factoring in the grueling stretch of miles needed to take him to the afflicted village and its refugee camp, due southwest of Mogadishu. Three events on the day's agenda, a long, hot twelve hours or more before him, and it was time to embrace death once again. The grim problem could prove the first order of the day's business, but, then again, he concluded, it was best to deal with the most troubling and by far the most hazardous of his three chores.

Listening to the soft hum of the air conditioner,

pumping out icy waves through the office of his command-and-control center, he knew that once he stepped outside, the sweat would start to flow free and unchecked. Discomfort he could live with, but uncertainty he wouldn't entertain, since not having answers to certain questions, not knowing who or where his enemies were, could kill. Indeed, the first outbreak of sweat, he thought, would be brought on by more than just the brutal hammering of sunlight.

He watched as Nahbat, his AK-47 leading the way, swept through the door.

"They are on Aboyge Street. Perhaps three minutes remain before they arrive."

Dugula grunted, a slew of questions about the visitors tumbling through his mind. He picked up his AK-47, chambered a round, aware of the numbers coming their way. "Assemble everyone in the courtyard. Same drill as before. Do it quickly, and may God pity the first man who is not ready to fight to the death, if necessary, because I will not show mercy to cowards."

"Understood."

White men in Somalia, Dugula thought. They were a rare sight. It was beyond strange—malevolent perhaps—how these whites had ingratiated themselves to a rival clan, even if they had thrown around large sums of both shillings and U.S. dollars to buy protection, gather information, carve inroads into their clans. But for what purpose? Who were they? CIA? Mercenaries?

The first time he had met them they had dropped off an envelope bulging with U.S. dollars, saying little, only that they would require his help, that he would be well compensated for, again, some unspecified act. Dugula had some idea what they wanted, catching the whispers from his various informants around the city, but he needed to hear them state it out loud.

Slipping on his dark sunglasses, he marched outside, grimacing at the first blast of heat. He was halfway across the courtyard, counting his own men, spread along both walls, a gauntlet of assault rifles and RPGs, poised to catch the visitors in a crossfire, when the first wave of the technicals rolled through the gate. The technicals were a common sight all over Mogadishu, he knew, the Toyota pickups or anything else on wheels, with roofs cleaved off to allow free and easy fields of fire for the .50-caliber machine guns or the smattering of TOW rockets. Truck beds, he noted, were crammed with gunmen, most of the them *mooryan,* teenage thugs. The glaze in their eyes from the amphetamine-like high of *qat* warned him they were edged out. Not good, no telling what they would do as he saw their fingers tight around the triggers of assault rifles, ready to shoot, he had to assume, for little or no reason.

He stood his ground, dust spooling in his face, the technicals fanning out. Twelve, no, thirteen technicals lurching to a halt then, nervous-sounding laughter, chatter among the *mooryan,* a few mouths still grinding away at *qat*. As before, the black minivan was last, carrying its mystery whites, two motorbikes with gunmen flanking the vehicle. Dugula waited, pulse drumming in his skull. The minivan stopped in the dust cloud, door sliding open.

Three men in brown fatigues stepped out, slow, sure of themselves. AKs were draped across their shoulders, spare banana clips wedged in their waistbands. Commando daggers were sheathed at their hips. As they cut the gap, Dugula found the black hoods concealing their identities unsettling for a moment. He wasn't sure what to make of this display, wondering if they were issuing some silent statement meant to unnerve him, or if their desire to keep their faces hidden was genuine, bore some special significance. If he chose, he could have them followed again, but the word from his trackers was that these men were bounced all over Mogadishu in the black van, changing vehicles, in and out of safehouses, able, or so he was told, to vanish into the air. It made him wonder how accurate—or deceitful—their report, whom he could trust, where did the truth lie. Money always had a way of shifting allegiance.

Blue Eyes, as he thought of the hood in the middle, held his stare. Dugula was certain he was grinning to himself. Arrogant bastard, he thought, stifling the urge to whip the assault rifle off his shoulder and blaze away. Dugula felt himself being measured, Blue Eyes laughing back at him, a private joke.

"We have to stop meeting like this, Habbie. Your little slice of hell on Earth, not high up on my list of hot spots to start with, is starting to make even me a little jumpy, and I've been down some dark alleys in my day."

"Perhaps you would prefer we do this on some sandy beach, sipping iced tea?"

"Right. After a nice dip in the Indian Ocean. No, thanks, but I'd rather swim with sharks of the human variety than what's out in those waters. And do me and yourself a favor when we leave here. Leave your own *mooryan* at home. If I start seeing a bunch of your shooters on my bumper, I'm going to begin thinking ours can never be a working and profitable match made in Hell."

"Perhaps if I knew exactly what you wanted? If I were to understand what is this working relationship to which you refer?"

"It's this."

The white with the scar on his hand spoke up, producing a thick envelope from behind his back, tucking it in his waistband. "Fifty thousand dollars, American. An advance, if you agree."

"But you need to understand the rules first, Habbie," Blue Eyes said before Dugula could ask the obvious. "Then we can play ball. You love money, you want power, you want to be top dog on the block. You're on every shit list from UNICEF to the White House. Thing is, what we are, we're your three wise men, come here bearing gifts."

"How magnanimous. To what do I owe this great honor?"

The third black hood got into the act next. Like the first time they met, the three whites ricocheted the verbal shooting match between them, leaving Dugula wondering if this act was scripted, and who, exactly, was in charge between them. Number three had blackness behind the slit where his left eye was, Dugula fairly assuming there was a patch covering some war memento.

"Here it is," One Eye began. "In the coming days there are going to be several very significant big events, within and beyond your borders. We prefer to not stand here in this heat and dust and with sky spies framing our every move, answering a bunch of questions that only time and decisive action will answer in the first place. First, we're taking the human cargo you have smuggled in-country. They're part of the plan. They go with us."

There it was, he thought, gut clenching, spine tightening. Before the thought they were some sort of international bounty hunters or CIA black ops, come to either kill or capture the holy freedom fighters he had been paid to grant safe haven to, Blue Eyes, as if he could read minds, cooled some of his fears.

"Relax. We're not here to kill or arrest those who are under the care of your golden umbrella."

"Truth be known," Scar Hand said, "their leaders are aware of our presence here. Call it a blessing from Allah, a strange union between infidels and Islam, but it's arranged. And your guests have already agreed to go the distance."

Dugula bared his teeth, a half smile, half grimace, and waved a hand. "This is all very mysterious, and suspicious. You talk, ten ways out of your mouths, but you say little."

"No time to stand around and gnaw on nerves or question what's damn near an act of God being dumped in your lap. You accept—on faith—and you'll be well rewarded," One Eye said.

"There is a number inside the envelope," Blue Eyes said. "Call it. A cutout to a very important individual in a country better left unnamed at this time, but an individual you know well through your own Web site. He'll back our story, and he's backing us."

"You are telling me, what, exactly?"

"Rule number one," Blue Eyes said. "You're on a need-to-know basis, that is, until the time comes when your role will become larger than the scourge of Muhammad's head-lopping converters. Then it will be defined, a blinding light that will grant you, shall we say, instant transformation. Super warlord. That could be you."

They paused, Dugula sensing he was supposed to be impressed or implore them to continue. "I'm listening."

"You recruit some of these fighters for your clan,"

One Eye said, "from other countries, some of them used by you to wipe out rivals, help keep the iron grip on your turf. They train here, they plan their operations when they're not beefing up your troops. Surprised? Habbie, we know everything that goes on in this neck of the woods. Hey, as far as some folks you know are concerned, we're the next-greatest thing to Allah. Think of us as damn near supernatural."

"The Alpha and the Omega," Scar Hand declared. "That's us."

"And we're here to tell you what is in motion cannot be aborted," Blue Eyes said.

"We don't need to spell out the organizations of the fighters you have in-country," Scar Hand said. "All you really need to know is they're with us. More truth— these fighters have already been contacted by their leaders, weeks back, and they've been ordered to accept our terms without conditions."

"They know some of the score," One Eye said. "Not much, but the truth will be revealed in due course. But their leaders know something of the endgame. All parties—down to you—have agreed."

"You want endgame speculation? What will go down could prove one of the biggest coups," Scar Hand said. "One of the most fearsome blows Islam has ever struck against the infidels."

"With or without you," Blue Eyes said, tone hardening, "it's a done deal."

"And Umir Hahgan? You come to Somalia, three

wise white men," Dugula said, putting an edge to his voice, "and you go straight to my main rival. How much did you pay him? And if I say no to this strange offer, ask no questions, go along, a blind man in the dark among the wolves and hyenas, what then? Do you set Hahgan's men against me?"

"It's like this," Blue Eyes said. "We hedged our bets, granted. Hahgan's giving up some fighters, and yeah, he's been paid, enough to keep the troops in *qat* and whores for a while. Time to put aside all this petty squabbling over some real estate. Fact is, you're stronger than Umir, more men, more guns, more contacts from Cairo to Karachi, but we'll pencil in the number-two man on the roster if we have to. Hey, you need to start thinking more about your future, leave the hand-wringing to the losing side. Now's the time."

"Think big, as in immortality big," Scar Hand added. "Your name could end up being glorified by the entire Muslim world, feared by your enemies, for decades to come. You're a rising star, could be bigger than Osama, if you want. Let me ask you, you don't want to just be a second-string warlord, creaking around this shithole in your golden years, or do you?"

"I would think," One Eye said, "your ambitions would be a little bit larger than 'exterminating' all those hungry mouths you and the twenty-something other clans won't feed."

"While you rip off planeloads of UN aid and resell

it across the borders," Scar Hand said. "Chump change, compared to what we're offering you."

"Now you insult me in front of my men."

"No offense intended. Just the hard facts," Blue Eyes shot back.

"We won't waste your time—don't waste ours. We're thinking you've got a big day ahead of you," One Eye said. "Probably heading out to exterminate some camp infested with disease."

"Or take down another UN plane," Scar Hand said.

How did they know so much? Dugula wondered. Or were they guessing? Perhaps his secured phones and fax weren't so secure. Or had Hahgan infiltrated his clan with spies?

"In or out?" Blue Eyes asked. "No is no, and we're fine with that."

"You can go back to business as usual," Scar Hand said. "Stay small."

"Decision time," One Eye added. "Dump or jump off the crapper."

Dugula took a few moments, peering into those slitted gazes, eyes, he decided, without emotion, no soul. It was true that he wanted far more for himself than remaining where he was, doing what he'd done. The suggestion on their part was that certain free-dom-fighting organizations—of which at least forty members were under his protective umbrella—had al-ready agreed to some undefined role for some al-legedly grand but mysterious big events. If he declined? Then what? Risk some long, protracted war with rivals who supposedly were ready to leap on board for this so-called big event? Let rivals grab the glory these whites were offering? What glory? Or was this some elaborate ruse, a trap being laid by rivals? He didn't think so; none of the competition was that clever or devious. His rivals were, for the most part, thugs with hair-trigger tempers, rarely, if ever, thinking through the consequences to their impulsive violence. If he was right, then being presented with some bigger picture...

Dugula felt curiosity and greed wrestle him to the brink of acceptance. "How much money?"

"Is that a yes?" Blue Eyes wanted to know.

"The money?"

"Two million, deposited into a numbered account in one of several European banks of your choosing," One Eye answered.

"Half on acceptance," Scar Hand said, "the other half when the curtain drops on the last act."

"I have a large clan," Dugula said. "Many men to feed, house, equip, arm. They say there are over two million assault rifles in Mogadishu, but, as you said, my ambitions are bigger than just having my men ride around in technicals with outdated Russian machine guns. You demand much, tell me next to nothing. I hear promises, words, big plans. I would like to hear how badly you are willing to enlist my services. Two million," he told them, shaking his head softly, lips pursed.

He watched them, no change of expression, their eyes cold, then Blue Eyes said, "Four. That's as high as we can go."

Dugula already had an answer to give them, but the fact that they had upped the ante with little hesitation told him they had come to the bargaining table prepared to lowball his services. So be it, he decided. Depending on what the future held, how great the risk, whatever his undeclared role in this big event, he could always ask for—no, demand—more money. If he was going to be allied with other Muslims for some glorious battle against the infidels, how could a mere three Westerners possibly dare to think they could deceive him into a course of action that would destroy him and the clan?

"When will you need these services of myself and my men?".

"Soon," Blue Eyes said. "Carry on with your day. You'll know when it's begun."

Dugula smiled back at the laughing eyes, unwilling to show fear or hesitation now that his decision was final. "Then…the envelope, please."

HUSSEIN NAHBAT was pained and baffled. Beyond that there was a fair amount of anxiety about the future, namely his own.

From the shotgun seat of his technical, he saw the village and surrounding camp of nomads rise up in the distance on the barren plain. The panorama of squalid dwellings, meandering camels, goats and black stick figures in rags struck him as little more than some hellish mirage, floating up on the slick heat shimmer. Judging the numbers of shabby stone hovels, the huts erected by sticks wrapped in plastic sheeting, he guessed four to five hundred Somalis. Whatever Ethiopian refugees had crossed the border, survived this far, he figured perhaps another hundred or so bodies would be tossed to the fires. If what he'd heard about their trek and their affliction was true, they were walking contagions, cursing the Somalis here with the same inevitable fate. Drought, famine, another round of civil war between rebel forces and the outbreak of some hemorrhagic fever had been driving Ethiopians across the borders into Sudan, Kenya, Eritrea.

It was their task, Nahbat knew, to cleanse the area, contain the plague these people had brought to Somalia. This land was not their home, and their leader, calling them leprous invaders, had issued the decree they were to put the torch to all homes and flesh, diseased or otherwise, Ethiopian or Somali.

As Omari, his cousin, bore their technical down on the northern outskirts of the first line of beehive-shaped hovels, he found the others were already hard at it, rounding up men, women, children. The shooting had started, rattling bursts of autofire coming from all points around the village, limp bodies already being dragged from the tents of various sizes on the western perimeter. Dugula's men, he noted, didn't handle the bodies. Instead, they forced Ethiopians at gunpoint to drag their own dead—or dying—to the pit. He saw other Ethiopians, weakened by disease and malnutrition, standing utterly still outside their tents, some of the women hitting their knees, pleading for mercy.

There was none.

And the pain bit deeper into his belly. This was madness, this was…what, he wondered—wrong? Evil?

Nahbat was unaware Omari had ground them to a halt, as he witnessed a small baby ripped from the arms of its wailing mother, a pistol leaping in the hands of her executioner, a bullet through the brain abruptly silencing her pleas. Though he had to follow orders under threat of execution, and related as he was to Habir Dugula—a distant cousin of one of the leader's countless sons and daughters by various wives and mistresses—what he felt whenever they cleansed a village went beyond horror and pain.

He felt his heart ache, a swollen lump in his throat threatening to shut off air the more he watched. He wanted to weep.

Nahbat fought back the tears. He suddenly longed to be a twelve-year-old boy again, a simple goatherd, ignorant to the horrors of his country. That seemed like only yesterday, when, in fact, it was just a little over a year ago his cousin had shoved an assault rifle in his hands, and life had changed forever. Strange, he thought, in this one year of being an armed combatant in the war for Mogadishu and the campaign of genocide against those deemed unfit to live, he felt like a tired, sick old man. He was too young, he thought, to feel such pain. Worse, he was helpless to do anything but carry out his part in the atrocity, thinking himself a coward for being unable to stand up and shout how wrong this was.

He tried to focus his distress on another baffling matter, failing to will away the nausea as the first wave of the stench of diseased flesh, the sickly sweet taint of bodies being doused by gasoline and torched, ballooned his senses. What was this business with the white men and the rival clan? Why were they involving themselves in some mysterious affair with foreigners that not even their great leader had the first clue was all about? They had lingered at the compound after the departure of the black hoods and Hahgan's *mooryan*, while he assumed Habir Dugula made some attempt to verify the existence of the cutout, their supposed marching orders. Then there was a briefing by their great leader, all orders, no questions allowed. Simply put, he recalled, Dugula told them they would do whatever the white men's bidding, that they would be paid in time, far more, or so promised, than their weekly handful of shillings. The future was more than just in doubt, he feared; the time ahead was in peril. He wondered if he would live to see his fourteenth birthday.

He was out the door somehow, Omari barking in his ear to get moving. The AK-47 began to slip from his fingers, bile shooting up into his throat. He heard the wailing, pleas for mercy, the braying of animals in terror. The din alone might have been enough to bring him to his knees, retch and cry, but the stink was overpowering by itself, threatening to knock him off his feet. The world began to spin, legs turning to rubber when a rough hand clawed into his shoulder, spun him.

"Take this!"

It was Omari, eyes boring into him over the bandanna wrapped around his nose and mouth.

The slap to his face rang in his ears like a pistol shot.

"What is wrong with you!"

"I…I feel sick, my cousin."

"Get over it! We have work to do!"

Omari wound the bandanna around his face, knotting it tight against the back of his skull with an angry twist. He had another disturbing thought right then, as the veil seemed to do little to stem the tide of miasma assaulting him, mind, senses and soul. What if he fainted, flat on his back, the vomit trapped by the bandanna, strangling him?

The screaming, shooting and the awareness Omari was watching him closely, perhaps questioning his resolve, put some iron in his legs. He was turning toward the Russian transport truck, where they were hauling out more ten-gallon cans of gasoline, when Nahbat spotted their great leader.

Resentment flared through him, another dagger of pain and confusion to the heart. Dugula was standing in the distance on a rise. Surrounded by twenty or more of his men, he watched through field glasses, making certain they did as they were ordered. When he appeared satisfied the job would get done, he hopped into his jeep, the others falling into an assortment of technicals, Hummers. That the great man wouldn't dirty his hands with this hideous chore inflamed him with great anger, leaving him to wonder if Somalia would ever know justice, much less peace.

He lingered by the technical, watching as the convoy kicked up clouds of dust, all of them gone to greet the UN plane flying in from Kenya.

Another wall of grief dropped over Nahbat. He knew what they would do when that plane landed. It sickened him. There was an answer, he believed—no, there was an answer he knew and felt in his heart—a way around this insanity, one far greater, a solution most certainly noble and humane and merciful, but the afflicted, the doomed he heard wailing around him would never see it.

All that medicine and food, he thought, on board the UN plane. Doctors, with skill and knowledge, who could, if not save the afflicted, perhaps ease their pain and suffering until a cure was delivered.

It would never happen.

He had seen it before, too many times.

"May God have mercy."

"What was that?"

Wheeling, startled, he found Omari glaring at him. He watched, holding back the tears, fighting down the bile, his cousin marching toward him, holding out a can.

Nahbat shook his head, muttered, "Nothing."

And took the can.

CHAPTER ONE

If it was true a man learned more from failure than success, Ben Collins knew he was in no position to test that theory. In his line of work, there were no second chances. Failure wasn't an option; failure spelled death. In black ops, he made it a point to see losing was for the other guy.

The stack of boxes stamped CARE, deep in the aft of the C-130, would be the last thing the warlord's frontline marauders saw when they hit the ramp. The ruse didn't stop with this first strike, but what others didn't know, he thought, wouldn't kill them. At least not yet.

It was just about time to get down to dirty business, murky waters, he knew, that had been chummed since the first bunch of al-Qaeda and Taliban criminals had been dumped off at Gitmo. There was blood in that water again, he thought, flesh to consume, but it all

went way beyond waxing a bunch of thugs and terrorists in some of the most dangerous, godforsaken real
estate this side of Hell. Sure, there were bad guys to
bag, chain, thrust under military gavel. There was a trial
to consider, arranged to go down in secrecy....

Whoa, he told himself. This was only the first giant
leap; the goal line was way off on the distant horizon.
No point in getting ahead. There were still details to
nail down and he could be sure, given the nature of
black ops, not to mention the usual chaos and confusion of battle, more than a few problems would crop
up along the way.

The ex–Delta Force major raked a stare over the six
black ops under his command of Cobra Force Twelve.
Seven more commandos on the ground were moving
in right then, on schedule to help light the fuse. According to radar monitoring the two Hummers' transpond-
ers, the sat imagery, piped into his consoles amidships
from an NRO bird parked over and watching the area
in question—AIQ—they were three miles out, closing
hard, with Dugula and twenty-one henchmen rolling
across the plain, the latest round of the Exterminator's
methods of population control framed, live and in color,
on another monitor. Behind his ground force, two Black
Hawks and one Apache were picking up the rear, covering all bases.

All set.

No blue UN helmets, doctors, or relief workers were
on board. This was no mission of mercy, or another

group of unarmed do-gooders from Red Cross or UNICEF, he thought, getting ripped off by Dugula.

He studied their faces, but there was no need to sound off with last-minute Patton speeches to shore up resolve. They knew the drill, briefed thoroughly for days, the details gone over one last time on the Company airbase just inside the Kenyan border, before he put the radio call on the special UN frequency to Dugula that they were moving, coordinate the drop-off. All of them were battle-hardened CIA men—specifically Special Operations Division—or ex-military, he knew, with more than a few Afghanistan forays notched on some of their belts.

It was reassuring to know he was wading into the fire with pros. To an operative they had on their war faces, togged in brown camos, M-16/M-203 combos the lead weapon. Webbing, combat vests, all of it stuffed and hung with spare grenades and clips, then on down to Beretta 92-F side arms on the hip, commando daggers sheathed on the lower leg. The blades were last resort, Collins stating earlier this was blast and burn, the faces of Dugula and a few of his top lieutenants committed to memory.

Once they blasted off the ramp it was going to be a turkey shoot for the most part, Somali thugs hemmed in, turning tail, unless he missed his guess, when the flying hammer dropped on them from above. He glanced at their own two armored Hummers, one mounted M-60 machine gun, belted and ready to rip.

The other vehicle, showing off its TOW antitank launch pad, would be out of the gate first. Altogether, plenty of firepower, muscle, experience and determination to win the day against a bunch of one-time camel herders who now had control of Mogadishu, and into the deep south of the country, because none of the other competing clans had the guns or the guts to stand up to them.

He took a moment next to ponder the sudden curve-ball thrown him by superiors. Cobra Force Twelve was his diamond, once in the rough, but with three successful missions under the belt, with his track record in Delta and later on working with the Company, he had made friends in high and powerful places. Hell, he was a damn hero, in fact, enough medals and ribbons to fill a steamer trunk, but this one wasn't for God and country. What was now in motion—at least the campaign given the thumbs-up by the White House—was pretty much his show.

But there was a wild card—the man's handle—out there with the ground team.

It wasn't entirely true he was solely in charge, Collins knew. There was this odd man out preying on his thoughts, some hotshot hardballer, according to his dossier, dropped in his lap at the eleventh hour. The order to put the thirteenth man on the team had come straight from the President, Wild Card inserted as coleader of Cobra Force. Beyond some irritation and anxiety, a dig to professional pride he was forced to share all tactical and command decisions, the tall dark man tagged Wild Card made him a little nervous, what with the question as to exactly why the White House shoved him onto the mission in the first place.

He wanted to believe the colonel—with a record full of deletions that left little doubt he was likewise black ops—was simply there as an extra gun, with supposedly all the combat experience in the world to aid, assist and kick much additional ass. Or was it something else? Was Wild Card a watchdog? Had the rumor mill churned at the Pentagon, spilling some seeds of doubt into the Oval Office? Had someone in the loop gotten cold feet, gone running to the higher-ups if just to save his own skin? Were his own people sharpening blades right then, poised to spring a trap?

No matter. If Wild Card had some personal agenda, if he proved a threat to the bigger picture, well, Collins knew there was an answer for that problem.

"Dragon One to Cobra Leader."

Collins strode to the intercom on the bulkhead. "Cobra Leader. Go."

"You boys strap in—we're going down. Show time."

"Roger. Stick to the plan, Dragon One, no matter how hot it gets out there."

"Aye-aye. Catch you on the flip side. Good luck. Dragon One, over and out."

Collins grabbed a seat, fastened on the webbing as the bird began to descend. Round one, he thought, coming up, but it was only the beginning. Shortly, if nothing else, one question about Wild Card would be answered. And if the odd man out couldn't pull his weight, wasn't as good as advertised, he would just be one less hassle to eliminate with a bullet in the near future.

The picture, small or large, both fuzzy at the moment, would clear up soon enough.

Spilled blood, he concluded, always had a way of separating the lions from the jackals.

IN A PERFECT WORLD all men and women, especially the poor and needy, would be fed, housed, educated. Beyond the basics even, the sick, the dying, the maimed, all manner of physical affliction would be cured, and they would rise to live, full, healthy, happy lives. In this world there would be opportunity for all, he thought, an even playing field where man could use whatever natural abilities and intelligence, not to attain wealth, privilege, stature or dominion over others, but to help his fellow man make the earth a bright, kind, gentle place. There would be mercy, compassion, tolerance. There would be peace, harmony, trust and understanding. There would be no crime, no killing, no greed, no lust for a bigger slice of everything at the expense of his fellows, no life wasted in self-destruction. There would be no famine, disease or war.

There would be no Habir Dugula.

Of course, wherever this place existed, it was only just a dream, Mack Bolan knew, and all too painfully well. For the man also known as the Executioner this

Nirvana or Heaven, this imagined place on Earth, where all men were free, created equal to follow the tenets of life, liberty and the pursuit of happiness was the stuff of fantasy and angst, best left to the poets and the songwriters.

He was a soldier, first and last, brutally aware after walking countless miles in the arena of the savage, that as long as animal man existed, preying on the weak and the innocent, going for number one, peace was just a word.

The latest in a long line of vicious warlords in Somalia was all the proof he needed that evil was alive and well on Earth. But Habir Dugula was only one reason Bolan had undertaken this mission.

They were almost there, in place to give Dugula's mass murderers and armed profiteers a dose of their own poison. Hearing the familiar thunder, Bolan spotted the C-130, coming in for a landing on the plain, due south, the giant bird vanishing from sight a moment later above the lip of the wadi. Fisting his M-16/M-203 combo, adrenaline burning, Bolan shot a look at his driver, a twist to Cobra Leader's original attack plan flaring to mind. On the surface, the strike could in all probability work, he reasoned. For openers, they were all seasoned pros, whereas Dugula and goons were accustomed, for the most part, to slaughtering their unarmed countrymen. Sure, there was the usual street fighting in Mogadishu with rival clans, but as a rule of thumb, Dugula's thugs outnumbered the competition, and any sustained shooting match was spurred more by hair-trigger impulse than skill and cold tactics on an even battlefield. Just the same, he knew a wild bullet, even one fired in haste or panic, could score flesh.

Timing was the key ingredient to get it started, the soldier knew, ground forces unleashing the lightning and thunder in sync. It was a brazen play, no two ways about it, Collins and company shooting their way off the ramp, Hummers rampaging into the stunned forces of Dugula, mowing them down off the starting line. The Black Hawks and the Apache, a mile or more to their rear, flying nap of the earth and jamming any atypical Somali substandard radar in the area, were a definite added bonus. If Dugula stuck to form, according to UN and CIA reports, he would hang back while his thugs boarded the C-130, then loaded up the APCs and transports parked at the command post of the warlord's airfield. They would stock their warehouses with food and medicine slated for the sick and starving, sell it to other lesser-ranking warlords or whoever else could pay the going rate. Bolan expected once Dugula found they weren't faced with well-intentioned UN or Red Cross workers, the warlord would bolt.

The soldier gave a moment's thought to the mission, the parameters, endgame, reasons why he had accepted. For starters, it angered Bolan deeply that in this part of the world, where those who needed food and medicine the most, cried out for a helping hand just to get through the day, were not only denied the basics, but viewed as a blight to be removed from the body whole. In other words, those unfortunate enough not to be able to defend or fend for themselves, whatever the circumstance, weren't worth protecting or sustaining, seen as deadweight, a possible contagion to the power structure, worthy of only subjugation or death.

Dugula had been on the soldier's removal list for some time, the warlord living up to his ghoul's handle given him by the UN for too long now. In a land where lawlessness ruled, where there wasn't even the first fundamental institution, bureaucracy, no media or government whatsoever, it was impossible for even the World Health Organization to state the number of Dugula's victims. Western intelligence could emphatically claim that entire villages had been wiped off the plains in a genocide campaign where Bolan assumed the warlord meant to do nothing but spread fear and terror.

The soldier had been around long enough to know that whatever they did here would make little difference in the long run. One less Dugula, one less army of murderers, though, terrorizing the countryside might tip the scales an inch or so in favor of the oppressed. What was true, in his mind at least, that all it took for evil to triumph was for good men to turn a blind eye, wash their hands of atrocity and man's inhumanity to man as long as it didn't encroach on their own world. If all of it boiled down to the power of the gun winning over evil, the Executioner was a proved old hand at the game.

A little over three days ago, Bolan recalled, he had

been standing down at Stony Man Farm, the ultracovert intelligence agency in the Shenandoah Valley of Virginia, and overseen by his longtime friend, Hal Brognola. Brognola, a high-ranking official of the Justice Department who was—in addition to routine Justice duties—a cutout between the President of the United States and the Farm, had presented the soldier with quite the unusual mission. How the channels ran through the various intelligence agencies to launch this mission and who, exactly, had brainstormed this campaign, not even Bolan or Brognola was sure. Assume Pentagon brass, CIA, NSA, but the Man—who greenlighted all Stony Man operations—wanted what he called the best of the best on board a black ops team called Cobra Force Twelve.

It seemed the President—or whoever had put the idea in his head—felt the need for a second holding pen outside Guantanamo Bay. Gitmo, or so Brognola had been told by the Man, Bolan recalled, had gotten a bit overcrowded with bad guys. And secondly, or so the line of reasoning went, there was too much spotlight glaring on Gitmo, thanks to the media, which, in the usual convoluted political thinking, could end up smacking Washington with a black eye. Prisoner mistreatment, abyssmal living conditions, individual rights of terrorists denied, and so on. It hadn't been spelled out one hundred percent, but Bolan's gut told him the next prison camp for international criminals wouldn't pop up on CNN.

Usually the soldier operated alone, or as part of the

two Stony Man commando teams. Working with un-known factors, CIA or bona fide military men with combat experience, had proved perilous to his health in the past. Brognola, however, had laid it out, convinced him to colead Cobra Force Twelve. Never one to unduly swaddle himself in the Stars and Stripes, the big Fed had told him twenty to thirty of some of the most wanted terrorists, depending on how many could be taken alive, could prove intelligence mother lodes in the war on terror. Somalia was first on the roundup list.

Not even Brognola had been told where this military tribunal would be held, and Bolan wasn't quite sure what to make on the lack of concrete details. It smacked of dark secrecy to the soldier, all around, and Brognola had as much as said if it blew up in the faces of those in the field doing all the hunting and capturing then America would take a verbal shellacking by the UN, her supposed allies, not to mention the Muslim world cranking up the heat for jihad.

And even with intelligence operatives all over the map, guiding them from hit to hit, they were on their own. The Executioner understood and accepted his usual role as a deniable expendable if he was caught or killed by the enemy. That was acceptable. What wasn't were a few nagging speculations tossed his way by Brognola before he headed out to Fort Bragg to introduce himself—Colonel Brandon Stone—to the Cobra troops. The file on Collins and Cobra was classified, but the cyber sleuths at the Farm had unearthed a few questions, framed as suspicion, about the man and his team. They were terrorist headhunters, with a trio of successful outings to their credit, only a "but" in caps hung over their heads. The thing was, they had been in the general vicinity when a spate of kidnappings and murders of American citizens in Egypt, Pakistan and Indonesia sullied their record. Coincidence?

Another reason to hop on board.

The soldier was there now, willing to let battle and time tell the truth.

He turned to the driver—Asp—the op's mane of black hair and facial scruff framing the portrait of a mercenary. The pager on Bolan's hip vibrated, the same signal transmitted, he knew, to the other ground troops. The bird had landed.

"Listen up," Bolan told Asp, turning to make sure the lone black commando on the team—Python—heard him loud and clear. "There's been a little change in plans."

DUGULA WAS beyond troubled, and he couldn't simply will away the gnawing in his belly. Something was shooting him to new heights of fear, a feeling so alive it had become a living monster in his face.

As the day ground on, everything appearing to go as planned, the worm in his belly squirmed harder, terror not far behind the unease, threatening, he imagined, to uncoil an adder in his guts, devour him from the inside out.

He had placed the call to the man in Saudi Arabia, more out of nagging paranoia than curiosity. Sure enough, the cutout who had arranged safe transport for freedom fighters he was harboring, so high up the chain of command in the Islamic jihad that disobedience was a death sentence, had confirmed what the whites had told him.

There was, so the middleman said, a series of big events about to unfold, fear not, perform the holy duty, whatever it was. The Saudi had instructed him to comply with whatever the foreigners wanted him to do, no matter how bizarre their requests seemed. Again he was told he would know when it started, but not knowing when or what disturbed him the most, visions of the noose once more tightening around his neck flaming to mind. He was to have faith as strong as steel, ask no questions. He would be an important, even a glorious instrument exercising the will of God in the coming days. He was being called, perhaps by the Prophet himself, a holy decree he was to carry out, once again, on faith. And he would be paid—the bottom line in his ultimate decision—more than he could ever spend in two lifetimes. Woe be to anyone who attempted to betray any of them, chisel out of the bargain, or so the Saudi told him.

Still, he had many questions, all of them bringing on doubt and worry that would see him thrash through one or many sleepless nights before this big event. Beyond that, he was angered that forces beyond his control had assumed he would obey their mysterious dictates, even order him to relegate his power to the enemy. Being on an overseas line, though, the conversation was brief, code words and phrases that should leave any enemy eavesdroppers guessing.

Dugula watched as the giant UN cargo plane descended from the direction of Kenya, touched down, hurled up spools of dust, began to taxi. For a moment, attempting to calm himself, he marveled at the naiveté of these relief workers. Surely by now they knew what became of their cargo. Were they stupid? Or did they actually believe one more attempt to funnel food and medicine into this region would buy the masses a few more days, even weeks before they succumbed to the inevitable fate of the weak? That he would actually distribute the relief to the surrounding villages?

Fools.

They had long since given up attempting airdrops, or trekking to the villages themselves, on foot or by truck, since a few relief workers had mysteriously vanished.

It occurred to him, the thought dredging up more paranoia, that perhaps this time they had brought along a few guns to test his will. If that happened, it would prove no contest at all. If they made demands at gunpoint, they were all dead, shot on sight, and he would simply load the trucks with the cargo, burn the bodies, destroy the plane, take his chances. This was Somalia, after all, and only a massive invading army would dare attempt to…

He was out of his jeep, standing his ground, ordering his clansmen to move up on the plane when the C-130 swung around, ramp lowering, the bay out of view. Strange, he thought, since the previous attempts were done in full view of the ramp coming down. It could have been paranoia, anxiety getting the better of him, but something felt terribly wrong all of a sudden. Dust in his face, he found himself easing back toward his jeep. It was a faint and distant rattle, buzzing in his head, but a chatter that blew the lid on his fear.

Dugula knew the sound of autofire when he heard it.

CHAPTER TWO

Collins wished he could see Dugula's face, the horrifying reality that this wasn't the usual candy raid doing far more than just ruining the warlord's day. He could well imagine Dugula right then, nuts going numb, knifing chest pains, pasta legs, a scream of outrage no one but himself could hear, much less cared to, the whole shrieking nine yards of terror and confusion over why and who had come to yank his ticket. It was a fleeting impulse, wanting to be there, grinning in the guy's face of fear, but any gloating, Collins knew, was on hold.

Collins had a full shooting gallery before him to contend with. Getting hands on the Kewpie doll was the ultimate prize, but since the moment at hand was no guaranteed straight flush, Dugula had to keep.

The Cobra leader flamed away with his M-16, Mamba on the starboard side, likewise clamping down with autofire on the stunned opposition. So far they were on the money, Collins thought, shock appearing on the verge of winning the opening round, but the going would get a lot tougher once they were off the ramp. Figure ten had ventured up the ramp, AKs not even up and out, their faces laughing, maybe a private joke bandied about between them in their native tongue, but the Somali thugs lost all arrogant composure when the first few rounds began chopping into their ranks. White caftans were shredded to red ruins before they were even aware they were chewed and screwed, Collins and Mamba sweeping long bursts, port to starboard and back. Somalis tumbled, screamed, sailed down the ramp, a whirling dervish or two losing a sandal in midflight.

"Go!" Collins roared, but he heard engines revving already, pedal to the metal, the Hummers streaking away from their starting line, amidships.

The Hummer known as Thunder Three was a blur in Collins's eye. Holding back on the trigger of his assault rifle, he gutted another Somali with a short burst. Diamondback, he saw, manning the M-60, cut loose with the heavy-metal thunder. Two heartbeats' worth of pounding of 7.62 mm lead erased the terror on the face of a goon peeking over ramp, head erupting, the shattered crimson eggshell gone with the vanishing corpse. Thunder Four was right on their bumper, the point Hummer, Collins saw, about to bulldoze through a bloody scarecrow rising on the lip of the ramp, his arms shooting up as if they were supposed to slam on the brakes or veer around him. There was a thud on impact, Collins catching the sound of bones cracking like matchsticks, the scream flying away with the ramp kill.

One, two, and both Hummers were airborne, tires slamming to earth a moment later at the end of the ramp, his drivers straightening next, cutting the wheels hard, whipping around and gone to charge into what Collins figured was fifty percent of what was left of Dugula's shooters. According to intel, there were twenty-plus more Somali gunmen, either moving from the command hut or sitting tight, depending on Dugula's mood, but those numbers would be handled, he hoped, by his Apache and the colonel.

Collins was picking up the pace, Mamba on the march, both of them feeding fresh clips to their M-16s when the Cobra leader sighted on a downed Somali. He was dragging himself through the pooling blood on his elbows, toward the edge of the ramp, head cocked. The spurting hole in the middle of his back, the way he slithered ahead, legs limp weight, told Collins he'd taken one through the spine. Paralysis below the waist would prove the least of his woes; Collins unable to understand Somali but believed he caught the gist of it. Sounded like the guy wanted mercy, he thought, or was trying to tell him this was all some hideous mistake. Whoever he was, Collins knew he wasn't one of the catches of the day.

"Welcome to the big leagues, son," Collins told him, then drilled a 3-round burst into his face.

Halfway down the ramp, Collins leaped, landing on hard-packed earth, M-16 searching out fresh blood off to the port side of the Hercules. The trick now, he knew, would be taking Dugula and a few top lieutenants alive. He already had that figured out beforehand, though, his hand ready to unleather the tranquilizer gun on his right hip just as soon as he made eyeball confirmation. The dicey part would be getting close enough to drop Dugula and trophies in the sleeping bag. As for his other commandos, the running scheme was to encircle them before they could bolt. Thunders One and Two would race in from the north, a sweeping left hook to their flank. It was a tactical page, he thought with a moment's pride, ripped straight out of Genghis Khan's war book. If one of his troops got close enough to Dugula first, they were ordered to lob a canister his way, where a cloud of barbituate-laced gas would disperse.

Collins saw three, then four technicals already in flight, dust billowing around the vehicles as they reversed away from the C-130, Thunders Three and Four charging to outflank them. Collins took a moment to watch the action.

Autofire chattered around the technicals, two vehicles sitting, shooters steeled to go to the mat, two more murderous goon squads on wheels rolling to break out, but the noose was tightening, he saw. Screams of pain lanced out of all that swirling dust, but Collins felt grim satisfaction it was nearly a lock. Still, he saw two technicals break out of the ring, racing across the plain. His commandos were alternating bursts between shooting gunmen out of their technicals and blasting out tires.

He was grinning to himself, his Black Hawks soaring overhead to run down the rabbits, the Apache strafing the troops and transports at the command post to the northeast when he found only one of his ground Hummers barreling in from the wadi.

"What the—?"

The M-60 gunner on that rig—Lionteeth—told him the colonel was engaged somewhere with Somali gunmen. Or had he broken off, purposely changed their role on his own command? If so, why?

Scouting the plain, Collins spotted the other Hummer. Thunder One was rolling slow, nearly creeping toward the fleeing Somalis. The Cobra team leader figured out the strategy. A lone figure peeled off from the Hummer, M-16 blazing at the profiteers who were squirming from an overturned transport rig, an APC near them demolished, swathed in leaping flames, treated, he reckoned, to a direct hit from the Apache's Hellfire missile.

Wild Card was doing his thing, Collins thought, and cursed. So he had a prima donna on the team, the guy might as well have told him to kiss his ass, he'd do it his way.

A few choice words, assuming the colonel survived, had to wait as Collins drew a bead on a Somali gunman still standing in the dust, and drilled a burst into his chest.

THE EXECUTIONER sensed Asp and Python weren't happy about being ordered to change the game plan right before the shooting started, but they did as ordered. The shift in strategy, at least on his part, had one goal in mind. Cutting off any retreat on foot, he knew, was a dicier proposition than simply allowing the Black Hawks and Apache to blow the enemy off the plain. Say the warbirds ground up the Somalis with lead and Hellfires from above, and any capture of Dugula was all but lost. If their job was to cuff and stuff the world's most wanted international terror mongers, then anything short of bringing Dugula and top henchmen to justice spelled mission failure.

Bolan left the Apache to its Hellfire-and-chain-gun demolition. The command post, with any radar and tracking goodies, was blown away by the warbird, six or so Somalis scythed by 30 mm doom as they were bolting from the flying rubble. Before that round of destruction, the warbird had plowed a missile into one of the transport trucks, dead ahead to Bolan's twelve, wreckage spewing out of the fireball bowling another canvas-covered transport onto its side.

The soldier cut a wide berth around the hungry flames and oily smoke, his M-16 leading the way, the stink of burning diesel fuel and toasted flesh swelling the air, grinding into his senses as he closed on the cries of panic. His vector, if he nailed the enemy before him in seconds flat, would land him directly in the path of two technicals charging away from the ring of Cobra lead. It was a dust bowl near the C-130's nose, armed combatants blazing away, he saw, commandos then chasing down Somalis who had decided it was better to flee than stand and fight. It was hard for the soldier to tell which was which and who was who, but a split-second assessment of the numbers of bodies flying from technicals signaled to him the Somalis were clutching the short end of the stick.

Maybe ten Somalis, he viewed, came crawling or staggering out of the bed of their dumped transport. They were lurching to their feet, punch-drunk from the hard topple, AKs jerking in different directions, uncertain where the next immediate threat would rear up.

Bolan took care of their confusion, finger caressing the M-203's trigger. He dumped the 40 mm fragmentation bomb into their ranks—no point in wasting precious seconds when the prize was maybe on the fly. The blast ripped out the heart of the pack, torn figures kicked in separate directions. Three hardmen with the quickest feet and the most luck, knocked down by the concussive force but clearing the fireball and shock waves, scurried to get back in action. The Executioner tagged the trio with a raking burst of autofire, left to right and back, bodies flung into tight corkscrews, dropping. Two of the warlord's goons then popped into the soldier's gun sights on the other side of the downed transport, running for the oncoming technicals, arms flapping as if they were hailing a cab.

Bolan shot them both up the back, flinging them ahead, their arms windmilling, faces hammering down with such force their legs flew up. Out of the corner of his eye, he spotted Asp charging the Hummer at a group of Somalis pouring AK-47 autofire from the bed of a technical, Python opting to help hose down those survivors still in the fight with his M-16.

Bolan cut his path hard and fast toward the racing technical, drawing target acquisition on three gunmen in the jeep's bed. Rotor wash from the Black Hawks, hovering thirty yards behind, kicked up a cyclone of grit and dust, obscuring confirmation until the technical was nearly on top of the warrior.

But Bolan pinned down their man, Dugula's face of terror and outrage framed from the shotgun seat of the technical, the soldier's attention shifting back to the M-60 gunner who swiveled the machine gun in his direction. There was a moment's hesitation from the hardman on the M-60, a spray of bullets flying wild past the soldier, before he hit him with a burst of 5.56 mm tumblers and sent him flying. Two Cobra Hummers then burst out of the dust storm, an M-60 roaring, other Cobra commandos racing on foot ahead to help lay waste to the pack of Somalis in the trailing rig.

The Executioner focused on the big catch charging his way.

Dugula, Bolan glimpsed, was flailing his arms, raging at his driver, when he hit the M-16's trigger. The windshield imploded, a crimson halo where the wheelman had sat bearing grim testament that Dugula was the last passenger. The Executioner sidled away from the unmanned jeep, one last Somali launched from the bed of Dugula's getaway, then he blew out the port tires with a long burst of autofire. He let it surge past, saw Dugula's eyes bugging out, mouth vented, a silent scream lost to the din of autofire from some point downrange. Deflated tread slammed down into a rut, and the jeep shot up and over a jagged rip in the land, sailing a few yards, before it flipped onto its side.

THE WORLD WAS a shattered hell of noise, foul smells and choking dust from where he lay, slumped against the door, spitting flecks of blood and glass chips from his lips. Dugula heard the bitter chuckle next, but the sound was chased away by the Black Hawks, the bleat of massive blades a pounding racket that washed fire through his brain. They were nightmare specters suspended in the sky, two giant prehistoric birds of doom.

American commandos! He hadn't clearly seen the faces of their attackers, but he had been there in Mogadishu when the infidel forces had come to supposedly restore order to a lawless country, when he had been on the shortlist of kill or capture. The infidels had returned.

Black Hawks. It was happening again, only this time it appeared the invaders would create a different outcome. The three white devils had maneuvered him into this trap; he was sure of it. But if they were working with his own Muslim handlers, why? It made no sense, a preposterous riddle without the first clue. He had made every accommodation possible to the freedom fighters, arming them, refuge inside his borders, food, women and *qat*. Or had they, too, been deceived? Beyond his sense of outrage over the betrayal, pure fear began writhing in his belly.

"You'll know when it's begun."

He ran those words through his mind again, hatred burning. Now what?

His clansmen, he was sure, were all dead. If there were any survivors, could they stand and fight while…?

What? Should he attempt to flee again, but this time on foot? That he was still alive was no guarantee he wouldn't be shot down in the next few moments. Where was his AK-47? And what would he do if he found the weapon? He was outnumbered, outgunned, alone most likely, autofire withering, no more screams, the lopsided battle winding down. There was a silence beyond the whapping rotors that sparked new fear. There really was no choice, he decided. Escape clearly wasn't going to happen. Best to die on his feet. If this was the end, it was God's will. So be it. The least he could do would be to kill as many of the enemy as he could before he was sent to Paradise.

Pinned by Muhmar's deadweight, he shoved him away, grunting with the effort before he had him wedged between the seats. He scrabbled his hands through the bed of glass on the floorboard, crying out as a sliver jabbed his finger. There. He plucked up the assault rifle, aware at least that one of his enemies was close by. He hadn't had a good look at the commando who had blasted out the window, sent the jeep careening out of control, trapping him now on his side, but he glimpsed enough of the eyes of the tall dark man to know his own doom was certain, the infidel probably circling the wreck even then.

How could this have happened? he wondered, rage clearing the sludge in his limbs. The attack had been unleashed, all thunder and lightning, instant death and destruction, so fierce it left little doubt they were there to kill him. It had been so easy before, intimidating the UN and Red Cross relief workers, seizing shipments…

It was over.

With the stock of the assault rifle, he punched out a jagged shard, groaning as pain knifed down his neck, reaching a point of fire between his shoulder blades. Nothing felt broken, but he assumed any pain was moments away from ending altogether.

Dugula squeezed through the opening, AK in shaky hands, the warlord unmindful of sharp glass tearing at his clothes. He sensed a presence behind him as he rose, the AK-47 swinging around, ready to kill whoever it was, however many were at his rear. He heard himself snarl, cursing all of this hideous misfortune, finger taking up slack on the trigger, pure murder pumping in his heart. It was the tall dark commando, rolling through the dust, coming out of nowhere, a floating wraith, right on top of him before he could act. The AK-47 nearly drew a bead, but Dugula knew it was already too late. There was a glimpse of the M-16, a question wanting to form in his mind as to why he wasn't already dead on his feet, when the fist plowed into his jaw and the lights winked out.

"YOU WANT TO MIRANDIZE that asshole, too, Colonel? Maybe find him a lawyer?"

The plastic cuffs were fastened to Dugula, Bolan wrenching the warlord's arms behind his back when it looked and sounded to the soldier as if this were where Collins wanted to assert his command in front of the troops. It was sheer luck on his part but earned, just the same, by audacity and determination that he'd gotten to Dugula first. Judging the tone he caught, Bolan could tell Collins didn't like getting upstaged, and on the first leg of the mission.

"I wasn't looking to steal anybody's thunder," Bolan said.

"Is that why you took it upon yourself to seal off their rear when you knew my gunships were supposed to do that?"

"It seemed the thing to do at the time."

"Is that a fact?"

Bolan watched Collins, holding his ground beside Dugula, the warlord groaning, coming around, legs twitching in the dust. The short right cross had branded a purple welt on his jaw, hardly the kind of punishment, Bolan knew Dugula deserved. There was a village of innocents being butchered right then weighing on Bolan's thoughts. The sky over the hills east had darkened, several more plumes of black smoke rising now since the battle here had erupted, bringing on a wide patch of unnatural dusk against the horizon. Time was wasting, lives being snuffed, Bolan sure they were being executed in droves by now. Up to then he hadn't heard Collins mention any secondary objective beyond rounding up Dugula. This, Bolan knew, would prove a defining moment, grant him some insight into Collins's true nature.

The salt-and-pepper flattop seemed to appear first in the boiling dust before six feet of muscled frame brought Collins swaggering out of the cloud, M-16 canted across his chest. Bolan read the former Delta major's anger beyond the tight smile. The other commandos were toeing the dead or dying, pleas for help or mercy bleating out from several wounded Somalis. Collins slowed his pace, head swiveling, the soldier following the Cobra leader's stare toward a commando—Tsunami—who was bent over a bloodied form convulsing near a technical riddled with bullet holes. Bolan panned on, found two more Cobra ops flanking a Somali who was on his knees, hands clasped, praying, it sounded, while in the same breath asking for mercy.

Collins shook his head. "He's nobody."

Bolan kept the anger to himself over the cold-blooded killing that followed, as the commandos drilled autofire into the Somali's chest. A kill in the heat of battle was one thing to Bolan, but when the enemy surrendered, execution on the spot was unacceptable. One act of outright savagery, Bolan knew, always led to another and even more brutal act. If a soldier couldn't separate the difference, he was lost, no exceptions.

"Major. Over here."

Again Collins peered at another Somali. His face was forced up and aimed at Collins, the commando named Roadrunner wadding up a handful of hair, a knee speared in his back. The Cobra leader gave a thumbs-down.

The face shoved away, the commando stood, drilled a 3-round burst into the Somali's back, abruptly silencing his plea.

Collins held up and rotated a clenched fist, signaling the Black Hawks to move off, presumably to recon the area for any gunmen who had managed to slip away.

"So, is this where it starts, Colonel?"

"Does what start?"

Something flickered through Collins's eyes, a darkness stirring behind the look, Bolan believing he sensed an angry animal presence of the savage he'd just seen carry out the executions.

Collins lowered his voice, edged with tight anger as he said, "I don't have time to jack around with you, Colonel. From here on, we map out a strategy. I'd like you to stick with the program. I need to know we're on the same page and not out here clashing cocks. We clear? Sudden interruptions in tactics, in my experience, have a way of proving hazardous to everybody's health."

"And improvising?"

Collins grunted. "Is that what you call it? Well, that depends on who's doing the improvising and why. I'm getting a sense here, Stone, that maybe you're not really a team player, or that you're a lot more than I've been led to believe. That maybe you're telling me I don't know how to do my job?"

Bolan nodded at Dugula. "He's in the net, but there's a few loose ends still running around over those hills, Major. This isn't over."

Collins glanced past Bolan. "What's happening over there isn't my concern, Colonel. They're not part of the mission parameters. And we're not some flying hospital or a bunch of Red Cross workers on a mission from God. Say we do what you're implying, say we're successful driving out the rest of Dugula's bad boys. Then what? We're looking at slews of wounded, dying, diseased, mouths to feed. We're not equipped for that scenario to start with."

"They're being slaughtered, Collins. Women, children. If they don't fit into your plans, chances are you could still put a few of Dugula's top lieutenants on your mantel."

"Hey, this isn't some game show to me, Stone. I'm not in this to land a seat as some military expert on *FOX & Friends* when I hang it up."

"Then let it be about something right."

Collins paused, considering something. "A part of me can almost respect you for wanting to be a decent guy and all that, Colonel. In other circumstances I might feel the same way. But do you know why whatever's left of Dugula's brigands are over that hump torching those people? They're carrying a plague, Stone, that's straight from up top. It's all been caught on sat imagery, and I've got the details in triplicate if you care to read the reports. The UN, WHO all know about it, and not even they will send in some relief help at this time. And we've been ordered to leave it alone. What's over those hills is a bunch of Ethiopian nomads who brought some sort of hemorrhagic contagion, some real wicked stuff that infected hundreds. We don't know what it is. It could even be Ebola. You think I want to risk the lives of my men just to play some kind of Mother Teresa to a bunch of people who are going to die anyway? Whose own countrymen will march in right behind us and kill and burn them even if we do take out the rest of Dugula's rabble? You want to be running around, shooting up bad guys with open sores and black shit flying out of their mouths and maybe getting doused in their infected blood? For all we know, this plague could be an airborne contagion."

"You don't want to do it, then let me handle it."

"I've got a lot to do, Colonel, before we move on to our next objective. I'll have to beg off."

"Then I'll go it alone. I won't just walk away."

Collins measured Bolan, bobbing his head. "Okay, tell you what. Just to show I've got some heart, take one of the Black Hawks, I'll even throw in the Apache, since my numbers show about thirty or more of Dugula's punks running around over there. I can spare four of my men, but that's it. You've got one hour, Stone, then I'm in the air. I'll take back my men and leave you behind if you're not ready to fly. Will that accommodate your sense of mercy and compassion for the oppressed?"

It suddenly sounded too easy, Collins relenting, handing over his own men even, despite his argument about the risks of infection. Bolan sensed something else had prompted the Cobra leader to cave, but Collins was already keying his com link, relaying the order, the Black Hawk coming back to pick up the soldier.

The Executioner watched as Collins snatched Dugula off the ground by the shoulder, then barked the handles of the four commandos who would ride with the colonel.

"One hour, Colonel. Clock's ticking."

No good luck, no kiss off, nothing. On his own, but he had been, pretty much, since accepting the mission.

The Executioner turned, forging into the dust as the Black Hawk landed. He couldn't put his finger on it, but there was a familiar churning in his gut, warning him that everything wasn't as it appeared with Collins and Cobra Force Twelve.

Bolan hopped into the warbird's belly. Time, he knew, would separate truth from lies, the righteous from the unclean of spirit. Right then there was another battle to fight, and hopefully a village, or part of it, at least to save.

One hour, he thought.

It could prove an eternity.

CHAPTER THREE

As anxious as Collins was to put Somalia behind him and set the stage for round two, it wouldn't hurt, he figured, to stay grounded for another hour or so. By then a few questions might get put to rest, or, perhaps better still, he could spare himself some grief in the future. No, it wouldn't cause him the first twinge of pain or regret if Stone—or the other four without the snake handles—didn't come back from the crusade. Stone the Merciful, he thought. What the hell kind of warrior went out of his way to play savior to people who were doomed to die anyway? The diseased of that village had never been on the itinerary of things to do, but it might just help his own scheme of things if Wild Card was aced in the next sixty minutes trying to play savior. Something about the big colonel was nagging him the more he pondered any number of possible scenarios. The SOB could be anything—a spy, a plant, a shooter with orders given behind his back to terminate all of them if...

There were calls over the satcom to make right then, last-minute details to be ironed out before the next incursion, a date with another homicidal megalomaniac that would go down inside Sudan's border. Hot spots to ignite, more bad guys to stuff or cuff, dreams to hold on to, he thought. Stone was on his own. He'd forget about him for the time being and let fate run its course.

Collins was up the ramp, kicking through a few boxes strewed before him when he heard Dugula squawking for answers as Asp and Python snapped on the leg irons, removed the plastic cuffs at gunpoint, then clamped the warlord to the cuffs on the bench.

He marched up to Dugula, slashed a backhand across his mouth.

"I'll say this one time only, Habir. Any more whining, any crap out of you at all, even give me that evil eye once more, I'll put one through your eye and dump you off with the rest of your garbage outside," Collins rasped. "You'll know what this is all about when I'm damn good and ready to clue you in. Not another goddamn word! So sit back and enjoy the flight." He stood, boring Dugula with his no-shit stare, found the warlord cowed into silence.

Where there was life, the guy figured there was hope, Collins thought, and left him to stew and taste the blood on his lip. He then passed out the orders, dividing up the duties between monitoring their consoles for any traffic in the area and securing the perimeter outside the Hercules. An all-clear from his commandos at the consoles, and he felt that insidious weight settle back on his shoulders.

Striding aft, he stared at the distant horizon. The warbirds were gone, Wild Card six minutes on the clock already. What the hell was that big bastard all about anyway? he wondered. Angered still the colonel had bucked the game plan, he recalled giving the tactical shift by Wild Card a long few moments' worth of spectating. Sure, the big guy could move, a pro, no doubt in his mind, but that transport truck had been indirectly dumped on its side by his Apache. It didn't take much martial skill or effort to plow a 40 mm knockout punch into badly mauled Somalis crawling out of that rig, but Stone had bored in, just the same, going for broke. The back-shooting of two on the fly he didn't have a problem with—hell, he would have done the same, all that honor and facing down the other guy, armed and on equal footing, just a bunch of Hollywood nonsense. It irked him, finally, that Stone had beaten him to Dugula, the new guy first to haul in a door prize, but he wasn't about to tip his hand that the old warrior pride had been stung. He knew a whole lot more than some glory on the battlefield was at stake.

BOLAN WAS UNDER no illusions he could save the village. Given the length of time Dugula's genocide campaign had been underway, the thickness and numbers of black clouds rising to blot out the landscape, and swarms of vultures that seemed to multiply out of nowhere the closer the Black Hawk bore down on the massacre, the Executioner had to assume saving any innocents would simply prove an exercise in futility.

If that was the case, Bolan had an alternative going in.

Whatever Collins's reasoning for not participating in what the soldier saw as the final solution to the Dugula atrocity, the least he could do for the dead was exact more than a few pounds of flesh from the savages.

His com link tied into the flight crews of the Black Hawk and Apache, he handed out the orders as soon as they soared over the hills. Bolan found utter chaos down there, black smoke cloaking entire areas of what he could only view as a vision of Hell. He made out brief bursts of autofire rattling throughout the village, screams whipped away by rotor wash, spotted men and women still being run down, shot. If this wasn't worth fighting against, risking his life for…

Whether Collins had shown his true colors as a savage remained to be seen.

Bolan put together his attack strategy based on enemy numbers, village layout, civilian body count. The majority of Somali thugs appeared to be wrapping up their grisly cleansing chore, a series of pyres confined to the far eastern edge of the campsite. He figured fifteen to twenty still torching the dead, that hardforce fit best for some Apache chain-gun pronouncement of their fate. There were still pockets of gunmen on the move as he sighted them lurching about between rows of beehive huts, combing for any survivors, skirting along a straight north-to-south sweep. With all the smoke taking to the sky, shielding the birds, and coupled with what he believed was their single-minded obsession to murder and burn, Bolan figured they had a few moments to spare before the enemy noticed they were about to be hit.

Bolan gave it to the pilots, ordered his Black Hawk crew to drop him off at the southeastern edge of the village. There was no time to lay it out, diagram tactics and such. The Apache was to strafe the pyre grounds and churn up anything that cropped up with a gun, take out everything on wheels. To his mild surprise they copied, but why wouldn't they? He shared leadership with Collins, but that alone was starting to make him wonder. There was no time to question motives or ponder all that Collins had done and failed to do as far as this leg of the mission fell. Bolan was on his own, and he told the four commandos Collins had handed over as much. They were to sit tight, help the M-60 door gunner with firepower from the air.

"So, tell me, why bring us along in the first place?" Roadrunner asked.

"We're supposed to just sit up here and scratch ourselves, Colonel?" Tsunami added.

"Contagion," Bolan told them, as the Black Hawk veered in the direction where it would drop him off.

"The good major seemed real concerned about his guys coming into contact with some unspecified disease down there. Consider this a favor. You want to cover me from up here or play with yourselves, that's up to you."

A shrug, a grunt, a soft shake of the head but Bolan could almost read the thoughts behind the body language. He wasn't looking to play hero, aware he could use all the help on the ground he could get. The problem was he wasn't sure he could trust them. And if he pulled it off by himself, say cuffed and brought back a few top henchmen to Collins? Perhaps, he decided, it was time to take a deeper measure of the Cobra leader. His suspicion was that Collins had hung him out here to burn. If so, then why?

"Have it your way, Colonel," Tsunami said as the Black Hawk lowered, the LZ clear of any hardforce as far as Bolan could tell. "Good luck."

The Executioner jumped off, M-16 out and ready to announce his presence. Bolan didn't have long to wait as two goons in skullcaps appeared from between a row of huts already ablaze. They swung his way, eyes wide, confused and shocked, but just in time for Bolan to wax them off their feet.

OMARI NAHBAT BELIEVED that not only were they doing a service for their country, but they also were performing God's work. Surely, he thought, God wouldn't want his children to suffer a slow, agonizing death from plagues that had no cure. Even if there was medicine to relieve their misery, it would only prolong a life that would end soon enough, flesh succumbing eventually to the ravaging dictates of plague. It was God's will, since any antibiotics or painkillers that found their way into the country always ran out—or were pilfered by the strong who were meant to rule. Why fight the course of nature? That was hardly murder in his eyes, as he watched the corpses dragged by Ethiopians or the more brave of heart of his clansmen, the dead flung or rolled into the leaping flames. This was containment, pure and simple, a way to save the healthy populace from plague, spare the strong and healthy. Who or what could fight invisible killers, anyway? Fire was the only cure, cremation on the spot of the afflicted the only answer, the way he and the others saw it. There were no regulated state-run hospitals in his country, and doctors usually came in from beyond the borders, provided, of course, they had the nerve, the cash or the medicine to sell just to stay long enough to waste their time on the walking dead. Disease was as monstrous and unforgiving a killer as famine in Somalia, and it was everywhere.

The shriek jarred him. Nahbat slipped the AK-47 off his shoulder. Two of his clansmen, he found, wrestled with what he assumed had been a corpse. Arms thrashed, a cry rang out, then they tossed the boy's body into the fire. One of them stepped back, chuckling, slapping his palms as if that might wash away any disease he might have come into contact with. The awful scream chilled Nahbat for a moment, shivering him to the bone, but he was grateful when it ended moments later.

He turned away, suddenly wondering, as he searched the line of clansmen, where Hussein had gone. There had been something in the boy's eyes he had found unsettling. What was it? Horror? Contempt for the rest of them? Judgment? He was young, unaccustomed to the harsh realities of life, but that was no excuse for Hussein to neglect his duties, to not pull his weight. The boy needed to learn respect, he thought, show gratitude to a cousin who had given him life beyond being a simple goatherd and who might have perhaps been destined to suffer the same fate as the afflicted in the remote regions of the country.

The shooting was subsiding now to the south, the stink of plastic on fire from that direction flung up his nose, compounding the queasy churn in his gut as he found still more huts being torched. He strode from the pyres, both to clear his senses of burning flesh and to find Hussein. He had been standing at the edge of the pit moments ago, but the boy's familiar short, spindly frame was nowhere to be found.

He needed to have a talk with Hussein anyway, find the truth of whatever was in the boy's heart. There was no room in the clan for weaklings. If he discovered Hussein couldn't cut it, he would have to kill his cousin, if only to save face.

He was forging into a wall of drifting smoke, searching the village, the fires spreading now, warping the plastic-covered tents, when he thought he spotted a large black object in the sky. It appeared to fly south, there then gone, but it was nearly impossible to make out what it was, the towering barricades of smoke all but obscuring his view.

He decided it was nothing more than his senses bombarded by the task at hand, eyes playing tricks, and went in search of Hussein.

"COME WITH ME, little one. Do not be afraid. I will take you from this place."

He heard himself say it, only Hussein Nahbat didn't believe his own words of assurance, much less feel any confidence he could pull off a disappearing act. If he did manage to escape into the surrounding wasteland, leading this boy to safety, then what? Where would he go? His parents were dead, and the village he had come from had perished recently from famine or disease, or so his cousin had said. Better to die, wandering in self-imposed exile, he decided, wasting away, step by step, hungry and thirsty, leaving his and the boy's fate in the hands of God than play any part in the evil around him. Beyond his flesh, he had a soul still to think about, to attempt to save in the eyes of a merciful God. And surely God would judge this evil, he had to believe, in a world far better than the one he so desperately wished to escape.

He wanted to think himself a coward for running, not standing up to them, fighting back, but what could he do? He was only one against a small army of murderers. Not only that, he wasn't sure he could even pull the trigger on his clansmen, despite the fact he knew they were evil men who deserved only death. And if he didn't participate in throwing the dead—and, God have mercy, the dying—into the fires or shoot down unarmed women and children, they would deem him unworthy to live among their ranks, brand then execute him as traitor and coward. Flee, then, leave it all to fate. Perhaps, at the very least, he could find a way to spare one innocent from this madness, even if that meant risking his own life.

The sudden chatter of weapons fire from nearby jolted him. Nearly gagging behind his bandanna from any number of ghastly smells, he stared at the child, figured he was no more than five or six. It was hard to tell how old he actually was, the boy little more than a dark, emaciated scarecrow, flesh hanging loose on a body that hadn't seen perhaps even a morsel of wheat, a crumb of bread, he believed, in days. The eyes were sunken, lifeless orbs, the face nearly a skull, that death's-head expression he had seen on children who were too weak from hunger to even speak. Hussein felt the tears coming back, the burning mist equal parts grief and air singed by heat and the sting of death. How the boy had been missed by his clansmen, he couldn't say.

Fate? Divine intervention?

Somehow he had gotten this far, managed to slip away, the others too consumed by their hideous undertaking, a few of them even laughing and joking about what they did, their callous displays somehow making the atrocity even more revolting. It had been an accident—or was it something else again?—when he had stumbled over what he had believed at first was a discarded bundle of rags.

He laid down his assault rifle. He had never fired the weapon, never would. He reached out a hand, swept away the debris the boy had hidden under.

"We must go."

Did he see a flicker of hope in those eyes?

The boy took his hand, too weak to stand on his own, Nahbat knew, so he scooped the child up, clutching him to his chest.

He looked around at the firestorms consuming their homes, searching, fearing his armed brethren would discover him now, just as he was moving. He coughed, the sound alarming him, afraid he would be heard by roving killers, but he hoped the drifting banks of smoke would help conceal his escape. Beyond two fires, nearly converging, he saw open land. He was skirting around the dead who had been shot where they stood when he heard, "Hussein! Stop!"

He thought he would be sick, felt his legs nearly fold as despair froze him in his tracks. There would be no rational explanation in the eyes of his cousin, he knew, for this action, much less forgiveness.

So be it.

He turned slowly, a nauseous lurch in his heart. As he watched his cousin step through the drifting smoke, the AK-47 up and aimed his way, he experienced a moment of blinding clarity, a strange peace settling over him. It was over; both he and the boy were dead, but he wouldn't beg for their lives.

"You disappoint me greatly, Hussein."

"As do you and the others, cousin."

He decided to try to reason with Omari, if only for the boy, even though he knew it was hopeless. "Do not do this, Omari."

His cousin laughed. "You would die for him? For what? Why? You would risk catching plague and infect the rest of us?"

He smiled at his cousin. "You are already infected, I am afraid."

"I have handled none of them, you fool, unlike you, who clutch that boy and are probably now infected yourself."

"I was referring to your soul."

The weapon was lowering, Omari considering something, baffled, it seemed, then Hussein saw the madness fly back into his eyes. Even before the weapon was up and blazing, Hussein Nahbat had a stark revelation, aware in his dying moment, as he felt the bullets tearing first into the boy, that he had only been dreaming a fool's dream for thinking he and the boy could have survived this chaos.

CHAPTER FOUR

They were teenagers, fourteen, eighteen tops, but Bolan knew all too painfully well youth received no special consideration in a world where anarchy and savagery dictated who lived to steal a few more years on the planet. With the average life expectancy of a Somali male roughly two decades, if famine or drought or disease didn't get them, they were snapped up by warlords to shoot it out with rival clansmen, profit somehow off the misery of their countrymen or marched out to commit genocide when there was no food or medicine to plunder from relief aid. An education on the hard facts, the dark side of life came by way of the sword. If they didn't want to fight, they were killed on the spot.

Simple as that.

But who was to blame in the final analysis? Bolan had to wonder. The one who handed them the weapon, or the one who freely accepted it? Both?

No matter really, he knew, since a bullet would kill him no matter who fired it, whether a raving sociopath, a frightened kid threatened by elders to do murderous deeds, or a warrior fully seasoned with the blood of other warriors on his hands.

One of the boys was dead before he hit the ground, cradling something, the other standing, capping off another and unnecessary burst into unfeeling flesh, then taking in what he had done, head cocked halfway toward the Executioner, oblivious to all else, eyes twinkling mirrors of the firestorms. Was that pride in the eyes? The boy satisfied? Whatever sick drama had played out here, Bolan would never know but he could venture a guess. The soldier glimpsed the shredded ruins of the small child, butchered alongside with what he assumed was his potential rescuer, then he pounded a burst of autofire up the back of their killer. The boy never knew what hit him, and it was just as well, Bolan thought. Mercy, if any was due, was reserved for the afterlife.

There would be time enough, assuming he walked out of here in one piece, to feel hot anger later. Even still, he knew there could never be any reasoning—or mercy shown for the guilty—for the madness he found here. The Executioner briefly felt a curious, distant, otherworldly sense, as light as the wind, slightly disembodied even as he waded deeper into this horror. It was as if he'd been here before, and he had, too many times, in fact, to tally. It struck him—as he heard the

Apache unload Hellfire missiles, the stutter of weapons fire from the Black Hawk mowing down illegal combatants—all of this murder of innocents strewed before him, a zenith of man's inhumanity to man, had always been here, somewhere in time and place, one way one or another, throughout the ages. Human nature was the only one constant, and sad but true, that went double for animal man.

The guilty had to be punished, no exceptions, no mercy. High time, he decided, for a little Old Testament vengeance.

Bolan melted into, then swept out of the drifting smoke, his gut knotted with a grapefruit-size chunk of raw anger, despite the intention to roll into this a stone-cold professional. Unless he was a psychopath or simply evil, Bolan knew no man could fully digest without the first flicker of wrenching emotion the atrocity that had happened here. With the full slamming force of death in his face, the bile squirmed in his gut for a moment, urging him on to wax as many armed killers as quickly and mercilessly as possible. Flies and mosquitoes swarmed the dead; vultures, brazen and impatient to gorge, descending now on bodies. He could ill afford to concern himself with unfeeling flesh, dwell on the full, hideous impact of all these lives snuffed out so callously. And if there was contagion here, he was willing to risk infection, if only to avenge this monstrosity, Collins be damned.

They were running everywhere dead ahead, trying

to flee certain death from above, haphazard human—
or inhuman—traffic rearing up in his sights as he came
out of the thickest patch of smoke. Closing on the hungry bonfires consuming diseased flesh, a few of the
gunmen fired wild bursts at the warbirds, squawking in
panic and confusion over this sudden final judgment of
their deed. Three, then four hardmen wheeled around
the corner of a firewall dancing up a hut that used to
provide the most meager of shelter, he assumed, for the
late occupants. They skidded to a halt, ten or so paces
from Bolan, sandaled feet kicking up dust. Figure the
horrific pounding of explosions and the sight of their
own getting a heavy-metal dose of their own poison
was too much for them to stomach, fleeing now to save
themselves.

There was nowhere for them to run or hide.

Two of them stared at the sight of the tall white man
who had marched out of nowhere, staring ahead as if
he were some avenging angel of doom that had
materialized out of the smoke. Their eyes wide, the
soldier read the looks, then heard the muffled cries
from behind bandannas. It sounded as if they wanted
their lives spared, a show of mercy from the lone invader. It was all just some terrible mistake. Two of
them were on the verge, it looked, of throwing down
their arms.

How could they expect that which they had never
shown? Bolan decided, and blew them off their feet, a
raking blast of steel-jacketed projectiles down the line,

flinging them back toward other running and doomed killing brethren being gored and gutted from the sky.

There was no point, Bolan knew, in engaging in a long and protracted sweep of the village and its perimeter. Fire was eating up anything left standing. The smoke was so thick, so putrid it left little doubt to Bolan the savages had completed their task.

What was left of the hardforce was pretty much chopped up or blown into the firewalls next as a Hellfire missile ripped through a motor pool, ten or more broken dark figurines taking to the air above the crunching blast. A half dozen far from the epicenter were sent staggering about from the shock wave, howling next, flinching, darting from renewed bursts of terror no doubt kicking them into high gear as wreckage hammered home.

Ducking under a winging slab of metal, Bolan hosed down a few more Somali killers, then changed clips on the advance, began searching the hellgrounds.

The evil fumes pouring into his senses was enough to nearly knock even the most battle-hardened soldier off his feet, and Bolan knew he wasn't above any queasy roil in his gut. He swiveled, searching, attempting to control any deep intakes of the foul air. He spotted an armed runner to his nine, hit the trigger on his M-16. The Executioner drove the gunner into his comrade, who was minus an arm just above the elbow from the Hellfire amputation. A mercy burst, and the amputee dropped in his tracks in an ungainly flop, face plastered to earth.

All done?

Bolan listened to raging flames, scoured the dead for wounded or live ones, bodies strewed and stacked in what was a fairly tight but wide circle where the warbirds had unleashed their final ring of doom, two or three flaming technical carcasses seeming to float back to Earth like some ghastly magic act.

Keying his com link, scanning the carnage, peering into the smoke and fires for any signs of armed resistance, the Executioner raised the Black Hawk's pilot. Sitrep. He barely heard Black Hawk One inform him it looked clear of hostiles from where he sat, sickened as he was by what he saw here. Perhaps it was because he'd been here before—other places, other times—but the end result was all the same.

Death. All gone on, both the innocent and the guilty.

Again, Bolan felt a part of his soul, his humanity collapsing on itself, a sorrow welling up from deep inside, wanting to take him down into a void of hot rage. He would suck it up, of course, aware this was only the beginning, that more monsters were beyond Somalia, their own rampage only just out of the gate to lay waste to whatever evil they didn't bag for some future trial. Perhaps, he thought, this evil he found here was simply a microcosm of the end. He was no doomsayer, no Nostradamus and certainly no John the Divine, but he had to wonder. Was this just part and parcel of the evolution of man speeding to his ultimate destiny? Would, could, such evil in a part of the world where life meant less than zero, spread like a cancer, spill from one border to the next, contaminate one country after the other? No matter what he did, no matter how much evil he destroyed, he knew the Four Horsemen would live on in Somalia—perhaps continue to thrive throughout the entire region known as the Horn of Africa—but at least a fat batch of homicidal maniacs could no longer scourge their own countryside.

Was it enough? Was it ever?

The Black Hawk was down, time to go, and the Executioner hopped up through the hatch. He wished he could have done far more here, spare at the very least a few innocent lives, but he would be glad to put this evil place behind.

Damn glad, but the nagging question lingered in his mind: what next?

"YOU'RE LATE. Sixty-five minutes isn't an hour, Stone. We're rolling, we're on a tight schedule here. I'm talking deadlines that are shaved down to seconds, or have you forgotten mission priority?"

"We can meet you back at Shark Base if your panties are that twisted up."

"Don't get fucking smart, Stone, and we're not going back to Kenya."

"News to me."

"I can believe that. By the way, quite the floor show I hear you put on. Too bad it didn't make a damn bit of difference, since I understand from my flying aces on

your Black Hawk loaner Dugula's *qat*-chewing shit-
bags had already wiped out that village. What was that
all about anyway, you going in alone?"

Bolan had turned off his hand radio, shed his com
link when boarding the Black Hawk, wanting only a
few brief moments with his own thoughts to bury the
weight of where he'd just been, what he'd seen. He had
begun to shed the ghosts of the hell he was putting behind, in the air, when Tsunami had pointed at his own,
then the soldier's handheld radio, Collins squawking
for him to shag his ass and pick up.

Now, if he didn't know better, it sounded to Bolan
as if Collins was disappointed he was still on the team,
alive and kicking. Collins pointed out their former
ranks in the military didn't mean squat in the here and
now, it was his show, the gist Bolan caught being he
was on board as a courtesy, that he had to have hu-
mongous muscular clout somewhere that the Cobra
leader would sure as hell like to have a face-to-face
with, since Colonel Stone didn't strike him as a team
player. Collins repeated his question.

"Concern."

"What?" Collins snapped.

"For your troops, since you were all worked up
about anybody coming down with some plague."

"Took the gamble yourself, I see. Appreciate all that
big concern for the men, but I tell you what, the first
sign you're sick from something you picked up back
there, I don't give a damn if you cough too hard or

break out in a sudden sweat, you're off the team. And if I have to, I'll strap a parachute on you myself and drop you in the middle of nowhere."

Bolan ignored the threat. "We're two minutes, maybe less away from—"

"I've got you marked on my screens. Just hustle the fuck up when you guys get dropped off—belay that, I want to see you sprint up the ramp."

Bolan grunted. Somehow he didn't picture himself sprinting on the good major's command.

"We've got a lot of ground to cover before the next round, and it's going down in a few hours. I'm assuming you've got a few jumps behind you?"

"One or two."

"You're shitting me, I hope."

"If you're worried about me breaking a leg or my neck, don't. But if you don't mind, I'll rig my own chute, okay?"

"I wouldn't see it any other way. Oh, and Stone? No more cowboy or crusader shit. We clear?"

Bolan hesitated, then said, "Yeah."

"You want to bleed for all the little people not even their own give a camel's steaming pile about, do it on your own dime or go find a church, light a candle and finger the Rosary. From here on, you better get acquainted with the concepts of team integrity and tactical cohesion."

Collins was off the air as at least three different remarks—two of which were smart-ass—leaped to Bolan's mind about those particular concepts. What the hell was really going on here? he wondered. With each passing minute and every exchange turning more brittle and heading toward volatile with Collins, the more the soldier was feeling the hairs wanting to stand up on the back his neck. Something about Cobra Force Twelve was out of tilt.

It wasn't the blinding light of any divine truth being revealed, but it damn near felt like a bolt of lightning hitting him between the eyes, seeking to jolt him closer to a dark reality. He searched the faces of the commandos Collins had wanted joined to his hip, but didn't allow the look to linger or penetrate. It was just a suspicion, nagging, growing, but one he decided to keep to himself until...

What?

That only four of the commandos carried serpent handles? That they were special to Collins, not essentially and integrally part of the team? But, if so, why? What demon lurked behind the masks of that tactical integrity, duty and honor they believed they showed him? His gut—rarely wrong—told him not only was there something shady, perhaps even sinister about his so-called teammates, but that this mission was set to come unraveled.

He'd play it out to the end of whatever the ride, the Executioner decided, aware now more than ever he was on his own, but one soldier up against who, how many and what?

HIS BLACK-OPS HANDLE for Operation Stranglehold—
the mission so tagged by Cobra Central—was Gambler,
but his real name was…

Who really knew? The name Harry Smith wanted
to come to mind if he chose to replay a childhood that
never existed. No one, not even himself, could remember his given name at birth. Even all the classified doc-
uments and disks at the NSA and the CIA were so full
of deletions on his past operations and his slew of assumed names and handles not even the superspooks
could accurately confirm his true identity, if put to task.

And who cared? Beyond whoever he really was in
name only, his legion, to be exact, very much gave a
damn, and they would follow his orders, or else.

No, he figured he couldn't state precisely who he
was, but he knew where he'd been in the world, what
he'd done. Most important, he had a full measure of
who the man inside was, and just what that warrior was
prepared to do. Oh, bliss to be, how sweet the light on
the horizon of tomorrow, he thought, oh, the riches to
be earned and enjoyed. Cobra Command, Pentagon,
White House, the members of the entire intel-military
infrastructure of the U.S. of A., would soon weep and
gnash their teeth in impotent rage when they were gone
with the wind.

Maybe, just for added chuckles, he'd leave behind
a photo or two on a body, a big dung-eating grin, a mid-
dle-finger salute leaping out of the pics, "See ya, don't

wanna be ya." Sure enough, the day was soon in coming when it would pay off beyond anyone's wildest imaginings, and ranting and raving that he was, essentially, nonexistent, so far off the official radar screen, so distantly removed from legitimate channels he didn't even have a Social Security Number. No sense in being a deniable expendable, taking all the risks all these years, if there was no reward, if he couldn't make the power players and pencil pushers and CNN camera hogs—who thought they jerked his strings, safe behind the lines, thumbs planted square up their rectums, denying they had killers out there in the world doing nasty things—swallow a fat load for all his blood and sweat. Deny this, he thought.

He had to chuckle to himself over what he viewed as a role that landed him as the next-best thing to being supernatural, up there with the greatest of saints or the most horrific of demons in human skin who had gone before him. After all, they, he thought—whoever the hell they were—claimed the greatest deceit ever played on the world by the Devil was making man believe the Devil didn't exist. And that, likewise, evil didn't exist, that it was only each and every individual human's perception of reality as it related only to his or her own world and all the wants and wishes that pertained exclusively to it.

He could live with that. He had to.

He was on the eve of pulling off some of the greatest treachery and rebellion, he knew, since Satan and his legion were cast out of Heaven.

Mogadishu was just an appetizer. Sudan, on the other hand, was a hunter's paradise, nothing but choice specials on the menu for their operation. It was a smorgasbord, in fact, of terrorists, suicide bombers, weapons dealers, assassins and so on. Hell, there were so many training camps spread all over the largest country in Africa, he figured nothing short of a few tactical nukes could wipe out the legions of international thugs and murderers that came here from as far away as the Philippines for R and R, sharpening skills, planning operations before they were shipped out for jihad.

It certainly bolstered his confidence, not to mention swelled the old pride a little more, that the moment and the trying times ahead would get handled together with the two other like-minded and nameless, faceless almighty black ops marching beside him.

He advanced down the narrow concrete corridor, gloomy light thrown about from naked bulbs powered by a generator. And there he was, the man of the hour, Gambler saw. The door to Colonel Ayeed Bashir's office was open, the lean hawk face in mustache and neatly trimmed beard glancing up from behind his desk. Gambler felt the grin loosening up now, decided to hold the expression, aware he—the three of them—held all the cards. Who was good or bold enough to call their bluff?

They were in lockstep with their escort, two soldiers front, two lieutenants pulling up the rear, AK-74s all around. Flanked by his comrades, Gambler shot them each a grin. Tim and Jim Smith—Warlock and Cyclops respectively—were likewise ghosts in the black-ops machine. He didn't have to question their guts when all backs were to the wall, their experience to deal with and blast or simply walk out the other side of crisis, nor their commitment to the endgame when the blanket was stripped away from over the pit and all good Cobras lunged out, biting. Too many past ops to count, much less recall all the history together, but both men bore the scars of war, badges of honor. For instance, the handle that Jimbo, he knew, gave himself had shot out of his mouth, no hesitation, as if he were proud of the land mine in Afghanistan that had cleaved off half his face, sheared off the left ear, with hot shrapnel tearing out the eye. Warlock had had a close combat encounter with a Yemeni terrorist who didn't like getting a light load of Semtex and Stingers and who was fond of knives. The purple scar ran from the knuckle of the middle finger, all the way to his bicep. It had been a rare occasion, not being there beside one or both ops, but the story went that not only had Warlock deflected the initial sweep of the Yemeni's blade, using his arm as a shield, but also he'd ripped the knife out of his hand before the guy had "Allah akhbar" out of his mouth. The follow-up counterattack left little to the imagination, but after, he heard, Warlock dropped the Yemeni with a right the pride of any heavyweight, and he'd gone to work, performing surgery on the poor bastard even as he nearly bled out himself. Warlock loathed and feared knives to this day, unless, of course, he did the cutting.

There would be no knife play tonight, Gambler knew, three Berettas to use between them when the vibrating signal came through on their pagers.

The three of them had been to the colonel's command post in southern Sudan twice before, ironing out the details for this third visit, where they were supposed to land Bashir some missiles, warheads packed with VX, which could be fitted on the Russian gunships outside. Unfortunately for the colonel, who was known in the region as Bashir the Crucifier or the Crucifying Colonel, he would never get his hands on the kind of hardware that would most certainly wipe out all the black rage against their Muslim oppressors.

Gambler had laid out their individual moves, redefined their roles while they were choppered out of Somalia by company liaisons. So far the setup was sticking to form.

He wasn't even through the door when the vibration trembled from the hip down. One minute and counting, and he knew their guy would be on the money.

Gambler watched Bashir glance up from whatever intel and maps he'd been perusing, no doubt planning tomorrow's massacre of Nilotes. The colonel sniffed the air, Gambler glimpsing Warlock checking his watch, counting off the numbers.

"Well?" Bashir stood erect, folded his hands behind his back. "I trust this time you bring me good news?"

Gambler ticked off the seconds in his head, Bashir darting a thinly veiled look of contempt over their faces, before anger broke through the expression.

"What? Why are you standing there, grinning like an idiot?"

"I bring you the best of all possible news, Colonel. You are the man of the millennium. We salute you, but we always did."

Bashir squeezed the bridge of his nose, sighed. "I do not have all night for these shallow attempts to curry favor. Spit it out."

He barked at Warlock, "You! Why do you keep looking at your watch?"

Warlock tapped the watch, shaking his head, frowning, then the three of them were grinning at Bashir, Cyclops giving his package a squeeze, stating his balls seemed to be itching and did the good Colonel have some kind of powder or salve handy?

Bashir looked at his men, grunting, appeared uncertain whether to laugh or scream in rage, fighting to keep his composure. "Okay. I watch your American TV sometimes, but the old videos, collector's items I believe you call them, before everything in your country became sex and violence. I get it, I can take some joking, strange as it is. I like comedy myself. Is this some sort of bad *Three Stooges* routine?"

"No routine," Warlock said.

"No act," Cyclops added.

"His nuts really itch," Gambler said, and chuckled.

"He's also got this thing about jars and collecting feces in them."

Before Bashir could pry himself from a clear state of confused revulsion, Gambler heard the rolling thunder next, saw the Sudanese colonel and his men freeze, dust floating from the ceiling, walls and floor shaking, as the first wave of explosions rocked the compound. Gambler briefly savored the sound of music that floated from the far eastern edge.

On the money.

Gambler allowed a moment for his AC-130 Spectre to spit it out for him, then he had the Beretta out and aimed squarely between Bashir's eyes.

CHAPTER FIVE

The gist of the Cobra leader's assault plan on the Sudanese colonel's garrison was a straight aerial bombardment followed by the troops blitzing into the smoke, dropping whatever enemy numbers popped up along the way. Bolan could live with that, as long as the key players were in place for the scooping, and the AC-130 Spectre smashed the bulk of the enemy on its first and only strafe of the fort. What he didn't much care for was Asp and Mamba assigned to his Blue Team. It struck Bolan as if Collins were glueing his serpents up his six, there to monitor his every move, made sure he followed orders, nothing cowboy, as the good major kept stating. Or was it something else?

No time to ponder any number of dark possibilities. Bolan was seconds away from plunging into the fires of combat, in charge of Blue Team, their role defined by Collins.

The Spectre was already wreaking havoc on the garrison as the soldier led Blue Team on a hard charge across the grassy plain, M-16/M-203 combo searching for live ones. It was always quite the fearsome sight, Bolan knew, to behold the devastating hell an AC-130 could dump on a target. Entire sections of designated walls were blown away, leaving behind any number of gaping holes through which to penetrate and make it up close and personal. He assumed the Spectre had razed the troop barracks inside those walls, catching most hands asleep at that hour, since Bolan spied any number of dark scarecrow figures sailing for the sky. It was a pummeling that shattered the senses, shook the earth under his feet as the 105 mm Howitzer, twin Vulcan Gatlings and Bofors 40 mm roared and flamed down from the port side of the flying leviathan. The Executioner knew that no matter how flayed and shocked and numb, there would be armed survivors somewhere near that firestorm.

Ideally Bolan would have preferred their seven-hundred-foot combat jump land them on the enemy's back door before the Spectre lowered the boom. A decent surveillance first, swathed in the blackness of night, assess numbers, machine-gun nests, any weak points around the garrison where they could slip through, quick and quiet. Collins insisted they do it his way. Sat imagery and Collins's HUMINT would have to cut it. While the Spectre soared in to pound the fort, Bolan and his teammates had jumped from the C-130. DZ was roughly two hundred yards west of ground zero, the night erupting ahead, the sky shimmering from the blasts marching through the compound. While Bolan was to bull Blue Team into the compound, Collins and his Black Team would mop up any runners, secure a number of vehicles to the east that were still intact. This was only round one of the Sudanese foray, as mapped out by Collins during the brief in the air. Colonel Ayeed Bashir, known as the Crucifying Colonel, having staked or impaled entire black Christian villages in the south, had been on Bolan's list of bad guys to take care of for some time. Opportunity now called, but the sort of justice Collins was bringing to the colonel and his top lieutenants paled in comparison to what Bolan believed the butcher deserved. From there, assuming they were successful in bagging Bashir and cronies, commandeered vehicles would take the team to a terrorist training camp, some fifteen miles northeast as the buzzard flew, where the second assault would be launched. Collins had a big surprise in store for that camp, a fuel-air explosive to be exact, but one that was packed with what he called NARCON-D.

That was up and coming, a long night ahead for all of them, so Bolan focused on the task at hand. According to his handheld monitor, the three black ops, their beacons flashing bright and strong on the screen, were in the command post, midway down and tucked up against the west wall, waiting to be escorted with prisoners to Collins. Whoever they were—Company shooters Bolan assumed—they had been engaged in some ruse to deliver chemical weapons to Bashir, stringing him along the whole time until the net could be dropped over him by Cobra Force. It sure seemed that Collins could make all the right moves, armed with all the answers, every critical piece of intelligence at his beck and call. For some reason that alone bothered Bolan.

Senses choked with a mesh of fumes, everything from burning fuel to eviscerated bodies strewed before him, the Executioner led Blue Team into the smoke. They were screaming just beyond the thinning pall, dancing around as rubble and bodies hit the ground when Bolan hit the trigger of his assault rifle. He fanned off to the left, directing concentrated 3-round bursts at armed shadows too shocked by the Spectre's hammering to get it together. Ten or more went down as Blue Team opened up in concert, Sudanese hardcases flung in all directions under the blistering autofire. Firing on the fly, waxing a trio of Sudanese hardmen scraping themselves up off the ground, the soldier headed for the command post. Whoever this vaunted trio the good major had bragged on, Bolan already had a mental picture of three more carbon copies of Collins. That, too, indicated not everything was as he was led to believe.

IT WAS A MOMENT to savor, all the sweat and blood to get it this far, seeing the light flare on in the colonel's eyes, Bashir standing there, torn between outrage and terror, the man looking set to soil himself. Gambler laughed, allowed his comrades their own victory jig as he heard their pistols barking, everything so far by the numbers. More music to his ears, the sounds of death as he heard the two soldiers—already deemed nonessential personnel going in—grunt, cry out as rounds tore into them, casting them aside, so much refuse. They were thudding to the floor, in rhythm to the beat of the ferocious thunder-doom of the Spectre, when Warlock and Cyclops both roared at the lieutenants to freeze.

"Do you want to explain yourself?"

"Nothing to explain, Colonel. We screwed you. On your knees, put your hands behind your back."

Bashir hesitated, so Gambler delivered a crack over his skull with the butt of his pistol, buckling his knees, then shoving him down onto the floor. Warlock and Cyclops were all over their own catches, relieving them of their assault rifles, fastening on the plastic cuffs, binding their hands behind their back. All set, or so Gambler hoped, aware they were hardly on their way, home free. With the compound under siege he could be sure a few of Bashir's more loyal following would have something to say about them skipping off with the Crucifying Colonel.

"I don't know what you think you're—"

"Yeah, yeah." Gambler fixed the cuffs on Bashir, jacked him standing. "You're thinking you've got a hundred men ready to cut us to ribbons when we walk out of here. But you hear that sound, Colonel? That's a Spectre out there. You ever seen one of those monsters at work? No? You'll see what it can do on the way out. And those hundred-plus soldiers you think will come running to your rescue? Most of them were blown to Hell where they slept in their bunks."

"They say even the Devil needs friends," Cyclops said, toting the AK-74.

"Guess you've been chosen to be our pal," Warlock added.

Gambler was hauling Bashir to the door when he heard, then saw the commotion. They were sliding into view, maybe fifteen Sudanese soldiers, assault rifles out, calling for Bashir, shadows in flickering light that threatened to wink out from the sheer shock rattle of the Spectre's pounding.

Bashir chuckled. "I believe you were saying?"

"Hey, assholes!" Gambler yelled, locking an arm around Bashir's throat, lugging his human shield into the doorway. "You can see I've got the good colonel, so I suggest you throw down your weapons and let us be on our way."

Bashir struggled, croaked out, "They are not to leave here alive!"

"Wrong thing to say, pal. Warlock!" Gambler growled over his shoulder. "Get on the blower, and please inform me Cobra Leader is in the neighborhood."

IF WILD CARD THOUGHT he was doing all the dirty work, he hadn't said it, but Stone's quiet compliance with the battle scheme still left Collins wondering. Blue Team was shouldering the brunt of the killing, taking on the greater risks by being, essentially, the first and only ones through the fort's door, but Collins and his Black Team weren't exactly looking at a stroll on the beach. It was a faint hope, something about Stone feeling more wrong with each turn on the mission, but Collins wouldn't mind if the man caught a bullet inside the walls. And he had almost given the order to Asp....

Patience, he told himself. Maybe later.

Collins veered in from his southeast vector, closing on the motor pool, pouring out a blanket of hot lead that mowed down the first wave of armed shadows beating a path for the smattering of APCs, Jeeps and Hummers. Like a well-oiled machine, Collins charging point, Black Team fanned out in a skirmish line, leapfrogging from vehicles, five assault rifles flaming away as the second wave of Sudanese soldiers burst out of the gate. Three well-placed warheads from their M-203s, Collins setting the example, and the triburst of fireballs ripped the heart out of the second batch. Whatever vehicles they didn't need would be wasted by the Spectre on a second flyby.

"Gambler to Cobra Leader! Come in!"

"Move it down the line!" Collins ordered his troops. "Find us a few rides and power them up!" They were gone next, Collins hunkering beside a Hummer, unclipping the handheld radio off his belt. He thumbed the button, acknowledged Gambler.

"I hope you're in the ballpark, Cobra Leader. We've got problems blocking our way out of the CP, roughly fifteen irate Sudanese."

"I'll handle it."

He was about to sign off, raise Stone when he heard the shouting and din of weapons fire blast out the radio.

"Looks like the cavalry just arrived, Cobra Leader. Appreciate your promptness."

"Then I'll see you in a few. Cobra Leader out."

No point in calling Wild Card—the damn guy was way ahead of him. Well, the night was young, and the contingent of terrorists on the backburner could prove a little more nasty chore than a bunch of shell-shocked Sudanese rabble. Not only that, but Collins kept thinking Wild Card just might have that accident by friendly fire yet.

BOLAN HANDED OUT the orders for Asp, Mamba and Tsunami to cover their backs. He caught a look in Asp's eyes, wondered briefly if that was defiance or something else, but the trio peeled off to comply with his order. Sons of bitches, he thought, what the hell was going on with them?

The Executioner heard the shouting inside the doorway, threats going back and forth between a number of Sudanese and who he assumed was Gambler. He gave the compound a quick search, a second's flare of paranoia warning him it would have been best to watch his own six, then found his rearguard take concealment behind a Toyota Land Cruiser miraculously unscathed. The trio of Cobra commandos began selecting the few armed runners on the loose, chopping them down with concentrated 3-round bursts, enemy return fire brief and wild, the night just about over for the enemy. Two more shadows, Bolan spied, were reeling in the smoking rubble of what had been their barracks, blown off their feet next by the Cobra triburst.

Bolan hand signaled Roadrunner and Brick to take flank on the opposite side of the doorway, Roller and Bulldozer to fall in behind him. A check inside the doorway, and the soldier found both sides locked in a standoff, each side trying to outshout and outbluster the other.

"Last time! Put the fucking guns down and eat some floor! I'll shoot this asshole colonel of yours and we'll take our chances!"

"You are not walking out of here!"

"I'm here to tell you, asshole, you are fucking with the wrong Yankees! I'll save you for last, honey, gut you like a fish!"

Bolan primed a frag grenade, figured a squad or so of Sudanese, dead ahead, twenty yards. They had split up, halving the force to each side of the hallway, he saw, a few muzzles of assault rifles poking out the doorway closest to their intended point of entry. The tricky part, he knew, would come if Gambler and pals decided to throw some rounds into the chaos, a ricochet or even a straight shot catching Bolan as he bulled into the fight.

No risk, no victory.

The Executioner told his teammates he would be the first one in, and rolled the steel egg down the floor. It bounded up, square in the heart of the Sudanese pack. Bolan hung back, hugging the wall as the blast erupted. They were screaming, a few bodies chewed, head to toe, by countless lethal steel bits. Two mauled Sudanese were scraping themselves off the floor when the Executioner charged into billowing smoke and cut loose with autofire.

A WARNING WOULD HAVE been nice, the grenade detonating before he realized what the plan was, but Gambler had human cover just in case some shrapnel came tearing his way. Bashir screamed, flinching, Gambler hauling him back deeper inside the office. He watched the smoke, Warlock and Cyclops squeezing beside him.

The smoke was hanging thick, Sudanese snakes writhing around, then the shooting started.

He was a big dark guy and he moved like lightning, a pro for damn sure.

Gambler watched him work.

Three commandos raced in behind the big shooter, combined autofire eating up whatever was crawling, kneeling or screaming. Blood spattered the scarred walls, bodies spinning, toppling, big shooter hitting the doorway where a few Sudanese rats might be hiding. No hesitation, no wasted moves as the big shooter flamed away with his M-16, sweeping the room, leaving no doubt in Gambler's mind their immediate problems were over. One Sudanese was crabbing his way, a big bloody slug sliding out of the smoke when the big shooter rolled over him and put a round in the back of his head.

"Sweet," Gambler called out, whistled.

"Nice work, guy," Warlock said.

"What I call grand slamming it," Cyclops added. "That damn near makes me want to cut a big fat steamer in a jar."

"You must be the Gambler."

Gambler was about to show the big shooter a winning smile, then saw something in those icy blue eyes that froze him. What the hell was he looking at like that? he wondered. Was that judgment? Taking a measuring of the three of them, not liking too much what he saw?

"That would be me. And you are?"

"Stone. Shake a leg. I don't want to keep your buddy Collins waiting."

Gambler looked at the big shooter as he turned away and melted into the smoke. What was that he just heard? A little tone in the voice? A badass and smartass package on the team?

Gambler shoved Bashir ahead, thinking things were just about to get real interesting. This Stone didn't fit the bill of a few of the black ops who had signed on for what was really going to go down. Gambler read the man as a serious problem.

And a definite liability, a walking killing thorn in the side who would have to be dealt with in no uncertain terms at some point.

"ASSUME ALL OF YOU have been introduced to the new guy?"

"You could say that," Gambler said.

"Sorta, kinda," Warlock added.

"Yeah, we got all warm and fuzzy together back at the CP," Cyclops said.

Bolan was making his way toward Collins when Gambler, Warlock and Cyclops handed their prisoners off to other Cobra commandos. The C-130 was on the plain, waiting to take the latest round of bad guys. It was time to shake things up a little, light a fire, the Executioner decided, his gut getting more knotted with bad instinct with each phase.

"You," the Executioner growled at Asp. "Next time I give you an order, you better shag your ass like it's on fire. We clear?"

Bolan watched the commando's jaw drop, Asp looking to Collins.

"He's clear," Collins said. "Move it out, soldier. What was that all about, Colonel?"

"You tell me."

Collins worked a look down the trio of black ops, then told Bolan, "Grab a seat in my ride, Stone. We've got a lot of work still to do. I don't want to have to hang around Sudan any longer than necessary."

Bolan hung back a moment as Collins marched off toward a Hummer, then fell in. He couldn't shake the ominous feeling the Cobra leader wanted him retired from the mission, and in permanent terms.

CHAPTER SIX

Abdulaziz Nayid believed he had endured too much pain and suffering, horror and humiliation at the hands of the infidels to now waste away in Sudan. Hate, and the hunger for revenge, had kept him alive up to that point, but he wanted more than burning in the fires of unsated vengeance, or wallowing in fantasy about all the death and destruction he wished to wreak on America. What he needed was blood.

Which meant he needed action, not sweating out the daily grind of PT and tactical exercises, sweeping stone hovels with his AK, shooting up paper targets or learning how to mix the components for pure TNT or how to build a dirty bomb. His pure anger and certainty he was chosen by God for greatness demanded far more than the sharpening of skills on hostage takedowns, or trying to stay awake and look interested during the long hours of classes given by their various appointed leaders on urban warfare, among other tactics in dispensing justice on their enemies. But when would he be called?

Sure, he knew he was one of the lucky to have escaped Afghanistan when the Americans had turned most of the country into a smoking crater with their ferocious and, in his mind, cowardly bombing campaign. He had lost and left behind slews of fellow Muslim fighters, many of whom, he knew, had been either buried alive or vaporized by incendiary bombs in the caves, holy warriors he now believed were in Paradise, smiling down, urging him to avenge them all.

Beyond the rage, he felt a moment's pang of sorrow, aware he had forsaken much, and so far achieved very little. He had a wife and six children in Pakistan, after all, wondered if they were even still alive, aware he would never see his family again unless he wished to risk venturing into Karachi, arrested by Pakistani authorities who had proved themselves traitors as they had thrown themselves in league with the Americans. Loss, he thought, seemed to be the way of his life, but he was tired of losing.

It was time to strike back.

It seemed like only yesterday, that harrowing trek northwest through Afghanistan, Iranian sympathizers whisking him and a band of fighters safely into their country. From the beginning they had been informed they would be shipped to Sudan, under the protective umbrella of Colonel Bashir, whose own loyalties to Is-

lamic jihad were suspect. Nayid was certain he was mo-
tivated to grant them all safe haven as long as the cash
kept coming. They had been told they were to train
harder, pray more and with feverish passion to implore
God to keep them strong and faithful.

That a big event was in store for all of them.

Their Iranian benefactor had said a lot, but told them
little.

He moved through the night, away from his camo-
netted tent, watching the deep shadows around the perimeter where light glowing from the few strung bulbs
powered by the generator was swallowed by the nooks
and crannies of the surrounding hills. Lugging his
AK-74, he looked up the hill, peering into the dark.
Softly he cursed the sentry he was going to relieve,
spotted the winking eye of a cigarette, a veritable beacon to any threat in the scrubland beyond their camp.

There would be no point in chastising the man, he
knew, rethinking his stance on the smoker, sure there
was no danger in this part of Sudan where they were
protected by Bashir and his soldiers. Sentry duty was
long, hard, boring. As long as none of them were caught
napping, a cigarette couldn't possibly hurt. They were
sixty-three strong, heavily armed, all of them brothers
in jihad, even though they came from various countries.

Their goal was the same.

Complete and utter destruction of America and Israel.

He decided he was brooding, wasting energy on

things he couldn't change. He skirted past the target range, felt the grin cut his lips at the sight of the current and former three American Presidents, paper targets riddled with bullet holes. Someday, God willing…

Quick but hardly quiet, flinching as stones rattled under his boots, he saw the sentry pitch away the smoke, ash and flame arcing away, the man there, then gone, melting back into some cubbyhole. Something felt wrong.

"In here."

The voice hissed out of the black hole. Closing, he strained to bring the face into view. There was just enough moon and starlight for him to make out the bearded visage of Musif the Yemeni.

"What is it?"

"Shh. Keep your voice down."

He followed Musif's stare to the south, looked back, found the Yemeni searching the black sky. "I thought I heard something. I thought I saw something move out there."

Nayid kept scouring the plain, the sky, the hill's ridgeline. He didn't see or hear anything.

"You've been up here too long. Go get some sleep."

Musif seemed to ignore his relief. Finally he grunted, "Perhaps you're right."

"Go, then."

Musif was climbing out of the hole, Nayid feeling the hackles rising on the back of his neck as he sensed some presence in the night, began scouring the ridgeline. For a second he believed he was simply infected by Musif's paranoia, then he heard the soft chug. It was quiet enough, but it sounded like a cannon shot in Nayid's ears.

Especially when he felt the hot gore splatter his face and glimpsed Musif toppling back into his hole.

Nayid realized what was happening, but he knew it was too late to stop it. It didn't seem right, and there was an instant where he wanted to curse this abominable injustice, aware he would never taste the glory of revenge against the infidels.

The tall black figure appeared to materialize out of the very earth when Nayid framed him through his haze of terror and outrage. He was taking up slack on the AK's trigger when he heard that dreaded coughing noise again, felt the hammer blow between his eyes that turned the night into impenetrable blackness.

THE EXECUTIONER used the smoker's cherry eye as his homing beacon. Two double taps from his sound-suppressed Beretta and they were down, crunching into the hole from where they had risen, lights doused instantly from one 9 mm subsonic round each to the head. If Collins's intel was on the money, Bolan was alone on the ridge, but he searched his surroundings just the same, senses tuned to any sound or movement all around. No point in getting carried away with any newfound trust in Collins, since he was the one hung out there to dry if it went to hell before the show started.

The decision for the soldier to go it alone and take down the sentries came straight from Collins on the ride in. Again the Executioner didn't trust the battle scheme, full of holes and any number of dire possibilities, but he was grateful to some extent to be the odd man out, trusting his own skills, breathing clean air away from the others. Which left him wondering if Collins was thinking in the heat of battle maybe he'd catch some errant friendly fire.

He had accepted his role, neither too eager nor showing any surprise, though he hid his suspicion that Collins was suddenly going against the grain, using Wild Card as a solo act when the man had been espousing the virtues of teamwork up to then. If there was something devious behind this sudden shift in strategy, then Bolan would treat his Cobra so-called teammates the same as any terrorist here. He might be getting paranoid, viewed as a lone wolf, not one of the guys, a loose cannon, but Bolan didn't think so. He couldn't remember the last time his gut instinct had been wrong.

They had ridden across the plain, two Hummers and one APC strong, coming up on the enemy's south end, the commandeered vehicles now parked in a wadi, all of them waiting on the C-130 to drop its package. All the maps, sat imagery and high-tech apparatus at the Cobra leader's disposal were paving the way, so far, so good, but this outing was meant to reel in the biggest number of human sharks yet. Aside from his weapons, handheld, spare clips and grenades, Bolan was also weighted down with a nylon satchel choked with plastic cuffs.

Sixty-plus terrorists were supposed to go down under a cloud of sleeping gas. NARCON-D would be released, a small fuel-air explosive that would disperse the potent tranquilizer over the entire camp. Or so the plan went. If it was up to Bolan, he'd just as soon bomb the place off the planet with a dose of thermite. Only he did understand Collins's explanation there might be a mother lode of valuable intelligence stored at the camp. The major talked about training videos, storehouses of explosives and other agents that might be used to build bombs. He went on about training manuals, the need to get inside their heads, "tune up the enemy" with Q and A, learn about any operations on the table.

He wanted facts and figures and every shred of intel on hand. He wanted a lot, as far as Bolan was concerned. Sudan, he knew, was littered with dozens of camps just like this one. What was to say there was anything even here remotely smacking of valuable intelligence? If there was—and Collins seemed certain the gold mine was in the camp—how did the major know? It was something of a monstrous bad joke, he thought, that terrorists could train, arm themselves and operate right under full view of Western eyes in the sky. They came here from as far away as Indonesia, the worst of the worst, and Bolan had to wonder why this particular camp was chosen. No mistake, Sudan was an outlaw nation, and the explanation from Collins for targeting this bunch was they were paying tribute to Bashir to claim real estate here. Bottom line, Collins stated he was looking to connect all the intelligence dots.

Well, he had been given his thirty minutes and no more to leg it in on the sentries, framed, according to Collins, by heat sensors in the hands of the latest addition of black ops. Aware the smallest beam of light could still reflect off his skin, Bolan had smeared his face, neck and hands with black warpaint. He had done his part, beating the clock by six minutes according to his chronometer. Two cashiered out, and it looked to Bolan as if he was all alone up there. Again Collins's intel was proving so good it struck Bolan as damn near divine. It seemed every step of the mission was orchestrated, contrived, or was the major really that good?

Bolan scanned the camp, his surroundings, waiting for the C-130 to release the bomb, which would be rolled right off the cargo ramp, floating to Earth by parachute. Wind, altitude, weight of package, rate of descent were apparently all factored in by Collins's supercomputers, the blast preset to go off a hundred feet above the camp. If the package sailed past the camp and detonated beyond the perimeter, if a roving terrorist spotted it coming down and they ran like hell, if they themselves had protective masks on hand...

Stowing the Beretta, Bolan snugged on his gas mask, then unslung his assault rifle. It was a sprawling camp, situated in a valley, ringed by low black hills. Tents, large and small, were all camo-draped, the terrorist training grounds complete with stone mock-ups, target ranges, a PT course, Toyota Land Cruisers and motor-bikes spread around the perimeter. Not much light, but Collins said his guys would arc a few flares over the camp.

Bolan was settling in beside the dead when he spotted several armed shadows streaming from tents. He sensed the agitation down there, silently urging the C-130 to show when the handheld radio on one of his victims crackled. They were calling for Musif, looking his way. What had set off their bells and whistles? Bolan wondered. Had they left behind a possum at the garrison who had radioed ahead?

The soldier gripped his assault rifle, scoured the sky south when he made out the faint rumble, spotted the black bulk of the Hercules. It was sailing in, maybe five thousand feet overhead, when he saw the canopy open. The way the enemy was scurrying about, Bolan suspected Collins was about to find the mother of all monkey wrenches hurled into his plan.

MUSTAFA ALZHARI found the order outrageous at first. That was two days ago, when their Iranian sponsor had called over the secured line, informing him they would be attacked, arrested, that they were to give up peacefully, the assault on the camp would be nonlethal. They were to comply, go along with whatever was demanded of them by whoever their captors were. The Iranian told him to fear not, keep the faith, that the most glorious victory of Islam to date was just ahead, and he and his comrades in Sudan were to accept what would appear to be an ominous fate.

God would take care of them, lead them to a glory they could never imagine. Or so the Iranian cryptically stated.

Two days to think about it, since the Iranian didn't seem willing to answer his questions, and the more Alzhari mulled it over the more he found the strange request absurd. Or was it? Naturally he had gone to Bashir, their guardian in Sudan, but the colonel had laughed off his anxiety and concerns. They were in Sudan, the colonel stated, why worry? Not even the Western imperialist warmongers dared to even set one foot inside his country.

He had wanted to push the matter, only quietly gathered his top lieutenants, put them on high alert. No point in shaking the nerves of the rest of the fighters under his command. He went about his business, training, teaching class, secure in the knowledge he was, indeed, in a country so isolated, so feared by even the most brazen of Western warmongers he decided to take Bashir at his worst. Even still, why would the Iranian—?

He heard the commotion beyond the flap of his tent. He was marching outside, taking in the numbers of his men suddenly up and flailing about all over the camp.

He heard how there was no response from Bashir when Habib had tried to call the garrison for their normal nightly check-in. He saw three of his men moving toward the hill, calling out to the sentry who was supposed to be up there. He felt the fear cutting through him, aware there was all of a sudden too much mystery swathing the night for all of this to be mere coincidence. He heard the rumbling overhead next, looking skyward with the others when he saw the object floating to Earth. The massive dark shape sailing overheard, even at the high altitude, was unmistakable.

He had seen enough C-130s, Spectres and B-52s in Afghanistan to know they were being attacked. And as a searchlight was framed on the object falling to Earth, he knew that long slender object was a missile attached to the parachute.

He shouted a warning to run, but if that was one of those fuel-air explosives coming down there wouldn't be enough time to flee the terrible fires about to be unleashed.

Still he had to try, bolting, sprinting for all he was worth, working on a feverish prayer to God to spare him the fires of the coming hell.

BOLAN TAGGED the threesome with a raking burst, left to right, the eruption of autofire confirming the fear he sensed from the camp proper that they were being hit.

The enemy was now on high alert, shadows racing out of the tents, weapons up and ready, RPGs wielded here and there. They were pointing at the sky, a few of them darting from the descending package, other terrorists holding their ground, firing their AKs skyward.

The night lit up next as the flares sizzled in, igniting an umbrella of white-red light, then the big package blew.

Bolan was selecting targets, out of the hole, sidling off toward the east. Return fire was wild at best, a swarm of lead locusts eating up the rock and the earth yards behind the soldier. The Executioner rattled off 3-round bursts, catching runners on the fly, then took in the cloud of NARCON-D. The way it blew, Bolan could be sure there would be more fighters than sleepers when the smoke settled.

The gray-white cloud ballooned, swelling out, but from the deep southern perimeter. Maybe ten to fifteen terrorists were falling, a few more reeling around as the wave rolled over them, but Collins's guys up in the Herc had missed their mark.

The Executioner knew all of them were in for a long and bloody night.

CHAPTER SEVEN

Collins feared the moment had all the earmarks of a horrendous disaster. Somehow his two guys on board the Herc had either misread their screens, miscalculated math that was nearly done down to the inch for them or a sudden gust of wind had blown the chute off target. Where it was supposed to blow dead center in the camp, the NARCON-D had nearly gone off in his face.

The truth was, it had. The shock wave of the detonation alone nearly dropped him in his tracks.

Collins heard the vicious curse trapped in his mask, a muffled roar that swelled and echoed through his head. His M-16 was out and ready, but he was nearly blinded in the cloud so there was nothing to clearly shoot. There was, however, shooting all over the camp, something—one of his guys—bumping into him, Collins aware Wild Card was out there, taking care of business or being taken care of. The cloud's dispersal would cover one square city block, which meant if the enemy spotted them when they finally burst out of the cloud, they had lost the edge. Communication, other than the handheld radios, was out the window since the com links couldn't snug on, much less allow for fitting the mike under the masks. It would take ten minutes at the outside for the cloud's tranquilizing potency to diminish to the point that they could shed the protective gear, communicate. By then, Collins knew they could all be dead.

It was a goat screw beyond his own worst miscalculations. He had a brief moment where he saw the future, felt the coming stab of bitter anger, wiping egg off his face, Stone standing there, looking at him, as silent as a statue but itching to say, "I told you so."

Whoever he'd jolted into, Collins shoved him in the direction away from the wrath of the most blistering retorts of autofire. West then, and with any luck...

He could see flare light now, armed shadows cropping up, his guys taking his cue on instinct and following his vector. Collins was drawing target acquisition, nearly out of the cloud when he heard the cry of pain beside him. Turning, he found one of his own, a spurt of blood shooting out his chest, spin then topple on his back.

IF COBRA FORCE WAS smothered in the NARCON-D cloud, Bolan knew for the moment he was one hundred percent on his own. But what was new? he figured. The longer the campaign ground on, the larger he felt that bull's-eye growing on his back.

No time now to concern himself with what Cobra did or didn't do, the Executioner was advancing down the hill, drilling precision bursts into the closest hardmen, spinning them around, human compasses dead on their feet, spraying blood. Bolan chose the RPG threats next as they popped into his gun sights. He nailed one rocket man as the terrorist swung his way, the missile sailing overhead, slamming into the hillside. The explosion rocked the night, Bolan then adding his own fireball into a group of maybe eight as they raced for cover behind a Land Cruiser. The blast took out the vehicle, the warrior changing clips, searching out some temporary concealment as lead snapped past his scalp. Bolan eased into a narrow depression and began to arm frag and incendiary grenades, hurling the steel eggs at armed runners, alert for any new players who showed up in masks or toted M-16s. Whatever Collins's original scheme, it was all but shot to hell. Everyone was, essentially, on his own.

A trio of detonations marched through clustered packs of terrorists, Bolan bringing up the M-16, hosing down anything he found in caftan, smock, skullcaps or headcloth. Forget any gold mine of intel, Bolan knew he and Cobra Force were in for the fight of their lives.

He chased down a pair of runners beating flight westward, stitching them up the spine, the rising bursts finally blowing off skullcaps in dark eruptions of blood and brain matter.

And Bolan sighted the first casualties for Cobra.

They were bulling their way out of the cloud, far to the west, a line of autofire punching out through the smoke, connecting enemy flesh. He spotted one, then two bodies in masks being dragged and dumped behind a Land Cruiser.

The Executioner decided to stick to the far eastern edge, aware that Collins would be in a state of perhaps mindless rage over the loss of two men. Couple that with bad gut feeling about the others, and Bolan figured it best to lone-wolf the action.

The Executioner lurched up out of the hole and waded into the slaughter zone.

ALZHARI COULD HARDLY be positive this attack was nonlethal, as foretold by the Iranian, since his own men were dying all around him. Either way, with all the shooting, screaming, the crunching din of explosions all over the camp, he wasn't taking any chances.

Not when the massive smoke cloud blew, a tidal wave of gray fumes sweeping his way, the night turned into day by flares, the glimpse of his own men cut down by unseen shooters telling him he'd better act or his number was up.

It was sheer dumb luck the AK-74 was within easy reach, one of the trio of his fighters who had been racing for the hill blown off his feet by an invisible shooter, the weapon flung back his direction. He was picking it up when the cloud washed over him, tentacles of gas—

tasteless and odorless—flung in his face. The assault rifle was in his hands, eyes tearing all of a sudden, when his legs began to buckle, head swimming in nausea, sight fuzzy. For a moment he couldn't believe this was happening, a gas bomb—it could be a nerve agent for all he knew—dropping over the camp. It was wrong to the point of absurd, even betrayal, he considered, that the Iranian had known about this assault, not clued him in on any of the finer details.

He knew the more gruesome particulars about nerve agents, VX and Sarin, having specifically worked with them in a laboratory in Afghanistan. If he was in fact dying, it was painless, quick and clean. There was no vomit spewing from his mouth, no convulsions as if he were hooked up to live electrical wires, no bowels cutting loose, no labored breathing. He was collapsing, a boneless heap of rubber, when he saw the masked invaders surge out of the cloud. A few of his men were holding on, firing wild bursts toward them when they were riddled with autofire. The world was turning hazy next, sight and sound fading fast, when he saw one of the black-clad masked shooters roll his way. It was a feeble attempt, senses going numb, but he scrabbled his hands for the assault rifle. He thought he heard muffled voices going back and forth, arguing it sounded, deciding, he believed, whether he should live or die.

"Looks like your lucky night, asshole."

The AK was in his hands, coming up, when the boot shot out of nowhere and slammed him in the jaw.

COLLINS CONTROLLED his rage as he stripped off the masks. Two of his men were down. His fingers were checking for a pulse, finding none. Asp and Roadrunner were history. He wouldn't leave them behind on the battlefield, of course, provided any of them walked away in one piece, then he considered secret knowledge. There was, after all, some good news here, but nobody outside the inner loop would need to know what the upshot was.

Collins found himself hunkered beside a Land Cruiser, his men raking the campgrounds with relentless autofire. Gambler, Warlock and Cyclops, sticking together like he knew they would, were nailing terrorists without discrimination, blasting anything that moved, crawled or was already out cold from the NARCON-D. Collins had just gotten into a brief pissing contest with Gambler over who and how many they should take when he'd recognized Mustafa Alzhari, a chemical wizard with connections to North Korean operatives who could land the Muslim world some very nasty ingredients for scraping together a weapon of mass destruction. One to the jaw, a satisfying and very resounding crack of bone, and Collins had Alzhari laid out and cuffed. Collins bellowed through the mask, tapping two of his commandos on the shoulder, ordering them to cease fire and start cuffing live ones—no more than ten if they could find that many. He had come in, wanting to haul off more, but he'd take what he could get at that point. Whether they were first- or second-tier terrorists didn't really matter any longer. Personal survival was tantamount to mission success. Besides, he had the camp commander, and if the bastard didn't want to talk, he could spill other guts or blood to loosen Alzhari's tongue.

He checked the eastern end of the camp where—lo and behold—Stone was proving himself a one-man wrecking crew. There were more bodies and body parts, more wreckage strewed around the unmistakable big masked shooter than even Collins could have believed the guy capable of racking up.

The sight of Gambler and pals wasting valuable HUMINT, pumping rounds into figures clearly punch-drunk and writhing on the ground, grabbed his immediate attention. He ran up to Gambler.

"Hey! I wouldn't mind a few live ones."

Gambler was consumed by blood lust, he saw, understandable given the circumstances and the fact they were up against the worst of the worst, but there were a few top dogs he needed found, confirmed dead or alive.

"Why don't you go help Stone," he told Gambler.

"And?"

He knew what Gambler was asking, but shook his head. "We just lost two men."

"Anybody on our payroll?"

"Asp. So I need every shooter—at least until the finish line is in sight."

Gambler grunted, marched off to assist Stone, who was having a field day butchering the enemy.

What a waste of superior talent it would prove, Collins thought. Ten ass-kickers like Wild Card and he figured he could conquer the world, then realized that soon enough he was going to do just that.

THREE TERRORISTS came charging out of nowhere, bellowing war cries of "God is great." Bolan, focused on waxing three mauled hardmen to his three o'clock, nearly missed the threat boring in from ahead. One lapse was all it would take, but their mouths alerted the soldier to the sudden new danger. A swarm of lead hornets chased Bolan to cover behind a Land Cruiser, slugs drumming the vehicle, blasting out windows, showering glass. He hit the ground on his stomach, extended the assault rifle flat out beneath the chassis and blew them down with a raking burst that chopped them off at the ankles.

The Executioner fed his M-16 a fresh clip, three wails flaying the air, and took in the furious action at the western end where Cobra Force appeared to have bailed themselves out of the frying pan.

Bolan was sliding around the front end of the Land Cruiser, looking to close in on the threesome, but they nearly punched his ticket when a masked shooter beat him to it. The gunner left him to it—glacier-blue eyes inside the bubbled holes of the mask telling him it was Gambler—and swept his compass.

Withering autofire lashed the air, Bolan tagging two rabbits fleeing for the hills. Collins, he heard, began shouting out the orders to his men.

"You want to give us a hand tidying up, Stone? No time to stand there and pat yourself on the back, even though you did some damn nice work here."

The black op's mask was off. Bolan was looking at Gambler, who was kicking at the dead trio, his mouth twisted in a grin.

On a slow turning march, Bolan began his own search of the campgrounds, a burning Land Cruiser coupled with another flare igniting in the sky overhead providing ample light to give the hellzone a walk-through.

"Any live ones you find, Stone, I want them cuffed and dumped into these vehicles. We're out of here and on the Herc in ten minutes."

Collins, mask off, signaling Bolan he could likewise shed his own protective gear, was marching out of a pall of black smoke. The other members of Cobra Force were toeing bodies, snapping cuffs on survivors, slapping drowsy terrorists back to reality.

It was over, at least here, the soldier knew.

Bolan went through the motions of an obligatory search for prisoners but kept one eye on the movements of Collins, Gambler and buddies. They had three terrorists on their knees, barking at them in a mixture of Arabic, Farsi and Pathan. Their knowledge of the languages didn't impress Bolan as much as it told him they knew the lay of those lands, had been around and down some dark and most likely dirty alleys. God only knew what they were really all about, but Bolan sensed a clear and present malevolence about the trio of black ops. Gambler lifted his M-16 when one of the prisoners protested he didn't know where any intelligence materials were hidden and shot him between the eyes.

"Anybody else doesn't want to give up what we know is here?" Gambler shouted.

Warlock repeated the question in Farsi, Cyclops in Pathan.

"Look at this guy," Cyclops growled, chuckling. "He's got a face you just want to slap. So, how about you, honey? Answer the question."

"Or," Warlock added, "you're the next one on the way to Hell to suck on…"

Bolan turned away, went on with his search, checking bodies, weapon ready for any terror Lazarus. He overheard Gambler snarling about booby traps as he manhandled a prisoner into the largest of the tents. Moments later, a shot rang out, then Gambler reappeared with a bulging nylon satchel.

Bolan slowly moved back toward the others, watched the action, listened. Prisoners were dumped into Land Cruisers, threats issued, interspersed with all manner of cursing. Collins ordering his Herc flight crew to bring it down on the coordinates he set on his GPS. Gambler next informed the major it looked as if they struck gold.

The Executioner gave the camp and the surrounding night one last search. Nothing stirred, groaned, twitched. He saw Collins walking up to him, met him halfway. Collins parked it, seemed to give the carnage an approving look, something new in the eyes, Bolan thought.

"You don't look too happy, Stone."

"You lost two men?"

"Yeah. Asp and Roadrunner."

"I'd think you'd be the one with the longer face, Major."

"Shit happens."

"Indeed it does. What next?"

"Interrogation once we get them chained down on the Herc."

"I gather that's where it all gets real interesting."

"Hey, maybe our methods for getting information from these scumbags doesn't gibe with most folks' sense of morality and fair play. What I'm saying, are you going to have a problem with how I let those three handle the Q-and-A session?"

Bolan probably would, since torture and cold-blooded murder wasn't how he handled business—at least as standard operating procedure—but there was some method to the madness he knew waited. If they were going to extract valuable information about terrorist operations, future plans for strikes and what the enemy had coined big events, some pain would have to be inflicted, perhaps even some blood shed. It was the way of the real world, Bolan knew.

"It's your show."

"Let's shake a leg, Stone. I've got a Spectre on the way. They're ready to burn this place off the earth with some nasty incendiary packages that made the trip. What we'll do when we board, I'm going to lay out the rest of the mission for you, including where we're eventually going to take this bunch for the trial. As far as I'm concerned, you've proved your mettle."

Bolan said nothing as Collins turned and walked away. Leave Collins to believe he'd just hung out the welcome-aboard sign, but Bolan was hardly flattered, much less about to embrace the change in attitude.

CHAPTER EIGHT

"Let me be perfectly clear. You aren't going to Paradise. You aren't going to a warm yellow planet. You aren't going to a sandy beach to work on your tan and unwind while you hatch your next chickenshit scheme to murder Israelis or Americans. There will be no flight schools, no lap dances in South Florida, no seventy-nine virgins waiting for you on the other end of this magic-carpet ride."

And so it began.

Bolan grabbed a cup of bad coffee, settled in, close to amidships, claiming one of several bolted-down chairs near the intel-planning bays, war tables and other high-tech apparatus. He counted twenty-six terrorists altogether, headcloths, skullcaps, turbans, tunics, African caftans and so forth distinguishing independent countries of origin. There would have been twenty-eight bad guys, but two prisoners came unhinged just as they were being ushered up the ramp of the C-130, and the terrible reality hit them with full sledgehammer force. As they lunged at their Cobra handlers, Cyclops and Warlock used the opportunity to put a 9 mm round from their Berettas through their brains, rolled them off the ramp, depositing still more enemy bodies on Sudanese soil. It was something of a monumental struggle after that, manhandling the others to the bench, between threats and beatings and blood spilled from rifle butts to the head and face, but Cobra got them chained down.

Bolan had silently begged off the whole brutal process, drawing funny looks from Gambler and cronies. It had been clear to Bolan the trio of black ops got the most jollies from abusing the prisoners beyond the necessary rough persuasion to accept their lot. Bolan filed them away as sadists. Whatever rotten else they were, he was sure in time they would reveal themselves.

Hands now cuffed to the long steel bench, feet manacled together, their expressions varied down the line, and Bolan read them in turn. Faces ranged from seething anger to utter disbelief to the sort of sociopathic hatred he'd found countless times before in the eyes of the fanatic. A few of the bad guys just appeared shell-shocked by the shellacking they'd received, thousand-mile stares fixed on the far wall. They might be in the bag now, but Bolan knew the real danger was just ahead, caged animals raging for a way to break out, devour their captors, whatever it took.

Collins had the intro session started; a slow pace, back and forth, hands behind his back, the star of the show. Gambler, Warlock and Cyclops stood behind the major, a few feet of space between them, looking pleased with the floor show so far. Asp and Roadrunner were getting zipped up in rubber bags. Bolan wasn't sure how they would be shipped back to the States, but was fairly certain Collins had allowed for casualties and had it figured out in advance.

They were ten minutes in the air, and the way the Hercules had swung around, Bolan believed they were heading south, figured the next stop was the base in Kenya. Beyond that, Collins had yet to fill him in on the next leg. While Collins paced and spoke in Arabic, Warlock and Cyclops translated in Farsi and Pathan when the major paused.

Bolan watched, sipped his coffee. A few of the Cobra commandos stood guard, M-16s out and aimed at the prisoners, while other commandos went to the computer bays, hauling out whatever intel had been seized at the camp. The one-eyed op worked on a smoke, a strange grin on his face, Bolan reading the glint in all five eyes, the major's ballyhooed HUMINT op edgy and eager, no doubt, to shake some more nerves with on-the-spot executions.

"You aren't heroes, you aren't martyrs, visionaries or divine instruments of God's will. What you are is camel dung, the droppings of Satan, cold-blooded murderers of innocent women and children. What—"

"Most of us speak near perfect English."

It was Alzhari piping up, the Sudanese camp leader wincing as he forced the words out from what Bolan could tell was a broken jaw.

"As for who is the droppings of Satan, it is a matter of opinion."

"I believe we have a smart-ass in the class, Major," Cyclops said.

"I believe you're correct," Collins chimed back. "Very well, then, people. I'll assume everyone will be clear on what I am about to tell you—in English. My mistake, since I know most terrorist scumbags learn to speak flawless English as part of their training. Pardon me the oversight, my first and last." Back to pacing, closing the gap to some of the prisoners, Collins fired up a cigarette, blowing streams of smoke in their faces. "You are now prisoners of the United States government. POWs, but stamped as illegal combatants. You will be questioned thoroughly and extensively and you will comply. I know you'll have many questions."

"Such as how you might relieve yourselves," Warlock cut in.

"The least of your problems," Cyclops added.

"Trust us," Gambler said. "You stink bad enough as it is, and the last thing we want is to smell you soiling your panties."

"Bear in mind," Gambler said, "as much as you believe your Allah knows your heart—"

"The Devil knows it equally as well," Cyclops said.

"Every dark thought, secret desire," Warlock added.

"Every malicious intent," Gambler said. "Bottom line, boys and girls," he continued, "you cannot fool us. You will give us what we want. We know you better than you know yourselves."

It was a sick singsong routine, Bolan throwing the trio a look. A picture of the Three Stooges, but with guns and malice and bigotry of sick heart, framed in his mind for a moment.

Collins held up a hand, glanced at the trio, then fell back into the act. "You are going to be detained. How long is up to each of you. How much information you provide may determine, in the long run, whether or not you are convicted of crimes against humanity. Depending on what we learn about you, depending on the nature of your evils, you may be hung at the end of your trial."

Bolan went back to his coffee when he heard the sudden outburst. Something about Collins and his manhood in relation to his mother, but Bolan couldn't spot the rebel tongue.

"Who said that? Who the fuck said that?" Collins roared, marching up and down the line, repeating the question. "No one said that, huh? Guess I'll just have to pick one as an example. Malcontents, smart mouths and foul language will not be tolerated on this joyride."

The nod was given, and Cyclops brought the Beretta out of his holster, walked up to a terrorist Collins jabbed his cigarette at, and shot him between the eyes. Blood and brain matter sprayed the prisoners flanking the body, then another captive was screaming, thrashing in his chains, three down the line.

"I thought the bulkhead was armor-plated," Cyclops growled.

"Ricochet. Use your knife from now on," Collins said. "Take care of that noise!"

The blade was out, Bolan feeling his gut clench. He nearly rose to put a stop to this insanity, but Cyclops already had fisted a handful of the wounded prisoner's hair. The face was yanked up, all defiance and hatred beyond the pain, as Cyclops slashed his throat, ear to ear. The soldier hadn't signed on for torture and indiscriminate cold-blooded murder of even the worst of the worst. It was far from any moral cowardice that froze Bolan from acting out his rage, putting an end to this horror show, and even at gunpoint.

He decided to let the sick drama unfold as it would. Beyond a scintilla of doubt—and there had been some up to then—he now knew Collins and Cobra were just as bad as the men they imprisoned. They were vicious, merciless predators. They could wrap themselves up in the Stars and Stripes all they wanted, but murder of helpless combatants, illegal or otherwise, simply ranked them as evil. The moment now also told Bolan he wasn't one of them, never had been, never would be, and they could write that in stone. He would keep it to himself, but he would hold them every bit as accountable to retribution and swift justice as they wanted to hold the enemy.

A wave of shouting and screaming erupted down the bench, the extremists going berserk, fighting to break out of their bondage, insane with outrage and fear. Collins was shouting for silence, his commandos rolling up to the bench, pointing assault rifles at the prisoners. A butt crack to a skull or two began to simmer them down.

"Any of you other sons of dirty milk mama whores want a taste?" Cyclops said, wiping the blade off on the caftan of the terrorist sitting next to the victim and getting sopped in geysering crimson. The cut had been so deep, Bolan could tell he'd nearly decapitated the terrorist. They left him there, chained and spouting blood.

"Now, I believe I was laying out your sorry futures," Collins said. From a metal table, the major picked up a yellow tablet of paper. "Whether you spill your guts by word of mouth, or if any of you fancies yourselves a wanna-be scribe," he said, and slapped a face with the tablet, then flung it at another prisoner, "you are going to tell us everything. How it gets done is up to you. But you are going to give up every mullah, imam or goathumping whore you have ever spoken with in your miserable lives. Your words will be eventually written down, and, no, for you there will be no six-figure advance out of New Yawk City for your tales of woe and sorrow through the narrow and rapidly closing windows of your former soulless murderous lives. You— each and every one of you—were not born and raised in the promised land. You have paved your own roads to Hell and Hell is where you are going. Do not worry. Soon there will be more joining you, so you are going to have plenty of misery loves company." Collins paused, grinning down the line, then flicked his cigarette, winging it off a bearded face. "Any questions?"

Collins spun on his heels, Gambler falling in behind the major. Cyclops and Warlock remained with the prisoners. Bolan watched as the two ops opened small pouches, began fixing patches with numbers on the shoulder of each prisoner, unable to resist a few more taunts.

"Enjoy the floor show, Colonel?" Gambler asked.

"Immensely."

"You being smart?"

"Never," Bolan told Gambler.

He was grunting, but moving on to the work bays. Bolan, alone with Collins, spotted something in the major's eyes he didn't think the man capable of. Was that sorrow or regret? Or was Collins about to attempt to warm him up with another act?

Collins shook a cigarette out of the pack, offered one to Bolan, who'd declined. When the major had his smoke lit, he said, "Some days—you ever wake up, Stone, and not like who or what you see in the mirror? You ever wonder if sometimes your life should have been different?"

"I've had occasion."

"But not too often."

"We're all only human."

"Or inhuman," Collins said, looking back over his shoulder.

Bolan said nothing, though he wanted to point out exactly who back there was the more inhuman.

"We've got a lot of work to do, Colonel. We hit Kenya, we'll iron out the details for the next stint." Collins worked on his smoke. "We're going on a little vacation to the Seychelles. Just you, me and Gambler. Come on, let's go see what goodies we grabbed up from the homeboys back there."

Bolan kept the suspicion off his face about the next round, but the itch between his shoulder blades just got worse. There was a whole lot of doubt in his mind a trip to the island nation of the Seychelles was going to be a day at the beach.

KHALIQ QUNANI WAS a long way from home, and he was disturbed.

It wasn't the first time he'd left his country, a cutout delivering intelligence, marching orders or money from his ayatollah to a group of fighters. Before, whether it was Chechnya, Kabul, Karachi or Paris, he had met with brother Muslims to outline future operations against the infidels, drop off money and intelligence, shore up resolve.

Now he had been ordered to work with the enemy, as different a mission as Heaven was to Hell. Precisely who they were he wasn't sure, his entire task swathed in grim mystery, anxiety sure to dog him for days to come. He had never met them, not even viewed a photo of these shadow men. The homing beacon fixed to his belt beneath his cashmere topcoat would lead them to him, or so he had been told. And the briefcase in his hand was bringing to the enemy that which they so valued, and was apparently their sole reason for, as his ayatollah put it, coming over to the right side.

Money—three hundred million U.S. dollars to be exact—was to be delivered to these nameless, faceless Westerners. It was all electronic funds, but he had the access codes to the bank accounts that would prove the transfers had been made.

It had been a long journey from Tehran, but jumping nerves and running adrenaline kept his weariness at bay. He had stayed in Istanbul for a day, then flown on by a private charter to Sicily. He had been ordered to take his time, shake any tails, proceed with cautious optimism, meeting with fellow Muslim cutouts who had moved him on safely to the next leg of his sojourn. In Sicily a boat had been waiting, hauling him the sixty miles south to the island archipelago of Malta. Halfway to North Africa now, he vaguely entertained the notion of sailing on from the capital city of Valleta, turning his back on some plan that not even he was privy to in detail. But he knew to shirk his duty was not only a certain death sentence, but also he would risk his immortal soul to eternal damnation by not carrying out the will of God as spoken through his ayatollah. He had never questioned the ayatollah's judgment before now, but he couldn't help but wonder about the sanity of working with the enemy. Then he recalled the holy man's final words before leaving Iran.

"These infidels will do as they told us they will, I assure you. They love money too much to not aid us in pulling off a big event that will shake the Great Satan to his knees. Go with God. Fear not. The future and our glory came to me in a vision."

Inspiration to carry on with the task wished to return but too many questions were suspended in his thoughts. What big event? When and where would this happen? What would be his role? Why join forces with the Devil to begin with?

Wishing he was armed, he shucked up his coat against the chilly morning air breezing in off Grand Harbor. A dirty light was just now breaking over the ships and boats of various size and duties. He was on schedule, according to his watch, as he continued his westward vector, angling away from the docks, melting into the shadows swaddling the first rows of grimy stone buildings. Shadows were coming to life all around him, his nerves talking back to him louder with each passing moment. He wondered when and how many of his contacts would suddenly move out of any number of alleys and courtyards in the fortified city of towers and ramparts, a maze of imposing architecture he was sure that had helped the Maltese drive away invaders over the centuries. He stopped as he suddenly felt a presence closing on him from behind. He jumped when he heard, "Are you enjoying your stay in Malta?"

It was his contact. Slowly, he turned, found a muscular dark-haired man in a black bomber jacket. Hard to say what nationality, his skin burnished by the sun and the sea, but Qunani assumed he was of Western origin. "That remains to be seen," he said, repeating the words he had memorized.

"This way."

He followed his contact into an alley. His heart racing, he braced to attack should he discover his ayatollah had been betrayed. The contact led him to a nondescript stone building midway down the alley. A door was opened, and the contact held his arm out. Qunani had come this far, he hesitated in the doorway, then ventured inside. He was met by another dark man, who beckoned to follow him down the hallway. Light flickered from a doorway at the far end, and Qunani was ushered through.

It appeared to be some sort of command-and-control center. Qunani took in the banks of computers, other screens with digital readouts, a computerized wall map of the world.

A big gray-haired man walked up out of the shadows, displaying a shoulder-holstered pistol. "I assume you have it?"

Qunani set the briefcase on a metal table, clicked through the dial, opened it up. He produced the CD-ROM, handed it to the gray man. The gray man handed it off to a subordinate, who inserted the disk into a computer.

"The access codes," the gray man said.

Qunani gave them the codes, watched as the fingers of the shadow man flew over the keyboard.

"Three hundred million. The down payment," Qunani said. "As agreed upon, another third will be deposited when this event is under way. Another third when I have returned to Iran with the merchandise, whatever that is. I was informed by my sponsor that the rest of the agreed-upon price of a billion dollars will be turned over in cash, in person, when the item my sponsor was promised is delivered to him."

Qunani felt a flash of resentment as the gray man ignored him, watching only the computer monitor.

"Confirmation, mister?"

"It's there, sir. Three hundred mil."

The gray man smiled, Qunani chilled for a moment by the lifeless eyes staring him back. "Okay. Looks like we're in business."

"May I ask—?"

"No, you may not," the gray man said. "You can call me the Contact. That's all you need to know. You will be our guest here, so why don't you go get settled in, grab some food, some shut-eye. A lot is going to happen very soon and I don't know when you—or any of us—will sleep or eat again when this thing starts."

The gray man turned away, and Qunani heard another of the shadow men telling him, "This way."

Qunani held his ground, the questions piling up now more than ever. He wasn't sure how much sleep he would get in the house of the enemy, as he felt a sudden urge to pray.

CHAPTER NINE

"Oh, man, welcome to paradise. Have I arrived or what?"

It was a murmur, thrown to the wind at ten knots, but Bolan caught it, checked what he believed was yearning on Collins's face, would have sworn next the Cobra leader was even getting a little misty-eyed beneath his black Blues Brothers shades.

Paradise.

The soldier, sitting at the midway point on a bench in the large motorized outboard, followed Collins's stare to shore. It was, Bolan had to admit to himself, a beautiful sight to behold. The sun was up, cobalt and blazing, peeking in and out of scudding white clouds, the calmest and bluest-green water Bolan had ever seen sparkling like a vast bed of diamonds. Palm and *takamaka* trees rose from the white sand, a kaleidoscope of exotic birds fluttering here and there among the lush tropical vegetation. Gulls strafed the surface for breakfast to the west, a school of dolphins to the east, sleek torpedoes glistening as they arced in and out of sunlight. Schooners and what had to be a seven-figure, hundred-plus-foot yacht were sluicing toward the harbor of Grand Anse, but, according to Collins, the three of them were going to beach the boat in a remote cove, their beachhead on the island of Praslin, where an SUV was waiting for them, dropped off courtesy of Company ops, Bolan assumed. Water sprayed in his face as Gambler guided them toward shore in the Zodiac inflatable boat. There was one thing about this heaven on Earth he nearly mentioned to his two traveling black ops.

This was about as close as they would ever get to the Garden of Eden.

It was somewhat unclear to Bolan how they were going to proceed, though most of the details had already been spelled out, at least as far as the numbers and strategy went. Most of the night had been spent at the base in Kenya, he recalled, viewing training videos, poring over manuals that covered the usual nightmare aspects of murder and mayhem being dreamed up by terrorists, but with a few new frightening twists that involved chemical and biological agents, both the acquiring and use, or how to brew the nastier stuff at a home lab. There were various and sundry concoctions even for developing bombs on the spot using flammable liquids and other precursors and materials that could be bought at any hardware store. There were videos where black-hooded instructors taught hand-to-hand combat, hostage takedown, fired small and large arms, wired C-4 to cell phones as remote detonators, displayed the proper and most aggressive way to use knives and other sharp objects on dummies with poster faces of well-known American politicians and celebrities. One especially disturbing video had shown a goat thrashing in death throes as a white cloud was pumped into a room, but there was no mention of what the chemical had been. With all the material they had seized in Sudan, Bolan knew it would take days, perhaps even weeks to sift through, decipher encrypted passages, uncover future operations. Never one to look beyond the next battlefront, but depending on how the rest of the mission went, Bolan decided he could have Brognola flex some official muscle, land the intel gold mine or copies thereof in the hands of the cyber team at Stony Man Farm. No telling really what might turn up, but whatever intelligence could be stolen and studied always put the warrior one step ahead of the enemy.

Then there was Collins, giving Bolan once again the distinct impression he was holding back, or holding on to something only he was meant to know. For all his talk about filling in Colonel Stone on the rest of the mission, clue him in as to the final destination of the prisoners...

It didn't happen.

Bolan decided to sit back, aware the next few mo-

ments could be his last in some time to come to relax
and take in the sights. If nothing else, the three of them
were certainly decked out as if they were going to while
the day away on the golf course or sip Mai Tais poolside at some resort. Dark aviator shades covered Gambler's and Bolan's eyes, and they sported wildly colored
aloha shirts with flowers, flamingos and scantily clad
island girls. Black slacks of Italian silk for Bolan with
wingtips. Gambler went with white pants and alligator
shoes, Collins sticking to khakis and white loafers, the
Don Ho wardrobe provided courtesy of the Cobra
leader. Beyond the tourist-playboy appearance, the
nylon bags on the deck would soon dispel anybody's
notion they were in Praslin for fun and games. The
hardware was basic—mini-Uzis all around, Beretta
side arms, commando daggers and a smattering of frag,
flash-bang and incendiary grenades, with two canisters
packed with NARCON-D, and three gas masks.

Collins stated his contacts on the island had nailed
down the location of Iranian extremists, had them under
watch. There were two hits on the scorecard, enemy
numbers totaling fifteen, could be more, Collins said,
split between a hotel suite in Grand Anse and a remote
rain forest pocket at the eastern edge of the island. Collins claimed they were going in hard and fast, two faces
committed to memory for the cuff and stuff, but said
during the final brief he didn't want to be running
around Praslin, shooting and blowing up the island,
drawing a lot of attention to themselves. They had left

their Gulfstream ride parked back on the main island of Mahé on an airfield the major had informed him, Bolan recalled, was an American intelligence base, but when the soldier inquired which agency, the major answered he wasn't even sure God knew. Out of all the 115 islands that comprised the archipelago in the vast expanse of the Indian Ocean, the question begged itself how Collins knew exactly where the Iranian fundamentalists were holed up. The Cobra leader had simply told Bolan they'd been working on it for some time. They just knew.

But of course.

Using his GPS monitor, Gambler steered them into a cove thick with swaddling palm trees. Birds cawing, the sun beating down on his neck, Bolan felt coral rock scrape the bottom of the outboard. They were out, the soldier helping his teammates haul the outboard up the sandy bank where Gambler took the mooring line and tied it around the base of a palm tree.

Personal weapons bag in hand, Bolan, suddenly feeling that itch between his shoulder blades as they were now stepping back into the ring for the next round, hung back. Gambler was giving him that strange look again, Collins staring down the shoreline, then out to sea.

"I tell you what, gentlemen," Collins said. "You ever feel like you've worked and sweated—or in our cases—shed blood and risked our lives for Uncle Sam for so long and so many times you've earned the right to cut yourself a slice of paradise? Ever feel like you deserve it, screw it all, I'm going to take what I can now and live the good life?"

Bolan said nothing, but his gut was rumbling loud and angry, instinct warning him Collins had just revealed something dark and hungry about himself.

"All the time," Gambler said.

"One of these days," Collins murmured.

"And one of these nights," Gambler chimed in. "There shall be an 'all the time.'"

The look melted on the Cobra leader's face, the dark hunger in the eyes back as he said, "Let's go kick some butt."

Bolan hesitated, Collins and Gambler moving past the warrior. They might be in paradise, Bolan thought, but he was sure in the coming hours the fires of hell would blow through the Seychelles.

"You want to join us, Colonel?" Gambler called back.

Something about that guy, Bolan thought, the tone, the look, the body language, and knew he wasn't about to take point or drive their car with Gambler sitting behind him.

Welcome to Paradise, the Executioner thought, or welcome to Hell?

ZARIK HAMADAN HAD a gut feeling the party was over, but he'd suspected that the good times were never meant to keep on rolling even before he set foot on this island paradise. It was strange, if he thought about it, how he'd been ordered—a top lieutenant in the global jihad—to essentially cool his heels in the closest thing to heaven on Earth he could imagine, wait for whatever his marching orders from their ayatollah.

So he was now far away from his homeland, surrounding himself with all the sinful pleasures his religion denounced and despised as trappings of the Devil. But he had been told to go to the Seychelles, enjoy himself while he could, that a big event was soon to happen, be patient, have faith, be strong. The usual mantra, yes, but who could disobey the ayatollah?

So he had played hard, bringing along European playmates, a few ounces of cocaine and several cases of Scotch whiskey flying with himself and his elite guards in the Learjet that had left Riyadh six weeks ago, their Saudi contacts making all the prior logistical arrangements and handing over the party favors. Trouble was, he was having great difficulty enjoying the good times these days when he was juiced with anxiety all the time. The Saudis, he knew, could get away with it, lopping off the heads of drug dealers and addicts, publicly flogging women of loose morals, all sinners guilty until proven innocent, then jet off for a weekend in Paris or Amsterdam or London, gambling and drinking, drugging and whoring. There had been a time when he would have found that an abominable hypocrisy in the eyes of God, an evil lie that betrayed the strict tenets of the Koran. Six weeks in the Seychelles, though, and he wasn't so sure any longer. He was only flesh, only a man, after all, with needs and wants. Could be, he concluded, the Saudis had the right idea—do as I say, not as I do. Anyway, who could fight or stand up to the power of money?

He was out of the pool, one of his Swedish playmates bringing him a towel and a glass of champagne. He dismissed her with a kiss on the cheek and a squeeze of buttocks. Playtime was over. He needed to go to the suite, place calls to various contacts and cutouts who would get in touch with their leader. He needed to know something. All the sex, drugs and rock and roll was fine, as the infidels referred to their sinful indulgences, but he was antsy for answers. And being a man of action, a fighter who both planned and carried out operations against the enemy, he needed to get back out in the battlefield.

Toweled off, killing the drink, he spotted Baluq, his big guard, mingling with some of the locals near the bar. He caught his eye, waved him over, slipped into his sandals and Hawaiian shirt and began walking for the back entrance to the lobby on the far side of the pool. He took his cell phone, dialed up to the suite. Four, then five rings and he found himself becoming angry, aware his men were up there, most likely huffing blow and perhaps catching an early-morning hummer from one of the Euro-strumpets.

"Yes!"

Hamadan froze, felt his jaw clench, ears buzzing

with rage as he tuned in to the party antics. Ahmad had to practically shout over the thunder of American rock and roll, Hamadan catching some giggling in the background. It galled Hamadan even more that Ahmad actually sounded annoyed he had to answer the phone. Oh, but it was time to put an end to the nonsense.

"Get rid of the whores!" Hamadan snarled, watching as Baluq rolled toward him, looking miffed that he had to leave his new lady friends at the bar. "I am coming up and I want them gone by the time I get there! And turn off that racket! We have work to do!"

Hamadan punched off, dropped the cell phone in his pocket. It was time to announce to all of them it was back to work in no uncertain terms. A warrior needed to stay sharp, focused, alert, aware his destiny was far greater than wallowing around in the sludge of self-indulgence.

He was moving past the bar when three men seemed to suddenly materialize out of the vegetation that jumbled around the cabana. It was just a feeling, but something didn't look right about the trio. For a fleeting second he had the feeling they knew who and what he was, that they had come looking expressly for him. Or were his nerves simply shot, too much of everything paradise had to offer dulling the warrior's senses, replacing martial talent with simple paranoia and fear? Right then, not even he could be sure what was real or imagined. They were dressed for paradise, sure enough, checking out the sights poolside, one of them easing to-

ward the bar as if to order. The one with the black sunglasses appeared to ogle a few of the bathing beauties,
but there was something in the way the tall dark one
moved that left Hamadan wondering if he was being
stalked as he felt the hackles bristle on his neck. Sure,
the island was a tourist magnet, and they came from all
over Europe, the Middle East, provided their wallets
were fat, and rich Westerners were a common sight.
Paradise, he knew, wasn't meant for the poor, unless
they bussed tables or cleaned rooms.

He looked away from the trio, picking up the pace,
sweeping past the gaggle of couples just rousing to hit
the pool or the hotel restaurant for a late breakfast of
Bloody Marys and stuffed lobster. He was somewhat
comforted by the fact Baluq carried a Browning Hi-
Power beneath his white sports coat, but suddenly
wished he was armed. He was tempted to look back
over his shoulder, but if he was being followed he didn't
want to betray his suspicions. If he wasn't, then he
would feel foolish, perhaps even look silly, or worse,
a coward in the eyes of Baluq.

The lobby was bustling with tourist traffic. In his
heightened state of anxiety, the polished chrome, the
white marble of countertops and floor seemed to drive
hot needles into his eyes as the sunlight knifed through
the ceiling window. He beelined for the bank of eleva-
tors, found one of them opening just as he stepped up,
the car disgorging a mosaic of peoples and cultures from
the island and the world over. He was inside, keying the

slot that would take him to the top floor, turning, grateful to be alone, on his way up top to shake up the troops when—

The trio of strangers rolled into the car. It was a frozen moment, one for the ages as Hamadan saw his worst suspicions and imaginings become reality.

A glimpse of the sound-suppressed weapon, the doors closing, and Hamadan heard the soft chug. He didn't have to look to know Baluq was on his way to true Paradise, as he heard the heavy thud of deadweight and tasted blood on his lips.

IT WAS CALLED the Hotel California of all damn things. According to Collins, it was recently built by a Saudi construction company believed to have ties to the bin Laden family. According to Collins the Seychelles were the favorite stomping grounds for Saudi fat cats, Islamic extremists or other fugitives with money to burn on the run these days. Collins, Bolan recalled, stated a good portion of intelligence had come to him concerning a connection between the Iranian fundamentalists and Saudi sponsorship. That, Bolan knew, at least gibed with his own experience since the Saudis were notorious for talking out of both sides of their mouths, saying one thing about America and doing another. Bottom line the Seychelles was expensive, remote and the local authorities had no problem turning a blind eye to suspicious visitors if the price for blissful ignorance was right. It all made sense in the way of corruption to

Bolan, but he knew there was no time now to debate where the truth ended and the bullshit began.

They were no sooner in the elevator than Gambler had the sound-suppressed Beretta out and coring a neat red hole between the eyes of Hamadan's bodyguard. Blood splashed the teakwood wall, gore spraying the Iranian. Before the body crashed to the floor, Collins was all over Hamadan in the next eye blink, his own sound-suppressed Beretta thrust under the Iranian's chin.

"Who are you?" Hamadan rasped.

"We ain't tour guides, fella, unless you want to take a trip into the twilight zone," Gambler said, hauling out the mini-Uzi from his open bag, attaching the sound suppressor, cocked and locked.

"How many in the suite?"

The bells chimed, Bolan arming himself, sound suppressors already fixed during the drive in on his mini-Uzi and Beretta 93-R. It would be awkward, hitting the enemy while draping the nylon satchel over his head, hanging it from the other shoulder, but there was no choice.

"Seven," Hamadan told Collins.

The seventh floor was where the action would take place. Collins demanded the elevator key, and Hamadan handed it over.

"Lock the car when we get there, and keep the key in your pocket," Collins told Gambler.

"Any guests?" he asked Hamadan.

"No."

"No whores?"

"I sent them out of the suite."

"The doors, they open in or out?"

"In."

"I'll need the keys."

"You won't need them," Hamadan said. "They are left unlocked."

"Cocky little shits," Gambler said, watching the lights and the doors.

"Yeah," Collins said. "Well, even terrorist scum needs to unwind once in a while, but all this lax time is about to get a few of them killed. Turn around, asshole. Anything cute, you shout a warning, and I'll pump one through your head. Makes me sick just to look at you, down here, pumping good-looking broads of European persuasion, good food, big suite, boozing it up, even doing a little blow, I hear, the time of your life."

Hamadan grinned, defiant. "I hear envy."

"You hear the voice of alpha-male pride, shitbag," Collins growled. "Something I'm sure you don't know a goddamn thing about."

"And if he's lied about the doors?" Bolan wanted to know.

"Then frag 'em," Collins said. "He lies, he ends up like his pal here, and I'm sure he can see this guy just had his last foo-foo drink down at the bar."

Collins spun him, fastened the plastic cuffs. "You know the drill, gentlemen. I laid out the specs I got on the suite. Stick to the plan, by the numbers. I get in position, I'll give you a three count. Let's hit and git. Look alive—if there's a jihad goon waiting when these doors open, drop him."

The doors opened, Bolan lifting both weapons, braced for armed competition waiting or lurking in the hall. It was clear, Bolan out and scanning the empty hall, taking point against his better judgment as he led Gambler to the main double doors at the far south end of the hall. As planned, Collins would go in through the north doors that led down an alcove to the kitchen and dining area. The living room was for the soldier and Gambler to sweep. If it played true to the blueprints Collins had gotten from his island contacts, the idea was to catch them in a scissors pinch.

Bolan flanked one side of the doors, wedged the Beretta in the waistband at the small of his back, Gambler on the other, the soldier eyeballing his black ops counterpart. He looked down the hall where Collins was in position, the soldier suddenly not trusting the setup in the least. For one thing, it was damn convenient that Collins was going in with human body armor, while plastering Gambler to his rear. That itch was back, so strong now, the soldier was hearing bells and whistles.

As Collins showed three fingers, counted off, Bolan told himself to watch his own back.

The Executioner grabbed the handle, twisted, opened and went in, both mini-Uzi and Beretta leading the way and searching for targets.

CHAPTER TEN

He was going to do it his way. Hell with it, if the major had a problem with the call he'd live with the end result, come to see reason why it was done here and now. First the body would have to be left behind in the suite, since they couldn't very well lug a bloody corpse all over Grand Anse with tourists and local babes gawking and gaping at them on their way out of town. Second they were so far away from the real world, the corpse might never see U.S. soil, especially if a few bucks could be spread around to some hungry Seychellois mouths to make sure the body was buried at sea. Last but certainly not least, he just plain didn't trust or like the damn guy.

He didn't have a problem with going through the motions of the mission with the other commandos who weren't on board for the full ride. In time, they would receive the same treatment, but he read the big dark guy as something way different, something else than a standard-issue black ops commando. What, he wasn't sure. Some Company or NSA plant, the head shed having sniffed out the real deal? Who knew, and what's more, he didn't care.

Gambler only knew he had to put one in the back of the guy's head, end of story.

They were in, advancing down the foyer when the big guy got it started. Man, Gambler thought, but he could move, breathing steady, blasting away with both barrels, scanning the room, cover and concealment wherever he could take it. Palm trees, couch, shooting, advancing, hurling up a fat mahogany table as return fire sought him out, thick wood absorbing rounds with a thundering drumbeat. There was a chance—a damn remote one, the way the bad guys were getting shot to feces in two shakes—his problem would get taken care of by the Iranians.

That didn't appear about to happen.

Gambler figured he could at least make it look good, marching down the short flight of steps, drilling a burst of 9 mm scorchers into a machine-pistol-brandishing fanatic on the far side where interior decorators had brought the jungle to the joint. He cored him with a rising burst, a giant-screen TV with a lesbian scene going full core—quadruple-X action if he glimpsed it right—in living color right behind the jigging extremist. The image was there, then gone, as the extremist hammered back through the screen, arms flailing in the smoking and sparking ruins as the lesbians blinked out to just another masturbatory fantasy.

Gambler sighted down on Stone, the big guy catching another fundamentalist too slow on the draw. The aloha shirt chopped to red rags, the body sailed and crashed down through a coffee table littered with all manner of party goodies. Gambler counted up four bad guys down and out, heard the din of weapons fire from the north end of the suite. If all went well, Collins would get bogged down for a few critical seconds, never see the curtain fall on this Wild Card character. If it played out that way, Gambler saw himself in the near future, shrugging it off. "Shit happened, Major, one of the bad guys nailed him."

It sounded like a solid plan, but Stone was alternating his attention to one Iranian dashing for a hallway across the suite and looking back his way. No way, Gambler thought, the guy was probably one of the best shooting ops he'd ever seen, but he was no mind reader.

Gambler let him get the chase started, allowed for ten or so feet lag time, then charted his own hunt on an angle to his right flank. He was lifting the Beretta, the big guy spraying autofire down the hall, when he spotted his TV star rising from the smoke and glass. How the...?

Gambler swung his aim, chugged two rounds into his forehead, shattering skull like rotten eggshell. Stone, he saw, moving two, three steps closer to his rear, was changing clips in his mini-Uzi. Never a better opportunity, Gambler decided, and swung the Beretta up, finger taking up slack on the trigger.

BOLAN KNEW it was coming, and he was ready. Time and again, pure and simple, gut instinct had paid off, saved his life. When the stakes were life-and-death, there were no second chances. And in the Executioner's world traitors were shown no mercy, no exceptions.

Out of the corner of his eye, Bolan read the look, the gun hand swinging up, no mistaking where it was aimed. One swift pivot, and the Executioner hit the Beretta's trigger, pumped a 9 mm Parabellum shocker dead center between Gambler's eyes.

The soldier had just cut down what appeared the last of the extremists, or at least those armed combatants within sight. The moment seemed to suspend itself before Bolan. It was no more than a second, two tops, but Gambler was a statue, a strange expression of confusion and betrayal paralyzing his face before he toppled to his back.

The soldier checked the carnage, scouring the vandalized furniture where crimson sacks littered the living room. The shooting had abruptly stopped, Bolan turning when he spotted Collins jacking his prisoner into the living room. The look on the Cobra leader's face told Bolan he'd seen what happened.

Bolan jerked a nod at Gambler, then aimed his Beretta at Collins. "Do you want to explain that?"

"WHOA, HOLD UP, Colonel!"

Collins didn't have to look real hard at Stone's face

to know his life depended on how he played the next few seconds, which, he knew, meant he had to lie. The big question was would the man know or even sense he had an inkling Gambler had wanted to take him out since first laying eyes on him.

"I saw it happen, Stone."

"You did."

Flat and cold, Stone standing there, eyes boring into him, measuring the soul inside the man, and Collins began to feel his knees shake. He clawed his hand harder into Hamadan's shoulder to steady himself.

"I think I can explain."

"You can."

He stared into the ugly snout of the sound suppressor. "You mind taking that off my face?"

"I do."

"Listen, that guy—and not even I know who he really was, or what agency he worked for—was acting on his own."

"He was."

"Goddammit, I had nothing to do with it. I didn't even know how much murder of heart he had toward you."

"Until now."

"Yeah!"

"Convenient."

"Goddamn you, Stone, I—we—are walking out of here now!"

"No, we're not. Not until I know why your boy wanted to shoot me in the back of the head."

"You'd have to ask him."

"Little hard to do now."

"No shit, unless you want to do a séance before we leave."

"What's going on here, Collins? What's this mission really all about?"

Collins managed to steady his breathing, held Stone's stare, unwilling to flinch, wilt under the penetrating drill of those blue eyes. He shook Hamadan some, then said, "It's about a bunch of murdering scumbags like this here beauty who wish only to kill Americans and Jews. It's about rounding up some of the worst of the worst to, one, be interrogated so we know what said scumbags are planning and, two, to stand trial for crimes and other assorted atrocities against the human race. Beyond that, hell, I might go on CNN with proof for anyone straddling the fence that the so-called religion of Islam is a sham, a whopping lie, little more than a doctrine of violence, hate and intolerance. Maybe I'll get my own talk show. That's it, end of story. Whatever paranoid fantasies you might be having, I'm here to tell you I'm an American, a soldier who is committed solely to his duty. I have a job to do and I am going to do it. Whatever that one over there was up to, I have not the first fucking clue. Take it or leave it."

"And his other two stooges?"

"I'll deal with them when we get back. I'll remove them from the rest of this mission if that would ease any fears."

"It's not them I'm thinking I should be afraid of."

"Me, then, Stone? Okay, if you think I'm some treasonous bastard out to wax your butt because we knocked heads at the start, then shoot me."

Collins waited for the chug, the look in Stone's eyes hardening, the guy, he believed, actually thinking about it.

"If you don't mind, then, I'll keep an eye open from here on. If I even see you—"

"Don't even finish that remark. Look, if I were you, I'd feel the same damn way."

"So, what happened here was just some…aberration of the mission?"

"We'll never know now, will we? But I'll stand here and look you straight in the eye and state emphatically and with all good clean conscience that, yes, it was an aberration."

"End of story."

"End of story, and discussion. You either believe me or shoot me."

Collins felt his heart pound, Stone silent, looking as if he were debating the matter.

"How many did you take out?"

"Two."

The Beretta lowered. "Then we're done here. Let's go, Major. We've got work to do."

"I'll lead the way."

"And drive."

"Whatever."

Collins held in his pent-up breath, but took his fear and anger out on Hamadan, shoving the Iranian toward the foyer. He knew it wouldn't happen, Stone with his honor and all that crusader crap, but he still waited for the bullet to core into the back of his skull, not sure if the man had bought his act.

It didn't come, and that left Collins wondering if and when it ever would. If he didn't trust Wild Card before, if he'd wanted him out of the way since first laying eyes on the man, knowing what he knew where it was all headed...

Stone, he thought, had to know his hours were numbered in single digits.

Collins knew what had to be done, the late and unlamented Gambler having already tipped his hand, but he would choose the right time and place.

EVERY FIBER in his being screamed that Collins was lying. Gambler had failed, a bad memory, an appetizer hung out there for a sample taste, but the main course would be served, in time, by Collins or another Cobra commando.

Fair enough.

In his world, where there was only blood, death and mayhem, Bolan had also encountered more deceit and backstabbing along the way by the so-called good guys than he cared to remember. Sometimes they did it for a twisted ideology, or revenge against superiors or a country they felt had grievously wronged them. But more often than not, it boiled down to love of money.

Forever living on the edge, a sixth sense about the darker driving forces of human nature had developed, and Bolan considered himself better than a decent judge of character. Collins had shown him all the right—or wrong—signs that everybody else had something to hide except him and the thousand-pound gorilla on his shoulders, that he fancied himself just a little smarter, better and tougher. There was the trembling he'd seen in the major's knees, the voice breaking just enough while it strained for cool, calm and collected, the brain churning in high gear behind the eyes, selecting the right words. There was the forcing himself past any hesitation when the spotlight hit him in the eyes, fighting through the terror he'd been caught, the blame dumped on Gambler. There was bluster, posturing, the defiance that was part and parcel of the liar attempting to create his own truth and sell it. There was...

Well, more than enough to tell the Executioner not only was everything not as it seemed, but also that everything about this mission had changed for the rest of the ride. A line, as far he was concerned, had been drawn in the sand.

Right up to Gambler's coup—whether it was personal or something else—Collins had claimed to know everything about every player on both sides, all the pieces falling into place at the right time, with the possible exception of the near fiasco in Sudan. It made no sense, to say the least, that Collins would suddenly claim ignorance, wash his hands of one of his illustrious HUMINT black ops, write him off as a bad seed. That in mind, Bolan was sure there was some darker agenda on the major's table, but the Executioner was stuck right in the middle of whatever it was, left with no option but to brazen it out, wait for whenever the hammer would drop, be ready.

With no choice but to forge ahead, Bolan would dangle the noose for Collins, watch without watching the man every step of the way, instinct so finely honed over the years he might as well have eyes in the back of his head. If the major hung himself, so be it. If it came down to taking out Collins, Brognola would shake the black ops roost back home, put him solely in charge, send the other commandos of Cobra packing, resume the mission with operatives of his choosing from Stony Man.

The soldier was on his own, but then again, he figured he always had been since coming on board Cobra Force.

"Okay, Colonel, this is where we get off. You got the game plan down?" A pause, Collins staring in the rearview glass, waiting. "We okay, me and you?"

Bolan was in the back seat, Collins at the wheel, Hamadan in the shotgun seat. The Iranian was looking surly but giving up the intel they needed during the hour-plus drive to hit the extremist outpost near the beach.

Eight fanatics, or so the Iranian told them, at the end of the trail, a hundred yards or so from where they were now parked. One Ghazi Khatani was framed in

Bolan's memory from the intel pics of their prime target. The only motion and heat sensors and cameras were at the edge of the clearing before the thatch-and-bamboo compound rose, a sandy beach bristling with palm and casuarina trees providing the backdrop. Bolan had already perused the sat pics. There was a wharf stretching away from the beach, leading to a speedboat and schooner, the soldier focusing in on land-sat imagery that picked up a narrow trail that ran parallel with the main road. Collins informed him when this was wrapped they would get picked up by chopper, flown back to Mahé.

Simple.

He'd see about that.

Bolan took his satchel, draped it over his head, settled it on his shoulder. The bag open, he took and deposited a frag grenade in his pants pocket.

Bolan met Collins's look in the rearview mirror.

"Stone? You with me?"

"I've got it."

"We cool? We back in business?"

The major was feeling him out, Bolan knew, wanted reassurance they were back on the same team, whatever happened with Gambler was all just some bizarre misshap he couldn't explain.

Sure.

The strategy, once again, had a few flaws, Bolan thought. Their prisoner was to march down the trail, cuffed, announce himself while the two of them advanced on opposite sides toward the compound. When the enemy showed, it was pop and drop, bag the big game, hit the beach for evac. Bolan pictured the Iranian shouting a warning, Hamadan figuring eight against two were pretty decent odds to cut them down, set him free. Once the shooting started, Bolan saw the enemy scattering into the jungle or bolting for the beach, driving away in the cigarette speeder. Beyond that, they weren't exactly camouflaged for a jungle hit, flaming aloha shirts easy bull's-eyes. And no advance through a jungle was ever soundless. There were twigs to watch, brush to evade, branches and hanging vines and such to avoid. There were birds and animals, spooked by human presence, that could suddenly sound the alarm. Bolan was an old pro at stealth striking, but it was Collins this time out that planted whopping seeds of doubt this would go down by the numbers.

"We're just peachy," Bolan said.

"Let's do it, then." Collins turned to Hamadan. "Get out. Anything cute, and you're the first one to go. I don't need you that bad."

Bolan was out the door, mini-Uzi and Beretta leading the way toward his point of penetration into the rain forest. Hamadan was shoved away from the SUV, he saw, Collins giving him a swift kick in the rear with another warning about consequences for getting cute.

Let more games begin, the Executioner thought.

And Bolan checked for the path of least resistance into and beyond the thick vegetation, found it and slipped himself onto the sliver of dirt path outlined on the sat imagery that was able to pick up the course due to large holes in the canopy overhead.

He scanned the rain forest, darting ahead, crouched, wings fluttering somewhere, a caw slashing the silence. A check to the road, and Hamadan was walking ahead in a sort of waddle-shuffle, glancing at Collins, who vanished into the forest.

Bolan kept moving, glancing from Hamadan to where Collins had melted out of sight.

"I don't need you that bad."

The Executioner couldn't help but wonder to whom the man referred.

CHAPTER ELEVEN

Ghazi Khatani was feeling grateful for the simple things in life. It was quite the pleasant change compared to the anxiety and worry that had gripped him during his first few weeks on the island. Before he had landed on Praslin he had many reservations about leaving behind the safety and comfort of the familiar surroundings of Iran for an island in the middle of nowhere, shipped off by their leader to some remote corner of the planet, their task undisclosed, shrouded in secrecy and mystery, as if he and the others were criminals in hiding. It took some adjustment then, whiling away the days, fishing and swimming, snorkeling and boating around the islands on pleasure cruises with the local women, feasting on some of the best seafood brought in from Grand Anse he could have dreamed existed. Sometimes the other half of the contingent on Praslin brought in Seychellois women to help them pass away the lonely nights in orgies he would have deemed sinful to the extreme back in Iran.

All the creature comforts and then some in the large beach house, including fully stocked bar and refrigerator, satellite televisions, videos, computers and high-tech necessities for contact with other fighters in the global jihad, both on the island and back home. So he had decided, why worry? Life right now was one big party.

Settled in and relaxed for the first time on this island heaven, he figured he could count his blessings, far away from the stress and strife of his holy chosen path, viewing it all as a vacation, praising their great leader for singling him out for this much-deserved R & R. He was on call, of course, and the strange orders from their leader were what had both puzzled and frightened him at first.

He briefly recalled the words that had haunted his sleepless nights when he had first touched foot on the beach.

"Some will have to die so that others will live. Bear in mind, the global jihad is God's will, and it is greater than the life of any one man. However, I tell you this, in private, away from the others. As one of my top and most trusted lieutenants, your life will be spared. Men will be coming for you where you are going, but they are part of the great plan. Not even I know when precisely they will come, but your time will be short, so enjoy the paradise I am sending you to while you can.

You must not be afraid, since it has already been arranged you will merely be captured, but only for a short time, then you will be free and you will see the full glory of Islam. I am asking you now, do you have the courage and the faith to obey me—and God—without question?"

What could he have said other than yes? Their leader had spoken, so his wish for the great plan would be carried out.

The weeks had crawled by in tension and fear in the beginning, he recalled, but prayer had buoyed his faith, calmed his nerves so that he could now accept whatever the future held. Island life wasn't so bad, after all.

He was indulging in a cigarette and afternoon brandy as he watched for the tenth time an American movie about five Elvis impersonators robbing a casino in Las Vegas. It was his favorite movie, but found it somewhat ironic that as much as he hated America and all things Western, he idolized their films. Any confusion as to how he really felt about Americans didn't last long whenever he watched the five Elvises shoot up the casino, killing anyone—Americans, of course—who got in their way, rooting them on to rack up the body count.

He was catching a nice buzz, revved up as the fifth Elvis began shooting up the casino, when he heard voices shouting outside. He considered arming himself, then heard the familiar voice of Zarik. He was thinking Zarik was merely coming to bring supplies or women, but the voice sounded nervous and tense, one of his own men asking Zarik...

What? Khatani thought, out of his chair and moving for the door. Zarik was cuffed? Was this a joke or was it something more insidious?

Khatani wasn't two steps out on the porch when he saw two, then three of his men dropping onto the trail, long fingers of scarlet jetting from their skulls. The explosion came next, two more of his men flying away on the fireball. Part of his mind screamed this wasn't happening, they were being hit, massacred and in paradise, no less. Then the calm voice of his leader broke through.

"Some will have to die so that others can live."

If this was part of the great plan, it still galled Khatani that he was supposed to stand by while his Muslim brothers were slain before his eyes. But hadn't he been told he would be spared? Even so, he wasn't taking any chances. The AK-47 was inside, a dozen long steps that would feel like an eternity the way his men were getting chopped down by some invisible assassin.

Khatani was wheeling toward the doorway when he heard "Going somewhere?"

COLLINS AIMED the sound-suppressed Beretta between Khatani's eyes. He had made the porch, just as Stone began chugging out the doomsday send-offs, kicking Iranians all over the trail, nothing but head shots.

"You are the one? You have come to take me away,

or so I was told. I am to be captured? I am to be spared?"

Collins made his decision on the spot. "I don't need you that bad."

"Wait! What do you—?"

Collins drilled a round between Khatani's eyes. He left him there, sprawled at his feet, a flimsy explanation forming in his head how he would answer to Stone about the execution. Maybe he didn't need to explain himself. Hell, he was in charge. It was damn good, just the same, that he had reached Khatani first. The Iranian had some idea, it sounded, about the future. Whatever he thought he knew had gone to the grave with him.

The old lion was roaring back inside, and that was good, Collins decided. Whatever the moment of danger back at the suite, it had passed, but he knew he'd still had to string Stone along. What better way to prove the man was in no imminent threat of death by his hand than by jumping into the fight and pasting the few runners scattering in flight?

Collins sidled down the porch, a few wild rounds seeking him out, slashing off a piece of wooden beam. He was lining up another Iranian beach boy when he saw Hamadan bolting down the trail.

"Colonel! Get Hamadan!"

THREE IRANIANS WERE dumped by rapid successive taps of the Beretta's trigger when Bolan saw them come unhinged. Torn between fight and flight, a spray of AK autofire ripped through the vegetation around the soldier, but he was already advancing to cut off any rear exit for the beach, bulling his course through palm fronds and brush. The Executioner armed his frag grenade, let it fly at the rabbits. It blew in a cluster of three hardmen, two of them sailing on for the motor pool of a GMC and two Land Cruisers. There was a headfirst hammering through the windshield of the GMC by one shredded extremist missile, the other mangled scarecrow thudding into the grille. Number three was scraping himself off the ground, a slab of raw meat, sliced and diced by shrapnel, screaming in pain. Bolan drilled a death tap into the back of his skull, the 9 mm subsonic round kicking him off his feet.

That left three. There was Hamadan, the mark they'd come to round up, and one runner racing for the wharf. Their own prisoner was in flight, Bolan saw, scurrying back down the trail just as Collins sounded the alarm from the porch. It didn't eat up too much time—no more than thirty seconds total—and Bolan charged up on Hamadan's rear. A clip of the Beretta over the back of his head, and Bolan began manhandling him back down the trail.

Homed in on the autofire, as the lone extremist backpedaled down the wharf, the warrior saw Collins giving chase. He left Collins to take care of the final problem, as he spotted the body on the porch, senses tuned to any sound from inside the large beach house. A glimpse of the action, and Bolan saw the major hosing down the Iranian with a long burst of mini-Uzi fire, the body spinning off the wharf, splashing down into the water.

Hauling Hamadan by the arm, Bolan peered inside the beach compound. The only sound was the television blaring with the sounds of gunfire and men shouting at one another. The carnage littering the grounds briefly struck Bolan as surreal as he watched the celluloid battle. It happened like that sometimes, he thought. Coming out the other side of any armed engagement was never a given. He sometimes counted his own good fortune when he found himself still standing, even gave the gods of war a silent thanks on occasion, but when the adrenaline began to slow, a strange dreamlike quality could descend on the world around him. It never lasted but a second or two, but the feeling of being temporarily drained, even numb or disembodied, was still there.

Bolan went to the body. Khatani. Shot once between the eyes. No weapon he could find. So why the execution? This was supposed to be the big game they had come here to snare. Why just gun down an unarmed enemy who had supposedly made the Cobra list? Bolan grunted, almost couldn't wait to hear what snow job Collins would offer.

The moment of wonder proved a mental lapse, Bolan feeling it coming even as his mind registered the escape attempt. The leg sweep came out of nowhere, the soldier taking the blow to the back of his knee. His leg buckled as the head butt was craning down. Bolan whipped his face away, but took the blow on the side of his skull. Bells and lights shot through his brain, and Hamadan wrenched free. Bolan exploded into a charge, angered over the brazen attack. Three long strides, and the Executioner clamped a hand into Hamadan's shoulder. He ran the Iranian another two steps down the porch, then bounced his face off a beam. He let Hamadan drop, the Iranian rolling over, staring up, eyes blazing with hate and defiance.

"Go on! Kill me! If you think I am going to be some prisoner of the Americans, you are wrong! Never! I will kill you the first chance I get! Do it! You murdered the others, kill me!"

Bolan felt the Beretta lift a few inches. He wasn't quite sure what was possessing him, bringing on a sudden murderous impulse, but he was tempted to shoot what he knew was a cold-blooded killer who lived only to create death and destruction. Perhaps he was infected by the evil he'd seen on both sides, whatever humanity he maintained during a mission eroded by the vile company he kept. It passed, as he knew it would. Being an animal was easy. It was being human that was more often than not the tough part.

"Get up."

The Iranian shimmied to his feet as Collins rounded the corner.

"Problems, Colonel?"

"Nothing I couldn't handle." Bolan glanced over his shoulder at Khatani. "Him?"

"I decided I didn't need him that bad."

Bolan was tempted to ask why, but skipped it. He wasn't in the mood for more lies.

"Grab our boy here, Colonel, I just called in our ride."

THE RIDE WAS a Bell JetRanger, typical, Bolan knew, of what flew tourists around the islands. It touched down on the beach, near the wharf, a black op waiting in the fuselage hatch. Bolan slit his eyelids against the rotor wash and whipping sand, boarding behind Collins and Hamadan. He half expected Collins to give Paradise one final wistful look, but the major simply moved through the hatch.

As the Executioner grabbed a seat, the chopper up and away, that strange dreamy haze came back, settling a mist over reality that was part adrenaline residue but mostly exhaustion. He was only flesh and blood, after all, aware that he hadn't slept or eaten…

Since when?

The time passed for the soldier in that murky film. Bolan felt every muscle sore and aching and burning, from scalp to toes, his empty belly grumbling, mouth and throat raw from dehydration. He was alert, just the same, but felt as if he were slogging ahead, running on pure energy reserves and will alone. So many questions unanswered, they were a jumbled echo in his brain. The miles of this campaign were already taking their toll, but he knew he would suck it up, the way of the warrior.

They were in the Gulfstream, what felt like an endless passage of time later, airborne from Mahé, Collins on his radio. Bolan heard a lot of monosyllabic grunting from the command center in the rear. Something very ugly, he knew, waited in the near future, and it didn't involve hunting down the enemy. He decided to hold his tongue from there on, let Collins call the shots, go with the flow.

One of the Cobra gang.

Collins walked up in his mist, offered a cigarette. Bolan declined it and the proffered shot of booze from the major's silver flask. Hamadan had been handed over to what Collins called his cleanup crew on Praslin. Whatever intelligence could be found at the beach house would become the property of Collins's cleanup ops. Whatever became of the body of Gambler...well, Bolan didn't much give a damn. It was a strange state of mind the Executioner found himself in, caring but not caring, patient but impatient to reach—discover— what waited at the end of the line.

"Warlock and Cyclops flew ahead with the prisoners," Collins said. "They're in charge of interrogation— that came from up top."

"If there's any prisoners left to talk to by the time they get them to wherever they're going."

"A Greek island," Collins said. "That's where they'll

be detained, and that's where the tribunal will eventually be held."

"Let me guess. The Greeks don't know anything."

"They know, or at least the ones who should. It was a hard sell, the way I heard it, but they finally agreed to let us in. The island—Camp Zero—is the sole property of the United States government. Black ops all the way, Colonel. This is something from beginning to end you won't see splashed all over world headlines." Collins took a seat, puffing, peering at Bolan. "You look like hell, Colonel. I got some sandwiches, bottled water and cold beer in the fridge. Why don't you eat, grab a nap while there's time. Lebanon is up next. From here on it doesn't get any easier."

Or perhaps any down and dirtier, the Executioner thought.

CHAPTER TWELVE

Hamid Bhouri wanted peace on Earth, goodwill toward all men. There was no animosity, no violence in his heart toward those outside the Muslim faith, no matter how much he might disagree with them, no matter how much they might despise him and his faith. It wasn't even part of his character to take up arms against foreigners who might desire to impose their will on the people of the Middle East, and in the name of oil, if he chose to believe the propaganda of the extremists. As far as he was concerned, the sins of other men were theirs to own before the judgment of God when they left the world.

Over the years, surviving in a war-torn land, he had come to believe there was nothing he could say, nothing he could do to change the hearts of men bent on violence and destruction. Even with the best intentions of keeping his distance from the extremists, he was forever hounded, even railed at by militant Arabs at times to join their ranks, strike down the infidel, even if that meant a suicide attack, which, he knew, was an abomination in the eyes of God. Live and let live, he believed—if only that were true.

He still had to live in Lebanon. And no man, peacemaker or warrior, he thought, was ever allowed the luxury of choosing not to choose.

He prayed five times daily without fail, all passion and feverish imploring for paradise on Earth, free of violence and hatred and war, even though he knew it was little more than a fool's dream. Considering the darker side of human nature, the present state of world affairs—what with all the wars and rumors of wars—he feared the future of mankind was bleak at best, dire at worst. His own country, for instance, was still a seething caldron of violence and ancient hatreds and religious intolerance, his land surrounded by other nations that could well push the entire region beyond critical mass, ignite the fuse to a cataclysm imaginable only in the very bowels of Hell.

With what he suspected was coming that night, he had to ask God one last time for help and guidance, his faithful servant, if not for the salvation of other men's souls, then to watch over, protect and insure the safety of his own corner of the world. He was a family man, after all, with a wife and four children whose futures and safety he had to consider. It pained him greatly that his decision, the deceit of his task might very well have put their lives in danger.

To his family and neighbors, he was a simple farmer, a herder of goats and sheep, the rumors of his brief affiliation with Hamas and Hezbollah chaff in the wind, gone with brutal men long since dead and unlamented. Those days, he recalled—when the rumors could be misconstrued and edged toward fact—had been merely a charade in order to survive in the Muslim quarter of Beirut, the younger Bhouri publicly espousing extreme fundamentalism, faking it, to be sure, never firing a weapon even in anger. For that he was grateful, his soul still unstained by bloodshed, the taking of life. So very long ago, but it seemed only yesterday when, at the tail end of the fifteen-year-old civil war, he had inherited fertile land in the Bekaa Valley from his father, removed himself and his family from the strife and violence of the city. The warring factions and the extremists might have laid down their weapons in Beirut, no longer slaughtering each other, but the danger had followed him to the Bekaa.

Choices once again.

Lately there were more guns, more black-hooded terrorists in the countryside than he could count, much less cared to have live so close to his home in the town of Basri just north of the Beirut-Damascus Highway. With what he knew was a growing threat to the internal security of his country, the dream was losing its glowing allure. He no longer felt such a simple man with basic needs, wishing only to plow his wheat, see his children grow to have children, the fear now mounting that his country would once again be fractured by civil war or feel the wrath of invading armies or shattered to oblivion like Afghanistan by bombs falling endlessly out of the sky.

Peace on Earth? His bitter chuckle was flung back in his face by a cold wind soughing down the mountainside. The awful truth, he knew, was that what he longed for was as worlds apart from reality as Heaven was from Hell.

He wasn't sure whether he had made the choice, or if the choice had been made for him. As he crouched in a gully, searching the black skies above the snowcapped ridges of the Anti-Lebanon Mountains, wishing for a moment he was armed, he pondered his fate and the past that had led him to this moment.

Long ago he had been an information broker for Mossad and CIA agents. It was dangerous work, spying on his fellow countrymen, but there had been a time when he wasn't sure how he was going to feed his family. He had believed that by relocating to the Bekaa he would never have to tread those shark-infested waters again. How wrong he had been proven, wondering if a man ever really escaped his past.

Roughly three months ago he had been approached by two men in Basri, one of them with a thick Israeli accent, the other foreigner with a hideous scar on his hand. He was to gather whatever information he could on the Arnous camp in the Bekaa. They seemed to know every detail about his life, from birth to present and that had shaken him to the core of his being. They knew he had cousins who were in Hamas and Hezbollah, both in Lebanon and Israel. They knew he valued his family more than anything in the world. They could make his life a living hell if he didn't cooperate, putting out the word that he was a Mossad informant, which would leave his life and the lives of his family numbered in hours. After listening to their spiel with the thinly veiled threats and what was demanded of him, he had agreed. It wasn't so much out of fear as he had been prompted by a growing sense of urgency that his country—a mass haven for international terrorists—had to be cleansed of extremists. Or his country, he feared, could well suffer the same fate as Afghanistan if America was attacked and the fists of retribution were directed at Lebanon.

So they gave him a small laptop with secured fax and e-mail, a promise of a cash reward if his services proved useful to them. They had given him a homing beacon, GPS module, night-vision scope to spy on the camp at night. He was to report in and check his messages daily, await further orders. He was to monitor the countryside, assess the numbers of terrorists, detail for them the easiest and quickest route by which to infiltrate a small commando unit, using his own canvass-covered truck to trek in the invaders.

He already knew about the sprawling Arnous camp to the northeast but, whether it was luck or some design of fate, he had discovered the cave in the foothills of the mountains at the southern edge of the valley. He had been ordered to monitor the comings and goings of the extremists in that cave. He had counted no more than five at any one time. He had no idea how deep the cave went or what was inside, but an e-mail had come back only last night, telling him to not worry about it, "they" knew. The last, cryptic message had told him tonight was the night, he was to hunker down approximately a mile south of the cave, three hundred feet up the slope of the foothills, and wait. Whatever excuse, flimsy or otherwise, he was to give his wife for his midnight absence was his business. Just be there.

So there he was, alone and shivering in the dark in his sheepskin coat, waiting on a group of foreign commandos, risking his entire world. It was a given these night invaders were coming to kill the terrorists he had been spying and reporting on. He was ashamed for a moment by the sudden flash of violent desire in his heart, hoping they left no one behind in the cave or the camp alive, the risk being that one of the extremists would discover he had betrayed them.

He checked the homing beacon, the module clipped to his belt. The light was flashing red, telling him it was on-line. The gnawing fear now was that he would be discovered before the commandos arrived, perhaps was even being stalked right then by the extremists in the cave. If found, he would be searched, questioned, the high-tech gear he carried nothing but red flags he was out there in the valley for more than just a midnight stroll.

He checked the foothills again, alert for shadows, wondering how the invaders would come to him. With all the checkpoints and Syrian military outposts, he couldn't picture them just driving in, not unless they numbered in the hundreds, came in tanks, the beginning of some dreaded full-scale invasion, life as he knew it over. No, they needed a vehicle he had been told. The sky, then.

He was looking up, peering at the scudding clouds, thinking he spotted some dark shape sailing high above. It was a glimpse of a massive object, there in the cloud break, then gone, then he felt the muzzle of a weapon jammed into the back of his skull.

"You'd better be Hamid."

It took a long moment, his knees trembling, but he recalled the password. "Welcome to my humble country."

"That'll work. You understand what will happen to you if you don't play it straight with us?"

"Perfectly."

Hamid turned, faced the big commando. His face, neck and hands, he saw, were covered in black war paint. There was a massive assault rifle in his hands with an attached rocket launcher, the big shadow nearly invisible in his blacksuit, the invader weighted down with spare clips, grenades, a side arm. The eyes peered through the dark, as if dissecting the inner man, searching for hidden motivations, Bhouri feeling the freeze ripple through him. Bhouri knew he had nothing to hide, but he couldn't help but wonder right then if he was on the side of the angels, or if these commandos would prove themselves devils in human skin, march him to his own death.

He offered up a silent prayer that God be with him, wishing only to get this over with and return to his family.

THE RECRUITMENT, grooming and handling of unsavory characters on the other side was how covert ops succeeded in thrashing the enemy inside their borders. They could be gunrunners, drug mules, even terrorists who had a change of heart, wanted out or were looking to turn a quick buck. In short, they were betraying their own, untrustworthy until they proved themselves, actors in a grim drama of death. Bolan knew it was the way of the black-ops world, gaining information on the enemy by using the enemy, and there was no point in standing around debating if Hamid could be trusted or was steering them into an ambush.

They were on the ground and moving.

The Executioner, the first one out of the C-130, had touched down at the end of the HALO first, using his GPS and homing beacon tuned in to the informant's transponder. He had reached Bhouri first, landing roughly two thousand yards south of the man, silently padding down the slope, using cedar trees for momentary cover and surveillance of his surroundings while on the advance. It ground up critical time, thirty-two minutes before the other Cobra commandos were gathered, Hamid grilled again, and they were off and stalking through the night.

It was 0334 by the time Bolan, leading Gator and Wallbanger down the rocky slope, reached the ledge over the cave's entrance. He took a moment, signaling his teammates to pull up, the sentry suddenly stepping into view, working on a smoke.

Bolan assessed the entire play, liking and trusting it all even less after the near fatal Gambler encounter in Seychelles.

Again, it was the major's show, Collins detailing the strike since the moment they were wheels-up in Kenya. Their latest mobile base was near the Israeli-Lebanese border, the commanding officer, Colonel Ben David Yehudin, having greeted Cobra Force with less than a warm reception. Apparently the IDF and Mossad had their orders from up top, though, and the Israelis were on standby with the Gods of Thunder ready to unload an air strike on the Arnous camp, paving the way for a Cobra ground assault.

It was Bolan's task to take down the cave and occupants, destroy whatever arms cache was buried inside. According to both Collins and Yehudin, the Syrian army, coddling extremists from all over the Middle East and inviting them into Lebanon, was using heavy machinery to dig out caves and tunnels in the Anti-Lebanon Mountains. Whether they were storing weapons and explosives or preparing to dig in and ride out some massive air assault, no one could be sure. A potential suicide bomber, though, had been snatched up in Jerusalem weeks before. He had been cooperating with both Mossad and American intelligence agents working in the shadows of the Cobra campaign, handing over information about the camp and the cave. Supposedly the tunnel ran some two hundred feet straight ahead into the foothills, veered left, a reverse *L*. Another thirty feet down, and militants—no more than six—were posted to guard a massive cache of assault rifles, grenades and explosives. Handheld heat sensors would paint the numbers, but Bolan was watching his own twelve and six again. It struck him as more than curious that Collins had pasted two nonserpent commandos to his hip, the soldier again disturbed by the feeling he wasn't meant to make it out of the country, the three of them sacrificial lambs. Penetrating caves for an armed engagement was no easy chore to start with. Any number of dangers—booby traps, land mines and so forth—could rear up, with nooks and crannies concealing the enemy. The would-be bomber, or so Collins informed Bolan, swore the cave wasn't rigged with mines or sensors and trip wires. A straight shot to the depot, allegedly.

Collins wanted the roof brought down on the cave, and Wallbanger lugged the C-4 and incendiary packages for the blast-and-burn job. Bolan didn't have a problem with that; the less destructive capability the enemy had the better. The whiff of trouble he caught again wanted to paint the bull's-eye on his back. One, he was peeled off from the bulk of the force moving in on the camp. Two, when they sealed the cave here, they would be forced to drive in on the camp, commandeering the Land Cruiser parked in front of the cave. They were supposed to link up with the others while the bombs fell and Collins was off and running. The air show should wipe out most of the militants at Arnous. Close to two hundred extremists, homegrown and taking refuge in Lebanon to train and carry out operations, were up for the doomsday touch. The standing order from Collins was to burn down every armed extremist. No prisoners, unless they threw their hands up and made their job that much easier.

Alone again, feeling it deep in his gut, the Executioner laid down his M-16/M-203 combo. Drawing himself onto a knee, he pulled the sound-suppressed Beretta 93-R. He pointed at the sentry, who flicked the cigarette away, unzipped to relieve himself. The whirl of a hand, the arranged tornado signal, and they knew it was a go after the sentry was taken out.

The Executioner drew target acquisition.

CHAPTER THIRTEEN

"Don't talk."

Hamid Bhouri looked over at the black-clad, war-painted commando, not liking what he saw or heard in the least. He felt his gut clench, heart sink, fear gripping him as he stared into eyes that held no life. He knew it was over, and he cried inside, aware he would never see his family again.

Such, he thought, was the cruelty of life.

There was something about this one—unlike the first commando he had laid eyes on—he couldn't trust. It was as if he were looking at a sack of flesh with no soul, unlike the other commando, who seemed to have something else beyond the war face, something far greater and far more noble burning deep inside. But what? he now wondered. Mercy? Compassion? Understanding? That the first one could discriminate between good and evil, draw a line that defined clearly what was human and what was not, act decisively when there was no point of return for the other, no remorse or hope for those at the end of his gun?

Hamid Bhouri couldn't say for certain, but he knew he was looking at his own death beside him.

The one time this commando in the passenger seat had looked at him—or through him—Bhouri felt a chill walk down his spine, a whisper of doom ghosting through his mind that he was expendable at the end of this ride. Or was it simply just fear talking back at him, the fervent desire to finish his task and return home to his family? Was there hope still?

No.

This commando, apparently in charge, had a cold voice and the dead eyes of a serpent, looked and spoke to him as if he were less than dirt, alive only to serve his purpose, so much garbage to be crumpled up and tossed aside when he was no longer useful. It was only a gut feeling, but he'd seen and been around enough cold-blooded killers to know when he was in the presence of evil.

He had been explaining the route, distance, how he'd tracked the safest passage to the southern edge of the camp, nerves getting the better of him, talking if only to hear himself talk, clinging to a fading hope he would see his wife and children again.

Fading fast, and gone. God—or destiny—was calling him now to accept that which he couldn't change. Had he not, he recalled, told his own children that violence only begot more violence, continued only a cycle of pain and suffering for all? That angry pride was the willful instrument of the Devil, serving only to drive man to self-destruction? That, to turn the other cheek, going against the willful and proud impulse of man, was the only way? That there was more strength in humility, that a savage act only made man less human, or worthy in the eyes of God?

Who could say, he thought, but knew he was moments away from discovering.

Lights off on the van, he was winding them ahead through the wadi, cedars dotting the lunar landscape up the slopes, the night illuminated in a ghostly green hue through his NVD goggles. Three of the invaders had been left behind to penetrate the cave, do whatever they were going to do, while he provided taxi service for the rest, a sudden wish the first one was here now with him, that he would see the dawn and be with his family.

A fool's wish, he knew.

Four of the commandos were in the van, with four more heavily armed shadows lurching in his rear and side mirrors as they trailed, scouring the ridgelines, he assumed, for any threat. He had been ordered to maintain a steady ten miles per hour, the near invisible rearguard clipping along, armed spacemen, he thought, with their NVD headgear, falling farther behind but keeping a pace that told him they were in top mean and lean physical conditioning.

"Don't look at me—watch where you're going. I won't tell you again."

Something in the voice said it all.

Silently Bhouri began to pray. They were suddenly getting themselves worked up, the serpent commando with some minicomputer in his hands, his fingers a blur as they flew with a fury over the keyboard. He was rattling off numbers, ordering one of the others in the back to relay a series of those numbers, call it in.

"Park it, kill the engine."

Bhouri did as he was told. The serpent commando was ordering the others to go. They were out, melting into the night, charging the hill that would take them to the camp. He stripped off his night-vision goggles, laid them down between the seats, afraid but strangely calm in some way that took him out of his body. The fire began to burn up behind his eyes next, as he prayed for his soul, the future safety of his family, but he wouldn't show weakness or beg for his life. He was sick for a second, painfully aware that he had not sided with the angels.

There was, yes, evil alive and walking in the Bekaa, he knew, but who was what? Perhaps the invaders had come here to erase an abomination that was simply on the earth to cause grief and misery. Perhaps, he decided, it took some form of evil to defeat a greater evil. Perhaps God, in his infinite wisdom, didn't need to explain his plan to a simple farmer.

He didn't see the serpent commando do it, sensed

instead the pistol coming out, a sound suppressor being attached. It was a flash before his eyes, as he stared ahead into the night. All that was, and could have been, the faces of his family, a mosaic of pain and joy, tears and laughter raced before him, a living vision that told him all he needed to know.

He could have fought the serpent commando, lunging over, grabbing the gun. Even if he killed him, there were other men of violence with automatic weapons who would turn back, murder him.

Bhouri shut his eyes, the smile tight on his mouth, Samira and his children dancing through his mind again.

All that never would be.

There was a warmth next, a glow, spreading with a paralyzing force through him, a light he could see inside his head. He felt a courage he would have never dreamed himself capable of, accepting what was. It was over, but someday…

Someday he would see his family in Heaven.

In Arabic he told the serpent, "May God have mercy on your soul."

"What?"

"May peace and mercy be unto those who seek it."

He heard the serpent chuckle. "You know, if God cared so much, the world wouldn't be such a fucked-up place."

He turned his head toward the serpent as the commando lifted the pistol and told him, "Appreciate the lift."

NO SOONER HAD Bolan leaped off the ledge, landed, flanked by Wallbanger and Gator after getting the all-clear hand signal from the Cobra commandos, then he sensed how wrong it all felt. Sure, they were painted in red, five stationary targets in all at the deepest end of the reverse L on his heat-motion sensor, but one look down the narrow cave and his gut told him it was about to go to hell. Were they lying in wait? No question the enemy had the advantage in this situation, and what was to say they likewise didn't have heat and motion sensors at their disposal? Well, he had to go to them, no matter what, one of several potential deadly problems, and if they knew he was coming...

Damn! Bolan would be the first to admit he hated armed engagements in a cave, turf the enemy had created with every advantage on their side. Nothing he could do about it now. A flamethrower would be nice, or better still one of those warbirds at the good major's beck and call simply cleansing the cave with a well-placed laser-guided bunker buster.

So much for wishful thinking.

Bolan motioned for Gator to guard the entrance, Wallbanger to lag behind during their penetration. Each ventured step was going to prove beyond hazardous, Bolan's gaze flickering from the heat monitor to the floor and walls in search of trip wires, booby traps but...

It occurred to the warrior that if Collins did in fact want him out of the way, he just might get his wish.

Not tonight, Bolan determined. There was, yes, something to be said about sheer willful pride and raw guts.

The hole was just large enough for the soldier to slip inside, a single naked bulb midway down providing just enough light to steer his advance. Wallbanger, he glimpsed, wasn't listening so good; Bolan shooting his arm back for the commando to keep his distance. The Executioner wasn't looking to take a bullet for the home team on a reckless whim, but if it went south he could tell Collins—assuming he walked out—that he'd taken point, done his damnedest to keep his men out of harm's way, Colonel Considerate.

He scanned the rocky floor, the breaks in the wall for wires, concealed explosives, every yard breached and earned with agonizing quiet care. The assault rifle was out, one-handed, Bolan maybe fifty paces from the bend when he saw the flurry of movement on his screen.

They were coming.

A heartbeat later he saw the mirror mounted on the wall where the cave cut back in its reverse L. More often than not, Bolan knew, low-tech could beat high.

"Fall back!" he shouted at Wallbanger, just as two skullcapped hardmen whirled around the corner, holding back on the triggers of AK-47s, blazing away and screaming in Arabic.

It was pure luck, but Bolan spotted and flung himself into a narrow crevice slashed down the wall. A swarm of projectiles screamed past the Executioner in sense-shattering ricochets, the deafening roar of auto-fire swelling his brain. He crouched, heard the sharp cry ring out. A fleeting eyefull, but he caught Wallbanger falling, blood spurting from his chest and forehead. There was no choice but to brave the storm, bullets snapping past his head, if he was going to turn the tide. He was swinging around the edge of the crack when he found one of the two shooters arming a grenade. A lightning shift in aim and Bolan stitched him up the chest, flinging him back in a one-eighty jig, the grenade rolling up beside the falling body.

THE NUMBERS WERE crunched. All they had to do now, Collins thought, was to wait for the compound to start going up in flames. One F-117 Stealth, four F-15Es, two Apaches and his trusty Spectre were on the way. A combo American-Israeli squad of fighter pilots, but there was no mistake in his mind they were the best of the best. The Israelis, he knew, wanted this camp erased off the map, nothing more than a smoking memory, as bad as the Americans.

Stretched out in a prone position, Collins surveyed the massive compound, his troops fanned out on their bellies. They were spread out on the lip of the wadi, a quarter mile due south of the terror camp. Cyclone fence encircled an area that was roughly three city blocks. It was electrified, but it would be cut with rub-ber-handled hydraulic shears. Guard towers on four points of the compass, watching the valley, the perimeter swaddled in areas by cedar. One look, and he knew the fighter jockeys would have to get it right the first time. Four massive concrete buildings, the sat dishes marking the C and C structure to the west. Figure the other buildings were barracks, training centers, classrooms, over a hundred terrorists to tackle. Then there were machine-gun nests, two tracked ZSU-23-4s that would have to go first, enough APCs and Land Cruisers to swell a giant parking lot. Right then it appeared most hands were asleep, a few stragglers hanging around, just the same, smoking shadows in the outer reaches of klieg lights.

A fearsome piece of intelligence had reached Collins about this batch of terrorists. According to the late Gambler, there were detailed papers about their mission—or, rather, the darker aspects of what would soon go down. If those fell into the wrong hands, he was faced with major problems, his own plans all but scrapped. That would leave him...

Hell, broke, hung out and hunted.

No chance, if he had anything to say about it. That was part of the reason he had dispatched Stone to take down the cave. Not only that, but wiping out a nest of fanatics hunkered down in a cave was no easy task. With any luck...

Something told Collins he'd see Stone again. Or maybe not.

The face of Amir Habikin, the camp commander, was

framed in his memory. He needed the Syrian bastard talking, and he had to take first what was suspected he had. There were to be no survivors, unless they were third or fourth tier, out of the deeper circle of the enemy intelligence loop, and threw their hands up, begging for mercy.

He was tempted to check the black skies, but looked at the illuminated dial of his chronometer. He would hear the explosions before he even saw the payloads on the way.

Collins did.

There was thunder and lightning, rocking the world out of nowhere, the sky falling on the compound with the laser-guided barrage. The night was on fire, one rolling, blazing wave after another, buildings blown to smithereens, but Collins knew it wouldn't get any easier once they were inside the fence.

BOLAN RODE OUT the blast, hugging cover, then charged into the boiling smoke, sweeping the cloud with spray-and-pray autofire. They were shouting around the corner, a glance at his screen painting them at the deep end of the reverse L but coming toward him.

Arming a frag grenade, Bolan let it fly in a low whipping motion, the throw angled, a sidearmed pitch. He was aiming for a ricochet, spied it caroming off the far wall, then vanish. The explosion, trapped in the tight confines of the cave, split his skull but he was moving hard and fast to mop it up.

Crouched, he hit the edge, caught the moans of walking mangled and wheeled around the corner, holding back on the trigger. Two were reeling about, trying to bring their stuttering assault rifles back on-line, but they were absorbing lead, the soldier nailing them left to right.

Bolan took in the stacks of crates, then toed all five bodies, pumping a round each into forehead or the ground hamburger of each face. He whirled, barely catching the scuffling through the ringing in his ears. Gator materialized out of the smoke cloud.

Bolan ignored the angry look on Gator's face, aware the commando was jacked up over the loss of his teammate, searching for a quick release for his pent-up aggression. The Executioner brushed past him, moved on to finish the task here. Stooping over Wallbanger, he checked for a pulse, but already knew the commando was dead.

Gator was cursing. "What the fuck happened, Colonel?"

"You saw it."

"What am I—you—going to tell the major?"

"That he's lucky he didn't lose all three of us." Bolan plucked the incendiary package off Wallbanger. "Get him out of here and fire up that Land Cruiser. Move it!"

There was just enough angry hesitation from Gator, but Bolan checked the tongue lashing, as the commando grumbled, then scooped up Wallbanger, draping him over his shoulder in a fireman's carry.

Bolan put him out of mind, then trekked back to ignite the fuse that would bring the roof down on this rat's nest. Five more bad guys down, one less weapons cache for terrorists to slaughter the innocent with. Whatever else had happened here, Bolan figured it was a decent coup, all things considered.

CHAPTER FOURTEEN

The written standing orders had been delivered by fellow Syrian cutouts one week ago from their Iranian sponsor. It was so incredible, preposterous even, that Amir Habikin had dismissed it as lunacy. Seven long days later, and he was still left wondering if the vaunted leader of the global jihad was either insane or was in league with the Devil.

Which dumped him into a quandary of dark and unsettling dimensions.

The questions alone were endless, agonizing, driving him to consume more alcohol than normal, smoke an extra pack of American cigarettes per day. There were no answers in sight, just a stream of questions that flowed in the same direction toward the waterfall that could send him plunging into the abyss of some monstrous conspiracy, a leviathan in the churning waters at the end of the descent, waiting to swallow him whole.

Not even his fellow Muslims, he knew, were above betraying their own.

He was sitting at his desk, perusing the aspects of the proposed plan, wondering once more where the truth ended and the treachery might begin. It had become something of a nightly ritual, alone in his office, chain-smoking, a glass of whiskey at his fingertips, sifting through dark thoughts, reading the report over and over, then staring at it as if a vision of the future would leap out of the pages and slap him in the face, showing him all the answers, divine guidance sure to follow. The more he read and pondered the standing orders, the more curious—and anxious—he became.

Scratch that. He was frightened, and as a leader of holy warriors committed to jihad, he wasn't allowed to be afraid.

Incredible as it sounded, the global jihad leader, it appeared, had cut some deal with infidels to capture what was more or less a who's who list of well-known freedom fighters. From Somalia to Lebanon to the Gaza Strip many of what were, in his mind, the best, the brightest and the toughest of holy warriors, were to allow themselves to be taken prisoner by some faceless, nameless force of Western commandos. The when, where and how was unclear.

That was only the start, however. The insanity got better, or worse, depending on who was chosen to be saved and who was destined to become a sacrificial lamb.

It was so written that a select group would be captured alive, while scores of other holy warriors were to virtually commit suicide in the face of overwhelming force. Personally he had no desire to end up like so many of his fellow Muslims now imprisoned in Cuba, much less slain by hated enemies he was sworn to kill.

The plan didn't end with detainment, but he had no intention of carrying out the orders.

It was time, perhaps, to cut the umbilical cord to Iran. Sure, their sponsor shipped weapons, the necessary cash to arm and house his troops, money and matériel that kept General Salidin happy and funneling still more freedom fighters and weapons into the Bekaa. But what he was being asked to do was madness pure and simple.

There were operations already on the table, and they took absolute and supreme precedence. It had taken too much time, toil, sweat and money to prepare the infiltration of his freedom fighters into Israel, Western Europe, the United States. Years of preparation, in fact, had gone into a jihad that would shake the entire world, carve his very name in stone forever as the most holy and fearsome warrior. In twos and threes his own warriors were slated to go within days, bogus passports stamped with Western names allowing them to slip into the targeted countries, too much money and training to see it all wasted at the last moment.

Amir Habikin had a dream to fulfill, too.

Holy human time bombs were destined to erupt all over the streets of America, Israel, Western Europe, and at the same appointed hour, day and night. He could see it, so clear in his mind after a few stiff belts of whiskey, that it was alive in running cinematic color, dozens of glorious moments of victory forever seared in the annals of Muslim history. They would stroll into shopping malls, restaurants, movie theaters. They would stand in lines at banks, post offices, carry briefcases or wrap themselves up with explosives, bring down entire courthouses. They would walk down crowded streets, take out hundreds of infidels in the blink of an eye. They would slip luggage, stuffed with explosives, onto Greyhound, Amtrak, jetliners. There would be mass death at the same instant. There would be horror and chaos, wailing and gnashing of teeth. Entire transportation systems—rail, bus, plane, highway—would screech to a halt, everything jammed, swimming in blood and terror. There would be no hope, no way out for the enemy, no amount of cleaning up ever restoring order. Their so-called civilization as they knew it would be over, finished, all of it, he thought, gone to Hell where it belonged. What he couldn't finish, well, the infidels would slaughter and consume one another in panic, internal anarchy sweeping their masses, riots, looting, murder in the streets.

It was a beautiful vision to behold.

And he wasn't about to see it all perish because some wild scheme was dropped in his lap by a questionable ally with an insane agenda. There were entire waves of martyrs, loaded down with explosives, willing to light themselves up in the targeted lands on his word. Key cells were already in place. The date, in fact, was already set, but it would take time to get the other martyr cells situated, final logistics ironed out.

Now this madness—or foolishness—staring him in the face.

The more he thought about the Iranian, the more he began to believe that the sponsor was perhaps setting him up, a pawn in his mad scheme, or perhaps he was viewed now as expendable, the Iranian wishing him out of the way, wanting all operations and all the glory for himself.

That in mind, he decided it was best if he began covering all of his bases. He was protected by the Syrian army in the Bekaa, and he was thinking he should take this crazy scheme directly to General Salidin, get his thoughts, gauge his reaction. If they were on the same page, then the Iranian had to be cut loose. He was safe enough inside the borders of Lebanon, even against Muslim assassins who might seek to impale his head on a stake if the Iranian felt snubbed.

Enough.

He rose, gathering the report, shutting it inside his briefcase. One last sip of whiskey, stabbing out the cigarette, and he was marching for the door, toting the plan. He was in the hall that led to the radar and communication stations, searching for a subordinate to drive him to Salidin's command post when it happened.

It was strange, this frozen moment, he briefly

thought, how he knew what that sound of thunder was, and why the entire facade of the C and C building was blown through the room in a tidal wave of fire and smoke.

The enemy had arrived; the dream was over.

Amir Habikin wanted to scream in outrage, but there was a blinding supernova in his eyes, then he was airborne, sailing through blackness and silence.

THE FIREBALL ROILED OUT of the cave. Bolan winced at the flash of light but his mind was on the next battlefield. Even still, as Gator manned the Land Cruiser and tore over the broken floor of the wadi, he gave a grim moment's thought to the campaign. He was under no grand illusions about their effort to strike back at terrorism, in this or any other mission. The new war had shifted tactics, going preemptive in world headlines, but it was still the same never-ending battle for the Executioner. No matter how many they took out, it was a monumental task to expect even the most skilled and determined force to rid the planet of what the administration tagged as evil-doers. There would always be more terrorists when the sun rose the following day.

It never stopped for Bolan.

Perhaps, he thought, killing a man was easy—it was the changing of his heart that seemed impossible. A warrior, he would leave all that to the priests, poets and philosophers. For him, there was always that point of no return, and when any man crossed it, became a savage, out for number one, he could expect no mercy from the Executioner.

Bolan focused on the grim chore at hand, scouring the darkness as the headlights stabbed into the night. Keying his com link, as he saw the sky lighting up with mushrooming fireballs to the north, he attempted to raise Collins. "Wild Card to Cobra Leader! Do you read me?"

Three seconds and Collins growled in his ear, "I'm a little busy right now. What?"

"We're en route. ETA maybe five minutes. Your cave's been taken care of, five bad guys and cache, burned and buried."

"Roger that. Good work."

"You have a second to see us painted on your monitor? I'd hate to get waxed by mistake this late in the game."

"Yeah, but how come I'm only reading two of you?"

"Wallbanger didn't make it."

Collins cursed. "You know where to shake and bake, so get your asses here and give us a hand! Out!"

Bolan fed his M-16 a fresh clip, dumped a 40 mm frag grenade down the chute of his rocket launcher. He knew the battle strategy, but that didn't mean Collins or the Gods of Thunder would stick to the plan. Friendly fire sometimes didn't distinguish between friend or foe.

Moments later, Bolan saw the van pop up in the headlights. A figure was slumped in the driver's seat.

"Pull it over a second."

Gator hit the brakes with some anger the soldier figured was hostile residue, jerking him in his seat. He started to bare his teeth, but he focused on the body in the van. Their Lebanese contact had taken one between the eyes.

"Any thoughts why your boss eighty-sixed him?" Bolan asked Gator.

Gator shrugged. "None leap to mind, Colonel. Maybe the major knew something about him we didn't."

"Why does that bother me?"

"You'll have to ask the major."

"Move it out, we'll bail at the bottom of the slope."

"What about Wallbanger?" Gator asked, throwing a nod over his shoulder.

"He's not going anywhere. We'll come back and get him later."

The Executioner was out the door and advancing up the hill, the din of massive explosions swelling the air, urging him on and into the fire.

Aware of where it was headed beyond Lebanon, Bolan knew he was close to the end of the mission now. But, he wondered, the end—or the beginning—of what?

"THUNDER GOD Red White and Blue to Cobra Leader. Let me know something if you'd be so kind."

Collins was in and running, angling for the smoking rubble of what was left of the C and C center when his Apache ace patched through. Thunder God RWB was on the way, he hoped, to help mop up and cover their asses in the wake of the Spectre's brutal touch, but he was a little too preoccupied at the moment to check in for confirmation.

M-16 flaming and dropping two terrorists on the intensive-care list at twelve o'clock, Collins pulled up behind the overturned wreckage of a Land Cruiser, hacking on smoke, flames dancing near his face.

The compound, he saw, was an inferno, east to west, north to south, firestorms spiraling in some bizarre tornado twist from fuel and munitions depots north, the heat so intense it wanted to suck the air out of his lungs, bitter smoke stinging his eyes, bringing on the tears. There were still plenty of armed problems to take care of, despite the pummeling by the Gods of Thunder, twenty to thirty strong, scattered about and scurrying by his first reckoning. F-15Es and the black and near invisible flat arrowhead that was the Stealth, he saw, were still swarming the skies overhead, screens sure to be tuned in to any MiGs brazen or stupid enough to take to the skies. Any Syrian or Lebanese patrols in the area were on the playcard to get the hook.

Collins was taking Python and Diamondback on the hunt for Habikin's intel. It would be a miracle, he knew, if he found it. If anyone after this night bothered to dig through all that rubble and found it, he figured they could have it, but only after the job was done. Whether or not he found the package by some miracle, the game plan just got bumped up either way. There were pressing calls to make, time frames to alter, accounts to verify.

First he had to survive the night.

"Go, Thunder God!"

"I've got you painted. One minute and counting before we're on the spot."

"Still lots of problems for you to take care of, Thunder God. We're still in a pinch."

And Collins spotted a ZSU still intact, muzzle-flashes stabbing the night from the east and north towers, the bulk of crazed wounded appearing to scrape themselves off the ground or materializing out of wreckage and smoke to his deep three. He told his Apache ace to stick to the east, and his men would hang back while he sanitized that area.

"Get my Black Hawk in the area, ten minutes and counting to pick us up."

The order copied, Collins broke for the mountains of rubble. Python and Diamondback got the next round of shooting started. Three terrorists, the ones Collins thought as wearing checkered underwear wrapped around their heads, poked through a break in the rubble, AKs chattering. With Python and Diamondback brandishing M-249 SAWs—squad automatic weapons—the enemy didn't stand a chance.

Collins held back on the trigger of his assault rifle, adding some punch to the whopping firepower of the

SAWs, each one fitted with a 200-round magazine, blazing away at 750 rounds per minute. Faces and headcloths were obliterated in crimson clouds before Collins's eyes.

He was climbing the rubble next, peering into the smoke, sparks and electricity snapping from several small fires touched off by the aerial bombardment somewhere in all the debris but guiding him, when he spotted the battered snake. Sliding down the hill of rubble, he thrust the muzzle of his M-16 into a bloody mask of hatred.

In Arabic, Collins said, "Habikin? You seen him?"

The terrorist was thinking about something, then smiled, jerked a nod over his shoulder. "Good luck."

"The strong make their own luck," Collins said, and shot him in the face.

CHAPTER FIFTEEN

The Executioner once again found the overwhelming force of air firepower had leveled another opponent, but controlling the skies had never been in doubt. Even still, the warrior knew no enemy was ever entirely obliterated by saturation bombing alone, and there was much recent evidence—mistakes made in the interests of keeping friendly casualties to a minimum—in that regard. It took trained and determined professional soldiers to wade in on foot and smoke the last rat out of its nest. Whatever he might think—or suspect—about Collins and Cobra, he could stand up and tell them to a man they weren't lacking in martial skill and guts.

It took five minutes plus to find the hole in the fence, and by the time Bolan led Gator onto the slaughter-ground he could tell it was winding down. The enormity of the thrashing he found before him told him two things. One—the scope of this operation, so classified

and so buried even from the cyber team at Stony Man
Farm, was well beyond anything he'd been briefed on,
but he couldn't fault Brognola for plunging him into
some black void of dangerous ignorance where he had
to figure it out along the way, prove himself to un-
knowns, ride with whatever program unfolded with
each round. Two—no punches were being pulled.
Damn any political backlash or UN harangue, so-called
sovereign nations harboring terror armies were not even
any longer on short notice.

This mission, Bolan had seen, gave new meaning to
"preemptive strike."

The soldier took in the death spasms of the battle,
spotting Cobra commandos, concealed behind strewed
rubble and wreckage on a north-by-northeast line in
staggered firepoints, busy hosing down the shattered
terror remnants. Whatever they didn't nail with sustained autofire, rocket-propelled grenades, Bolan found
the Apache gunship hard at work. Hellfire missiles pep-
pered the ruins, east and north, the tank killer hovering
over the cyclone fencing, rotor wash shooting dust and
debris across the carnage, the warbird blazing away
with the grim works. The 30 mm cannon was pounding the standing guard towers to shredded matchsticks,
the nose swinging to rake a few runners, all but pulp-
ing them to flying goo, dismembering a ZSU and a
batch of vehicles in the process.

It was a dangerous moment, nonetheless, as Bolan
moved up on their rear. He keyed his com link, an-

nounced himself, his closing advance, Gator on his right flank.

"Hold your fire to your six!"

Even still, he braced himself for impulsive reaction. Tsunami whirled in his direction, eyes ablaze with ad- renaline. Two other Cobra commandos were swinging M-16s their way, Bolan shouting a warning, Tsunami bellowing at the others, "Hold up! It's Wild Card and Gator!"

Doc Holliday shouted at Bolan, "Where the fuck is Wallbanger?"

Bolan simply shook his head. Holliday grumbled something the soldier couldn't hear over all the racket, swung his multiround launcher toward the rear end of his wreckage concealment and popped off another mis- sile toward a pack of shooters firing away behind a Land Cruiser.

There were a few staggering targets left, Bolan sighting down, hunkering at the demolished nose of a Hummer beside Tsunami. The Executioner joined the others in a long sweep of autofire, dropping whatever shadows boiled up or reeled in the smoke.

"Where's the major?" Bolan shouted in Tsunami's face.

"Over there!"

The Executioner noticed Python and Diamondback were missing, tracked Tsunami's scowl toward at least a city block's worth of rubble.

Interesting the three of them were AWOL from this

melee, Bolan thought. Combing the demolished building for live ones? Or was it something else?

The Executioner decided to investigate. He was up and moving, rolling in a three-sixty, scanning for hostiles. Clear on the enemy front, but he figured it might be smart to announce to Collins he was coming to join whatever the party.

THE MIRACLE HAPPENED. If he was a believer in God he would have hit his knees, clasped hands and given thanks for this moment. He was far from saved regardless, but, hey, he was thinking as he tugged the briefcase out from between two concrete slabs where it had wedged—that the strong really did make their own luck. But that was life and life was tough. Only the weak and the foolish, the poor and the desperate, he thought, believed in the mythical nonsense of an almighty supreme being.

The strong survived, they won, they created their own destiny and they did indeed inherit the earth.

With his commando dagger, he pried the clasps open, threw back the lid. Rifling through the top sheaf of papers, right away he knew what he was looking at. He was spared for now, for sure, and praise be, just the same—at least to himself.

The sounds of withering autofire and crunching muffles of explosions beyond the rubble, Collins threw Python and Diamondback a glance, ordered, "Keep your eyes peeled. No one comes in. No one."

"Our little problem solved, Major?" Python asked.

"For the moment. And, believe me, this isn't little."

He couldn't believe what he read, his heart thundering in his ears. Part Farsi, part Arabic, there were eleven pages, clipped together, laying out the job beyond the mission. The great ayatollah—and this was not part of the original plan, as far as he had been led to believe—had detailed for Habikin the finer points, weaving in the usual Islamic line about keeping the faith, obedience to Allah's will and so forth.

Bastard had named names down the line on both sides, cited sat and other eyes in the sky, those open windows through which safe passage was already outlined and guaranteed in advance. Ran through each leg of the mission. Spelled out, bottom line, what the hell it was really all about from beginning to end.

"Un-effing-believable."

Collins was shaking, his face running with sweat. Damn right there were calls to make, find out if any nervous types, growing either a patriotic or moral conscience, were abandoning ship. He didn't think so, since it had come this far, and the plug would have been pulled by now if cold feet were shuffling off in the other direction. He had to believe this was simply some insurance policy, in case their own side didn't come through, and that made sense to him, as far as the twisted thinking of fanatic Muslims went.

"Rotten son of a…"

The other stack of papers, he discovered, was an operational manual. Keep that, he decided, to maintain the smokescreen, give it up—Israelis or the CIA, it didn't matter, play the big shot who had saved the day for the Western world. One fast but hard perusal, both anxiety and relief propelling him into speed-reading mode, and he knew he was looking at routes, times, operatives, strategy, the whole logistical ball of wax for a coming massive jihad. All of it was enciphered, of course, but this particular mathematic code had long since been broken by Gambler and a few other NSA operatives, passed on and learned by himself and a few of his own people. Some of what he read gibed with he'd learned about the great ayatollah's own vision of holy war, only matériel a little nastier than C-4 and dynamite would be used.

Collins was clacking open his lighter, putting the torch to the evidence when he heard Stone patch through, announcing he was on the way inside.

"This fucking guy again," he muttered.

It was all Collins could do to stay calm, respond.

"Glad you could make it, Colonel Stone."

Now Collins cursed, Python nearly shouting the bastard's name, a warning to hurry, wrap it up. Why not just hold the guy's hand, escort him in, have a peek inside the briefcase or toast marshmallows over the burning evidence?

Collins set the rest of the evidence on fire, a few pages at a time to be sure he got them all, then stowed the lighter. Then he slammed the briefcase shut, began to retrace the tortuous path back through the maze of debris. He sucked in a deep breath, tried to will the trembling out of his hands.

"WE'RE COMING OUT, Colonel. Hold your ground!"

It was Python doing the shouting again, the tone edged up and harried, striking Bolan as if he were being warned to sit tight. Something smelled, he thought, and it wasn't the stink of death in the air.

Bolan spotted the Black Hawk touching down for evac to the south edge, inside the fencing. Cobra commandos were now shuffling in a backpedal formation toward the dust storm, preparing to board, weapons fixed and sweeping the ruins for hostiles. No takers to be found, and Bolan watched, slow but moving ahead, as Python and Diamondback reared up over the rubble. They came down the hill, their SAWs aimed in opposite directions. There was something different in their eyes, but Bolan wasn't sure if he read relief or concern.

"Major says to hop aboard! We're outta here, Colonel! Company's on the way!" Python shouted over the rotor storm, not looking at Bolan as the two commandos passed by the soldier.

Standing his ground, Bolan saw Collins pop into view. The assault rifle slung around his shoulder, the Cobra leader worked his way down the rubble in a clumsy descent. The briefcase stoked the soldier's curiosity, the major glancing his way while he barked into his com link. Another intel gift from Heaven, Bolan figured, had mysteriously dropped out of the sky and into his lap.

"Hit 'em hard! Yeah, yeah, the same run you did here, all of you! I lift off, I want to see the bastards blown clear out into the Mediterranean! When it's done, peal off and cover my Black Hawk. Do it! Out!"

"Problems?"

Collins pulled up beside Bolan. "Only an armored Syrian convoy on the way."

"General Salidin?"

"Yeah, guess all the noise shook him out of his wet dream."

"Your aces have enough juice left?"

"Four T-72s, two APCs, three Hummers and a couple of raggedy-ass open troop transports, they might as well bend over and ask how deep."

"What did you turn up?" Bolan asked, nodding at the briefcase.

Collins smiled. "The holy grail of jihad."

"The holy grail, huh? For some reason, Major, you don't strike me as the religious type."

"An expression, is that okay with you? By the way, what happened to Wallbanger?"

Bolan gave Collins the short and bitter.

"You took point, huh? The kid wouldn't fall back?"

"You don't believe my version, ask Gator. I just gave you chapter and verse."

"I didn't say that, Colonel. Where's his body?"

"Down in the wadi right where your team bailed."

Collins was moving, hesitated, then scowled back at Bolan. "What's with the tone? Oh, I get it. You saw my goodbye kiss to our Lebanese contact. What? You want an explanation?"

Bolan shrugged.

"He was dirty. It had come to my attention, Colonel Stone, he was playing both sides. It had come to my attention he had assassinated two CIA operatives in Beirut recently and my orders were to use him like a Kleenex and throw him away. Yeah, if that's news to you I can't help it. Anything else troubling you?"

"I'll let you know."

BOLAN HEARD the distant thunder, the world strobing beyond the black ridgeline to the west. Again that strange dreamlike haze of adrenaline meltdown and bone-numbing fatigue weighed in, body, mind and soul, all one and the same, it felt, flowing together. That floating sensation was back, but stronger than before.

He was numb, but not comfortably so.

The Executioner stood near the starboard M-60 gunner, glimpsed Collins shaking free a cigarette, lighting up as Gator lumbered aboard, Wallbanger draped over his shoulder.

"Get us outta here, ace!" Collins hollered into the cockpit.

Bolan emptied his mind of all thought, grateful, if nothing else, for a moment of silence despite the roar-

ing of the aerial bombardment, the curtain call and re-
minder that still more bad men were dying. Gone to
meet...

What? Reward? Punishment?

Bolan knew it wasn't his place to make that call.

They were up, nose down, and soaring south for
Lion Base. The holocaust consuming the Syrian patrol
was a shimmering veil in the corner of Bolan's eye. He
watched as Collins admired the view, puffing, a strange
relaxed smile freezing his expression.

The soldier looked away from Collins, ran a gaze over
the others. They were either smoking, staring straight
ahead or slumped back with eyes shut, all of them chew-
ing on their own thoughts, most likely, just glad to be alive.

Natural and understandable. They were all warriors,
Bolan knew, would go the distance in battle, but only
the reckless fool or the suicidal really wished to die.
Even the savage clung to life.

The air was solemn, just the same, another of their
teammates going home in a rubber bag. The wind
whipping through the cabin did little to wipe away the
heavy fumes of sweat and cordite and smoke residue
pasting their skin and blacksuits.

"What's in that briefcase, Colonel," Collins said,
"has more than likely just preempted a full-scale jihad
from Tel Aviv clear to the U.S. West Coast. I'm not sure
if we got lucky or... You say you think I'm not a religious man, but I'm thinking—if there is a God—he was
on our side tonight."

"You wouldn't mind if I took a look?"

"When we hit Camp Zero, you can plow through it all you want. There's going to be at least two to three days of debriefing by the head shed. SOP. Interrogations of prisoners, like that. Unless, that is, you're in a hurry to get back to the States?"

"No rush, when this is wrapped. I'll take you up on your offer." Bolan paused, then said, "When we get there, Major, who gets to play Torquemada of the Grand Inquisition?"

Collins lost the smile, and Bolan felt the man measuring him, something savage again lurking behind the eyes. "You're a funny guy, Stone, and you know what, you've sort of grown on me."

How come, Bolan thought, he felt as if the man were saying so long, no longer needed his services, visions of getting tossed out with no parachute flaming to mind?

Bolan chuckled. "I was thinking of Mo, Larry and Curly."

"Mo—as you call him—is gone, as you know. I'll keep the other two under control, trust me. What happened on the Herc…"

"An aberration?"

"Exactly. Get some rest, Stone, if you can. One more stop to lend our Israeli friends a helping hand with their Palestinian headache…hell, it's fourth and goal on the one-yard line. Another touchdown, we're in the wind."

Bolan turned away and stared into the passing black heart of night.

CHAPTER SIXTEEN

"The Compound Intifada? They might as well hang out a shingle—Terrorists 'R' Us. Oh, gentlemen, I can tell you now, I'm going to leave the promised land a little more hope than it had before."

They were in the war room at Lion Base. Bolan had done a brief tour with Colonel Yehudin and the Cobra major, both given pass and magnetic swipe cards, but granted access only to the main and second levels. Bolan knew they hadn't seen every hidden nook and cranny. They were now one floor below main, one of several nerve centers, the operation here striking Bolan as similar in terms of computer banks, radar and tracking stations, digital wall maps and video screens; the works, supertech, gizmos and gadgets. He was certain, that only the best and the brightest need apply to handle. He had been informed by the Israeli colonel the base came complete with tunnels, armory, bunkers, certain there was much more than the eye could see. Pretty much all of it—down to the long table in the war room that could fit twenty or more comfortably at a time—reminded Bolan of the Farm, but on a much larger scale. The narrow elevator door with keypad in the far corner told Bolan there was at least one more level belowground, a combination bunker and command-and-control center. At one time Yakov Katzenelenbogen—Stony Man Farm's former tactician and both a former colonel in the Israeli army and intelligence operative—had told him there were seven such fortress-command centers housed at strategic intervals around the country. If the small nation came under siege by ballistic missiles packed with chem, bio or nuclear capability, the military, intelligence and political elite could live in what were small cities far beneath the earth's surface, enough provisions for six months, twelve tops if rationed properly. There were also silos with nuclear missiles in each of these compounds, enough thermonuclear megatonnage on tap, Katz had told him, to vaporize the entire Middle East, North Africa and Central Asia.

That, unfortunately, included hanging a radioactive cloud over the promised land if the megaton arrows began flying.

When choppered into Lion Base, Bolan had seen that, unlike the Farm, the Israelis didn't bother to conceal SAMs. Entire batteries of missiles were in full view, machine-gun nests choking a perimeter sealed off by electrified twenty-foot-high fencing. When marching into the building, it had been pointless to count all the main battle tanks—American M-1 Abrams—F-15s, Apaches, Black Hawks and APCs, tracked carriers with rockets ready to fly and God only knew what punch they packed. All told, there was enough on hand to hold back and counterpummel whatever wanted to strike the compound, hardware, he was sure, that could reach well beyond the borders.

Shaved, showered, fed and with a thirty-minute combat nap behind him, Bolan and the other Cobra commandos—together with a squad of Israeli shooters—were gathered at the table. Collins and the short, stocky, bald Colonel Yehudin shared the head of the table, both of them having clicked through a series of mug shots of the bad guys in question and their Compound Intifada.

The initial brief was forty minutes under way, coffee all around, Collins chain-smoking up a storm. Blueprints of the CIQ had been thoroughly detailed on the wall screen, the strike plan laid out. On the surface, it looked and sounded solid to Bolan, but, as usual, once the shooting started it was a roll of the dice. This time they were going in with a squad of Israeli commandos. For the Gaza hit, Bolan and Cobra had togged themselves in the standard-issue light brown of the IDF. Same hardware as before, Collins having already informed Bolan they would simply re-up on ammo.

Bolan was perusing his intel package when Collins growled out the remarks.

Yehudin nodded, the old warhorse striking Bolan as a soldier who knew what he was doing from firsthand hard experience.

"Yes," the Israeli colonel said, "they are becoming more brazen with each mass murder they commit. Sad but true, we are a nation that might never know peace. Not even I am sure what the solution is. All I know, as a soldier and a Jew, I cannot allow my people to continue to be murdered by terrorists. We will never be safe until every last one of these criminals is exiled, imprisoned or killed."

There was argument on that score to spare for both sides, Bolan thought, and against his better judgment. He always left the politics, religion and diplomatic currying of favor out of his equation. Right was right; wrong was wrong. Yes, sometimes there was gray, sometimes compromise could work. For Israel, he didn't see that happening. The killing had gone on throughout the ages, both Jews and Arabs the same blood, the offspring of Abraham, each side vehemently staking their own claim to this ancient land. Revenge against each other, though, had become a never-ending cycle, the only constant hatred and intolerance. They claimed it was a complicated situation, but in Bolan's mind it was very simple, at least in terms of conflict. It all boiled down to one side telling the other side that if they did what they wanted they could all get along. Pretty much, he knew, the way of the world.

Sad but true.

"Yeah, well, that said, all I want to know, Colonel," Collins said, blowing a thick cloud over the table, "are my suspects inside?"

Like a deck of cards, Collins flipped out five 8x11 mug shots in front of Yehudin. Yehudin rattled off the names of the terrorists, stamping them as two Egyptians, two Syrians, one top Palestinian lieutenant supposedly in line to replace Chairman Asshole, as Collins called him.

Bolan looked at Collins, read something darker, harder and meaner than ever in his eyes. They might be in the home stretch, but the Executioner knew this strike would be no stroll through the park. Again they were going through the front door, square up the gut on the enemy's turf. This time, however, the opposition was ready, knew they were coming.

Yehudin clicked on a shot of the compound.

It was a two-story white building, scarred by bullets, a gaping hole from a 105 mm at the far west edge. As more shots, both ground and aerial snapped by, Bolan counted at least six M-1 tanks, the armor having encircled the compound. Other shots displayed buildings, some completely demolished, others simply gutted empty shells from either air strikes, 105 mm M-1 pounding or both.

"We have had the compound under siege for four days," Yehudin said. "Electricity, water cut off. This mess splashed all over world headlines, we—the Jews, defending our homeland—are the ones at fault, pity the poor Palestinian butchers. My men have come under sniper fire from the second floor. I've lost two soldiers already. Starving them out does not appear to be a viable option. We have the UN attempting to insinuate themselves into the situation, demanding to take food, water and medicine inside to these criminals. The usual nonsense heard by diplomatic paper pushers who know nothing and understand even less about the situation. These terrorists have already stated they will fight to the death, to the last murderer. We know several of them are directly responsible for the recent spate of suicide bombings, marching out young boys—no older than ten—to do their bloody work. We suspect they even have a bomb-making factory in the basement."

"Saying they might take us and them out in one big bang?" Collins asked.

"It's always a possibility."

Collins scowled. "I've seen a few shots of the usual howling mob and stone-throwers in the neighborhood," Collins said, lighting another cigarette off the end of his gnawed butt. "That going to be a problem?"

"Not if we have to spray them with rubber bullets or hit them with tear gas," Yehudin answered. "When we attack, I assure you, my men can and will hold them back."

"I like your style, Colonel," Collins said, grinning through his smoke.

"To answer your question, Major, there are twenty-one terrorists inside. My orders were to hold off with an air strike until you arrived. At first, I must confess, I had reservations."

Collins lifted an eyebrow. "Really?"

"You have changed my opinion with your work. The intelligence you brought to me from Lebanon will greatly help us. Perhaps we may even turn the corner against these criminals."

"Glad I—we—could be of such invaluable assistance."

"Speaking of that intelligence, Colonel," Bolan said.

"I promised Colonel Stone," Collins jumped in, "a copy of what I gave you."

"It shall be done."

"Okay," Collins said, "full-frontal assault, front and back, top to bottom. Colonel Stone hits the roof, he moves down, we pinch them in. Me and my guys, we take point, Colonel Yehudin. Since you've been so kind as to give me free rein, I'd like twelve of your best shooters at my disposal, I'm talking room-sweepers, to go in behind us. Standard peel off, seal 'em up, room-by-room clearing. Frag 'em, go in blasting. If my targets want to come along for the ride, fine. If not, they die where they stand. They live, we get something from them, you'll get it back."

Yehudin nodded. "Understood. And the men you see here before you are some of my best."

"I'll take Tsunami and Gator," Bolan said, "with me."

"Just the three of you?" Collins said.

"I'd like to keep my end of it as simple as possible. That a problem?"

Collins seemed to ponder something, then nodded. "I can live with that." Collins paused, shook his head, then turned philosophical. "You know, I've been thinking, Colonel Yehudin, there seems a simple solution to the Palestinian problem."

Bolan watched Collins, couldn't wait to hear this.

"Which is?" Yehudin said.

"The other Arab countries cry about the deplorable, oppressive conditions the Palestinians live under," Collins said. "If they're that concerned, why don't the Lebanese, Saudis, Jordanians, Syrians just open their borders, let them in?"

Yehudin's brow furrowed.

"If," Collins went on, "they're some sort of…wandering plague, a displaced and disenfranchised blight on Israel, why don't the other Arab nations throw down the welcome mat? Why not give their Arab brethren the shot at the good life they claim the Israelis are denying them?"

"Good question," Yehudin said. "But I already have the answer. Remember, though, at one time the children of Israel, of Moses, dispersed to the four corners of the earth, were likewise viewed as this wandering plague you mentioned. Well, to answer your question, the other Arab countries want the Palestinians kept right here. They want them to wreak havoc, they want to kill us Jews, all of us, or drive us into the sea. They will not be satisfied until they have taken everything we have. Yes, I could stand here all day, tell you the history between us, the sibling rivalry between the first offspring of Abraham, how he cast out those of Arab heritage who can trace their roots back to him. I can talk about Moses, how the children of Israel have returned to the promised land as it was deemed by God."

Yehudin fell silent, end of discussion.

"This is your home, and you're going nowhere," Collins said. "I can respect that. Okay, how about we all meet back here at 0900 for a final brief? Gentlemen. Stone and the rest and my team are dismissed—they can grab some rest in the meantime, Colonel Yehudin. I've got some calls to make."

Bolan saw Collins pick the aluminum briefcase off the floor, motion for Python to follow him up the stairs. Something, Bolan sensed, was eating at Collins, had been, in fact, since he reemerged from the demolished C and C area in the Bekaa.

The soldier was out of his chair, intel packet in hand, trailing Collins and Python up the stairs. The steel door slid open as Collins swiped his card.

Hitting the hallway on the main floor, Bolan saw Collins and Python picking up the pace, a sense of urgency in their strides.

Calls, huh, Bolan thought, keeping his distance but watching as Collins and Python marched ahead, talking to each other in what appeared hushed tones. They veered around the corner, Bolan heading toward the quarters allotted to Cobra Force. He stopped, found Collins and Python moving out the door that led to the helipads.

Curious, Bolan gave it a few seconds, waited until the rest of Cobra Force had moved past, then followed in the major's wake.

He was outside, squinting against the harsh sunlight, when he found Collins and Python hopping up in the cabin of the Black Hawk. Collins slid shut the port then starboard doors. If the major had seen him watching, then Bolan figured he was being ignored. If ignored, then why?

Calls, huh, he again thought, and felt that itch grind harder than ever between the shoulder blades.

Bolan turned and accessed himself back into the building.

"WE'VE BEEN wondering when you'd call."

"We may have problems. There's been a change in plans, effective immediately."

"You're making me shiver and shake. What's up?"

Tim "Warlock" Smith felt his heart lurch, spine stiffen like a piece of steel, the whole package of rock tightness forcing him to sit upright in his bolted-down metal chair. Collins sounded edged-out, ready to blow a gasket, but there was an undercurrent of suspicion in the major's tone. Warlock wondered if maybe he'd done something, the sliver of accusation not escaping ears trained to pick up the smallest sign of deceit in the voice.

He was in the com cubicle on the Hercules, monitoring his state-of-the-art NSA prototype Dragon computer for communications from the others. Com link on, he looked over his shoulder at Cyclops as he slipped on his own headphones.

Warlock heard silence, Collins wanting to say something, choosing his words. Finally he said, "Okay, I'll bite. What problems? What change?"

"First, what's your situation?"

"Grounded. Incirlik," Warlock answered. "We're still waiting on the Marines. Snafu. Must have caught a ride with the Navy."

"Goddammit. How much longer?"

"I was told their briefing should be over soon."

"Soon? Define soon."

Warlock was feeling his nerves stretching taut, snapping back at him like frayed electric lines over this sudden intrigue, the agitation loud and clear in the major's voice. He shook loose a cigarette, Cyclops helping himself, lighting them both up.

"I was told roughly two to three hours before we're wheels-up."

"That might work to our advantage. Okay. I came across a nasty little surprise," Collins told him. "I'll bypass the particulars, but it's under control. It involved the bigger picture. It spelled it out. Our—or rather—your boy in ER station," he said, the code for Iran, "may be hedging his bets."

"How so?"

"I don't know, you tell me."

"Nothing to tell."

"Are you, Mr. C and the others still in the game?"

"I've been in contact with the others. All systems are go. What is this? You think…"

"I don't know what to think. But I'm booted up, so why don't you show me something?"

Warlock was snapping his fingers at Cyclops, but he was already punching in the access code on his own computer, fingers flying away.

"You can't explain your nasty little surprise?"

"Not in so much fine detail," Collins told him.

That made sense. No communication was ever guaranteed one-hundred percent security, not with all the latest in microchip supertechnology, the new NSA satellite, Warlock knew, that was recently put in orbit and designed specifically to intercept satlink coms, e-mails, and was even capable of eavesdropping on conversations inside a building.

It took a good thirty seconds for the information to be relayed, then confirmed. Finally Warlock heard Collins say, "Sweet. Looks like a party. Seychelles, here I come."

"You've had your look, you know it's there. I need to cut it off."

"So do it."

"Talk to me."

"Stick with the plan. We're almost there. Prep our pigeons at your earliest convenience. When they're locked down, uncuff them. Do not wash them, do not have them change into uniform, do not pass out Korans. Stall the head shed, make excuses, whatever, you're in charge of getting them situated. When I touch down, set your watch to two hours and ticking."

"This could alter…"

"Everything, I'm aware. Speaking of that, do you have everything on board?"

"Yes."

"Everything?"

"It's all here."

Warlock glanced at the large metal bin on the floor, against the bulkhead, the hair on the back of his neck standing up as he thought about what was inside.

"I was thinking," Collins said, "when you prep the pigeons you might want to ease them into it with the legend of King Groethe and Attila."

Warlock chuckled. "Way ahead of you." He paused, his own anger stirring. "What about Colonel Asshole?"

"His time is short."

"It damn well better be," Cyclops cut in. "G was the only—"

"I know how tight the three of you were. It will be handled and I will tell you how and when. We clear?"

"Got it," Warlock said.

"So then, I'll see you when I see you."

"Wait a second. I see a brick wall in our future."

"And?"

"I'm thinking we could all bail, just walk away,

leave them stewing. You saw the numbers. There's plenty, and with two of our own out of the game, the split just grew a little fatter."

"You sound real broken up about your buddy and Asp."

"Just being a realist."

"The answer is no. The full ride. I make a commitment, I keep it. Besides, we still have something to collect. And they're holding on to two of ours as collateral. What could be worse, they could aim the guns our way, knowing what they know. If that happens…well, I don't need to be sitting on the beach, jumping at the shadows of seagulls flying overhead, straining to get a hard-on for my island girl because my nerves are screaming at me. Read me?"

"Loud and clear."

"Later then."

Warlock stripped off the com link, his thoughts racing with questions. Problems. Nasty surprise. Change in plans. It was the last thing they needed when the brass ring was right there in front of them. He knew all about loss, the usual rug getting yanked out from under him as a black op whose duty, career—life—meant more to him than wife, kids and a home in the suburbs. He had risked his life for his country for years now, his eyes long since focused on retirement. As far as he was concerned the men he worked for—and America—could go straight to Hell. It was, anyway, too many changes, and all of them for the worse, having swamped America with a political correctness, a pseudoculture that turned his stomach. If glory was never in the equation—book deals, the hot seat on all the talking-head shows, telling the world how much he knew—the least he could do he was walk away with a fat wallet. Bottom line was he was in it for the money, and God pity any poor bastard who would deny what was rightfully his.

He glanced over his shoulder at Cyclops, could tell the man was seething over Gambler getting popped by Stone. Or…

What?

Cyclops had to have been reading his thoughts, as he said, "You're not thinking the major pulled one over on us?"

"No. I mean, we weren't there…"

"But?"

"I accept the major's version."

"I want a piece of Stone's ass to hang on my belt."

"You'll get it."

"I'd better."

"Fuck it."

"What's that mean—fuck it."

"It means we're too late in the game to start sweating."

"Ride it out."

"Take it to the limit."

"And beyond."

"They can kiss our asses."

"We did our time—hard time—for Uncle Sam," Warlock said. "Time for Uncle Sam to give us back a little something. Collins isn't the only one around with big dreams about an island paradise."

"Amen."

CHAPTER SEVENTEEN

Faisal Hussein was ready to go to God. He had been, in fact, prepared to martyr himself for years, but he had been hanging on, hoping to unleash one last massive wave of martyrs before the Zionists killed him. Either way, it was time, he knew, to stop marching out others in the cause, have them die, doing all of God's work in his place, blowing themselves up in the discos, restaurants, marketplaces, weddings. He needed to do his own no-small part, if nothing else than to bolster courage, shore up resolve in those warriors he left behind, his death only meaningful if they continued to fight the Jews until all Zionists were dead or driven into the sea.

Standing at the window on the second floor, peering through a crack in the curtain, he braced for the shelling to begin, or that massive rocket attack by helicopters that would bring the roof down. It wasn't a question of if, but when.

Four sleepless days now, and the anxiety was building all around, his men gaunt, reeking of sweat, unwashed flesh, the strain clear in red eyes that had seen virtually no sleep. With no running water, the toilets were backing up, the air foul with the fumes of body waste. The stink was the least of his concerns.

Hussein watched the tanks, hulking armored monsters parked out front, itching to cut loose his AK-47 if one of the soldiers stepped into view. Two days ago, and he'd gotten lucky, his patience rewarded as a soldier finally stepped into his gun sights. A clean head shot, no question the soldier was dead, and he found himself surprised the Israelis hadn't responded with instant retaliation.

So they were tired, hungry, anxious. They had to be patient—the fight would come to them, he had told his followers, prepare to meet God. A true believer accepted his lot, whatever it was, as a test from God, no matter how hopeless the moment seemed. A warrior, he believed, accepted his inevitable death, a sign he was chosen by God, and who among them could question his will?

There could be no other way than martyrdom.

The good news was they had at least another week's worth of food, bottled water on hand, but the meats and fruit would begin to rot soon. Empty bellies, he knew, made even the hardest of fighting men crumble. Surrender wasn't an option.

This, he thought, was the moment he had been waiting for, full-scale battle with the hated Jew oppressors, kill as many of them as he could before he soared to Paradise. He could see it now, aware he would go down with the ruins of the Compound Intifada, his own martyrdom simply a ringing statement the Palestinians would someday prevail, no matter what it took, no matter how many Jews were killed. His death would be remembered, hailed a victory, even, his face on posters flying high and proud as they mourned him in the streets of Gaza, the West Bank.

In death there would be glory.

It pained him, just the same, slated to take over the PLO, the successor to the Hero, but it was an honor he would never know.

He glanced at Namir as his cousin stepped up beside him.

"If they storm us, as you anticipate, I have prepared quite the surprise for them," Namir said.

"They will be coming," Hussein said. "It has been too quiet the last day. How many are ready?"

"Three. One upstairs, one to the back. One in the dining room, as you ordered."

It was a shame, he thought, they only had so much Semtex and dynamite left, having used up most of what the Syrians had smuggled in the past three weeks. The way it felt, Hussein believed the Israelis would encircle the compound, commandos storming inside, shooting, hurling around grenades. He had survived one such attempt before, despising the memory of himself surrendering instead of dying, imprisoned, beaten, tortured.

He would erase the feeling of cowardice forever this time. He would never again see the inside of a Zionist jail.

He heard the pounding of feet, voices raised in alarm. Turning, he found the Egyptian, Tuballah, racing into the room.

"Helicopters! Soldiers…"

He didn't hear the rest of it, as he flinched and hit the floor at the tremendous boom. The walls shook, the bottom floor rattling and rolling so hard he was sure the floor would cave beneath him.

"They're here! Go with God!" he shouted. "No one surrenders!"

THE EXECUTIONER had three live ones painted on his heat-seeking monitor. They were marked, just inside the concrete housing of the rooftop stairwell, Bolan the first one flying past the door gunner, finger curled around the trigger of his assault rifle when all hell broke loose. A forty-or-so-yard charge to penetration, the Black Hawk lifting off, and Bolan suspected what was coming next.

Tsunami and Gator, brandishing SAWs, trailed Bolan as the fanatic burst onto the roof. He was wrapped in packets and sticks, a shuffling mummy ready to blow them off the roof with a mixed wallop of Semtex and dynamite, screaming out the familiar martyr's cry.

"Allah akhbar!"

"Hit the deck!" Bolan roared, his full-bore autofire pounding the wanna-be martyr, driving him back in an ungainly jig step, the fanatic's finger on the button of the radio remote and—

Depressing doomsday.

Even as Bolan pummeled the fanatic back and down into the stairwell the blast erupted, fire, smoke, rubble and invisible hammering of shock waves tearing across the roof.

It could have been the giant sat dish, or the concrete structures dotting the roof—surveillance posts—that saved Bolan and Cobra company. No time to ponder good fortune, the Executioner nose-dived for cover behind Tsunami and Gator, debris and smoke shooting past them, the air suddenly choked with any number of foul odors. A look back, and Bolan found the Black Hawk was soaring away, the M-60 door gunner ducking as wreckage sought to bring down the warbird, the hull taking a few hits but flying on.

Bolan lurched up, peering into the thick clouds of smoke, the stairwell housing little more than smoking trash, when the thunder of a 105 mm shell echoed from below. The roof beneath Bolan's feet shuddered, signaling to the soldier that Collins, Cobra and the Israelis were making the bull rush inside.

"Stone!"

Bolan keyed his com link. "Yeah?"

"I didn't like the sound of what I just heard up top!"

"All present and accounted for, Major. I suggest we abort the mission."

"What?"

"We just had a close encounter with a suicide bomber. I'm thinking there's more inside, probably waiting behind a closed door or two. There's no fighting back against that kind of play."

"Keep going—that's an order."

"I would strongly suggest bailing. Bring the house down with a good 105 mm shelling or some Apaches, then see what's left standing."

"This is the home stretch, Colonel. Stick to the goddamn game plan. Now get your ass in gear."

"This is a bad idea, Collins."

"Hey, Stone, how about a little courage, huh?"

Bolan gave the orders for Tsunami and Gator to lag behind, ready to arm a frag grenade on his word.

"I go left, you two go right," the Executioner said, then led them across the roof, eyes fixed for anything that moved in the smoke.

For the moment Bolan found his screen clear of targets. Soon, he figured, that would change. There was no time to argue with Collins. He would help take down the compound, but getting too close to the enemy wasn't an option. This was worst-case times a thousand. If a man was hell-bent on committing suicide to kill his enemy, there was little that could be done to stop him.

Collins and the Israelis, Bolan feared, were going to

lose a few men on this one. There was nothing to do, he thought, but ride it out, hope—and, yes, offer up a quick silent prayer to the gods of war.

COLLINS WAS LOOKING at gutted fanatic sacks, body parts and slick puddles of goo when he barreled through the smoke. The 105 mm shells had pulverized half of the bottom floor. The beams were hanging matchsticks, doors and walls blown to hell, a torso with legs and dripping intestines hung in a gaping maw dead ahead. In this mess, Collins knew there was no telling how many fanatics had been blasted off the planet, how many left standing. They had taken a direct hit right up the sphincter.

What worried Collins now were those suicide bombers, grateful Stone had clued him in. He had figured a wicked surprise or two coming in, factored in his own play, which was why he waved for Doc Holliday and Lionteeth to take point, start kicking down doors. No sense in getting himself smoked now, not when the brass ring was hanging in his face.

The choking smoke of explosives and raining plaster nearly blinding him to what was down the hall, Collins claimed the edge for temporary concealment. Sticking to the script, half of the Israeli shooters branched off in both directions to his side, a few of those commandos weighted down with enough Semtex, he figured, to take out two city blocks. The other six Israeli commandos were already announcing their presence to the north, autofire steady, the crunch of a couple grenades telling Collins they were making quick work of militants with some heavy-duty room sweeping.

Collins glanced at the Israelis to his flanks as they pasted small globs of plastique to doors, priming the charges, when doors ahead burst open and another sense-shattering barrage of autofire erupted down the hallway, voices screaming in Arabic, fanatics hell-bent going down with the Compound Intifada. Collins figured why not give the suckers what they so desperately wanted, searching for targets, but suddenly wishing this was wrapped so he could be on his way when Lionteeth kicked in a door and a fireball blew out into the hall.

There was no sense in checking for pulses, since they had both taken the blast right in the face, but this was part of the scheme, anyway.

Two more out of the way who wouldn't have to be dealt with in short order. It was hell, he thought, to lose—or sacrifice—good fighting men like this, but he'd raise a toast to them at some point when he was sitting on a beach, sipping a cold one. He hadn't wanted this particular stint to start with, but he was under orders. To bail might have wafted a bad whiff Washington's way. He didn't plan on bagging any bad guys here, but what Colonels Stone and Yehudin didn't know wasn't his problem. Just blast, burn and hang back while everybody else did the dirty work.

"Move, move!" Collins barked at Python, Mamba, Diamondback and Brick, throwing a few rounds into the bedlam.

If only just for show, he thought, God love America.

He was just about home free, and then and only then maybe in God he could trust.

THE HACKING, shouting and cursing in Arabic alerted Bolan to their presence even before Gator looked up from his screen and flashed four fingers.

Three steel eggs lobbed down into the smoke, and Bolan jumped back with Tsunami and Gator as autofire stuttered in the cloud. They hugged the fangs of what was left of the concrete housing, rode it out until the triburst of flesh-eaters ripped below, screams lost in the thunderclaps.

Bolan led the charge down the steps, choked by cordite and blood, forging ahead. The blasts bought him a few critical seconds, as he whipped around the corner and spotted a fanatic sans arm. The militant was backpedaling, thick crimson spurting through the smoke and dust when the Executioner waxed him with a 3-round burst to the chest.

According to the blueprints, six rooms on the second floor had to be cleared, including a large area for war council.

Bolan signaled for Gator and Tsunami to move rearward—north—and start sweeping half the rooms.

Using the sensor on his handheld, Bolan turned up two targets, roughly fifteen feet away at ten o'clock. Hunkered down and waiting to galvanize into a suicide dash?

Whether they fired in blind panic or heard his approach Bolan couldn't say. The door was blasted to Swiss cheese, wood slivers slashing Bolan's face. He waited them out, crouched to the side, the sounds of autofire and explosions from below shaking the floor beneath his boots. When the shouts of panic replaced their firing—clips burned out—Bolan flung himself low into the doorway, pumped out a 40 mm frag bomb, ducked back.

Heart pounding, adrenaline coursing through his veins, the soldier swung back, peering into the smoke. His screen was clear where he aimed the sensor. Another grenade punching still more needles into his eardrums, Bolan whirled and found Gator and Tsunami hard at work, blazing away, screams and shouts fading moments later.

Combat senses on full alert, Bolan watched each door, glancing at the heat sensor. No red specters were framed on his screen.

It was over, he could tell, at least up top. Moments later, he spotted a figure, partly buried in slabs of wall blown down by frag blasts. Nothing left of the face, but one look at the diminutive corpse, and he could tell the body of a small child when he saw it.

He listened to the withering autofire from the first floor, watched the hall.

It was a done deal for the Compound Intifada, probably nothing left to do but clear a few more rooms. For a moment, he wanted to ponder the horrible dilemma that kept this country from ever knowing peace, how men who claimed to believe in God would send out children to commit suicide and murder the innocent.

Who, though, he figured, could fathom evil? In the final analysis, he concluded, perhaps it was enough a few good men were around to at least fight back.

OPERATION STRANGLEHOLD was over, at least as far as covert incursions into countries harboring terrorists went, but Bolan hardly felt satisfied with the results. Five countries, almost twice as many engagements, and all they were bringing back to Camp Zero were twenty-four terrorists. None of the major's targets inside the compound were left breathing to spill intelligence. Had it been worth the effort? Bolan wondered, and knew the answer was affirmative. Whatever they could learn from the prisoners could prove invaluable in stemming the tide of terrorism, perhaps even someday erase its dark stain from the world forever. And a few less butchers on the loose today made tomorrow a little safer place for those who only wished to live their days in peace.

The Executioner was standing out front near an M-1, waiting for Collins to emerge with what was left of the latest Cobra casualties in a bag. In the distance he made out the howling of mobs getting worked up into a frenzy. Just another day in the war-torn promised land. The sky, he saw, was choked with Apaches and Black Hawks, Israeli soldiers hopping out of the bellies of several of the birds, gone to join their comrades-in-arms to hold back what he could be sure was a raging Palestinian mob. The soldier maintained vigilance for any snipers lurking on the rooftops or claiming shooting holes inside the windows of surrounding apartment buildings.

Bolan saw Mamba and Diamondback wend their way through the rubble, a body bag each draped over their shoulders. According to Collins, Colonel Yehudin had lost two of his own men. Collins followed his commandos outside, keying his com link, Bolan spotting the Black Hawk coming in for pickup.

Collins walked up to Bolan, teeth gnashed. "We lost Lionteeth and Doc Holliday—one of those suicide bombers. I hope this isn't where you're going to tell me 'I told you so.'"

Bolan simply shook his head.

"Good. Because Colonel Y. isn't in the mood, either, thinking I somehow fucked up."

Bolan kept his expression neutral as Collins peered at him.

"Nothing to say, Colonel?"

"No."

"So let's get out of this lousy country. We've got a ride to catch and some suspects to start grilling. I hear there are snipers in the area still, and I'd hate to get waxed now that this thing is over."

Why was it, Bolan wondered, every time Collins opened his mouth he was sure the man was lying?

CHAPTER EIGHTEEN

Habir Dugula knew he was staring into the faces of something so cold, deadly and lifeless the two white men were perhaps not even human, or so they at least appeared in his fear-addled state of mind. They were a malevolent presence, no question, he thought, inhuman creatures with no regard for human life, unless they were served, obeyed, could take. What was this? he wondered. He shivered next as the voice whispering deep in the caverns of memory seemed to want to tell him something. But what? That he was…looking into a mirror?

No. He was different, certain they had no families to support, nurture, care for, no allegiance to even their own, thinking and craving only themselves, the sating of the dark force raging inside their souls. He might have taken life himself, killed scores of his own people, but it was in the hope, he told himself, that someday he would rule and save Somalia.

He preferred the two whites with their black hoods on. On second thought he didn't prefer looking at them with or without the ghoulish concealment, but there he was, and there they were, in the frightening flesh. Their silent laughing eyes seemed to want to tell him something, left him wondering if the future was now. Which, he feared, meant he was about to be executed.

The anxiety—the same churning in his belly he had felt since first encountering them—hit deep again, nearly paralyzing him when they unchained him from the bench, beckoned him to follow.

He rubbed chafed wrists, felt bowels rumble, his bladder swollen from endless hours of sitting in one position. Soiling himself now, he thought, would be the least of his concerns.

"Need to take a leak, Habbie, before we start?"

He balked, thinking One Eye could actually read his mind.

"Relax, Duggie."

The scarred mind reader, with those reptilian eyes boring into him, made Dugula believe this one didn't think the fires of Hell were all that bad, that he could take whatever he dished out, and then some.

"Don't look so constipated," the Scar went on. "We're here to help. Sort of lay out the future for you and the others."

"What we call show time. About that leak?"

There was an open commode in the rear, and he had watched as the others had been unchained, one by one, led by gunpoint to stand or squat over the stainless-steel bowl. Several times One Eye had undertaken the task. Whereas the others flushed the waste out of the ship, the One Eye ghoul left it, stinking air that was already vile with hanging fumes of sweat, blood and fear. Dugula gave relieving himself brief consideration, but the hideous spectacle of One Eye grinning at him in front of the others, and he figured he could hold on until they landed wherever they were going.

"I can manage."

"Good," Scar said. "Do follow."

One Eye chuckled. "Hey, but if you feel the urge, let me know."

They passed the cubicles where a few soldiers were hunched over consoles. They were airborne once again after hours of delay on unknown ground. More soldiers with assault rifles—twenty in all, he counted—had come up the ramp, most of them now standing guard over the others.

They led him deep to a dark corner, port side. He became uncomfortably aware they were moving him far away from any sign of life. He saw another cubicle, more computer consoles, communications equipment, a soft green light dancing off the partitioned walls. Out of the shadows, One Eye slid a large footlocker across the floor, placed it in the open area in front of the cubicle.

"Take a seat, Duggie. There is where you get the dreaded 'we need to have a talk' moment."

He hesitated, then sat, watched as One Eye slid the pistol out of his holster. His heart lurched, the sick grin staring him back, but One Eye set the weapon on the edge of a table. Scar settled down on a table opposite his comrade, one leg dangling. They lit cigarettes, both blowing thick streams in his face, his eyes tearing at the harsh sting, lungs hacking, then the clouds thinned enough where he could breathe.

Scar held out his pack. "Want one?"

One Eye swiveled the seat on a bolted-down chair. "Go on, might help you relax."

Dugula shook his head. One Eye hit him with another cloud between the eyes, but Dugula began to feel something moving, around or beneath him he wasn't sure, looked at his feet. Was it the floor? he wondered. The plane shimmying, up and down, as it hit turbulence, rocking the bin beneath him? Was that a thud he heard inside the box?

"The Exterminator, huh," One Eye said, cigarette locked in the frozen grin.

"I'm here to tell ya', you ain't no Attila, Duggie," Scar said.

One Eye scowled. "Nor any King Groethe."

"You ever hear of the Dark Ages king of the Groethe clan?"

"Called the Snake-eater?"

A pause, twin waves of smoke rolling over him and for a moment the two whites vanished in the clouds.

Scar glanced at One Eye, frowning. "Didn't think so."

"Yeah, why would a charcoal-colored baboon know anything about European history? Doesn't even know about his own. How it was Arabs, the rejected offspring of Abraham, by the way—and not Europeans—who were the greatest enslavers and oppressors of blacks. Kind of ironic, don't you think, they claim Islamic names and wrapped themselves all up in Muslim brotherhood back in America?"

Now the racial insults, he thought, keeping any expression off his face, but felt the anger now cracking through his mounting fear. Were they simply taunting him? Did they want him to erupt in a rage, give them an excuse to kill him?

They smoked in silence for several moments, staring him down, shrouding themselves in clouds, then Scar said, "It's called the secret history of the world. It's locked away in a vault deep beneath the Vatican. I know of a close personal friend, once assigned to guard the Pope after the assassination attempt.... Well, I'll spare you the details, but he's seen it."

"It has it all, from what the Garden of Eden really was, where man—and woman, excuse me, my political incorrectness—was first born, what his original sin was, meaning what Eve actually did, entire history of the human race. Every sad or gory or proud or vainglorious or supernatural moment down through the ages to the present and future. Even spells out the exact date of the end of the world, events leading up to, the horror…"

"And the rapture." Scar lit another cigarette off the dying butt. "What that particular event will be is a UFO. Covers the entire sky, four corners of Earth."

"Blinding light show, then poof. The chosen vanish into the mothership."

"King Groethe is in this book," Scar said.

"The Dark Ages king, remember, Habbie. Listen up, this is important."

"What it was," Scar said, "Attila, king of the Huns, made several massive incursions into Eastern Europe."

"The original Exterminator, Habbie, not a pretender like yourself."

"Anyway, Duggie, they swept through Poland several times, got to the border of what is now Germany with every try, then got thrashed by King Groethe and his barbarian hordes. Real tough guys to a man they were, I'm talking they doled out a shellacking that was beyond epic. Picture a bunch of little arrow-winging Huns on those little ponies charging thousands of Conans, decked out in leather and fur, swords as long as you are tall...what were the numbers?"

"The Huns always invaded with nothing short of two hundred thousand strong. Groethe's force was one-quarter that size. Amazing stuff."

"Kicked the Hun crap out of them, chased them nearly a thousand miles back into Russia, a river of blood the whole way." Scar chuckled. "You're talking a trail of hacked-up, decapitated, amputated, castrated

Huns that not even the two of us can fathom or picture in our wildest wet ones. Love that guy Groethe."

"You want to take our food, you want to fuck our women, assholes?" One Eye laughed.

"You're going to have to earn it, because if I lose I won't be around to see or feel the shame and disgrace. Nothing but big swaying balls all around. Except for the two of us here, they don't make 'em like that anymore."

Dugula was becoming more unnerved, but felt his anger rising over their sick nonsense. He felt his lips move, uttered, "The point?"

"We're getting there," Scar said.

"Jirvic," he continued, "the hill in Poland was called. The last try by Attila was a few weeks before he died. He gave it one last shot, give the man credit where it's due, and it was a whopper. Groethe and men charged down the hill, same sad story for Attila. This time, Attila makes a fast exit, and Groethe holds back…"

"Figures by now Attila's seen the light."

"But on their way out of Poland," Scar said, matching his comrade's grin, "they leave behind a very nasty surprise. They brought cobras with them from the Far East and India."

"Cobras?" Dugula said.

"Cobras," Scar said. "It nearly changed the entire course of human history."

"Fifteen-thousand-plus serpents, carried in sacks, all the way from home sweet home," One Eye said.

"Most of them impregnated females, ready to pop. Devious bastard, Attila."

Dugula felt the grin nearly cut his lips, then checked it as twin scowls, forming as if on cue, stared him back through the smoke.

"I see you, Mr. Skeptical," Scar said. "Thinking it's too cold in Poland or anywhere in Europe for serpents to live. Easy enough to explain. It was summer. They could manage a few more months, but that's all Attila was hoping for. By then, he figured enough of his enemies would be killed off, countryside crawling with cobras, ride back, shoot with arrows whatever was left slithering about."

"Didn't work out that way, Habbie."

"See, Attila had torched so much of Poland, destroyed all their crops…"

"No one, not even the Groethe clan—who had a few bad years farming because they were busy running around and massacring Huns and saving Europe—had anything to eat."

Scar let the silence hang, then smiled. "Yeah, I see you, Mr. Wondering. Don't wonder, Habbie, the Groethe clan did it, it happened. See, they had never seen such a creature, awed and afraid, the hood, the fangs, all that, basic human reaction to snakes."

"Perfectly understandable, the fear, revulsion. Even the Devil is a snake, or so we hear. Me? I don't believe there is a Devil."

Dugula shuddered, thinking, Then you need to take a look in the mirror.

Scar cleared his throat. "At first, naturally, they didn't realize its bite could kill, then when a few of them keeled over, they knew they had a serious problem, suspected even they were faced with extinction."

"Near perfect form of genocide. Let the snakes do the dirty work."

Scar smiled around his cigarette. "They hunted down the cobras, thousands at a time, had to. Save themselves from getting bitten first, but you've got Groethe and clan starving—a man's got to eat, right—so they hacked off heads with swords, stomped them, whatever it took."

"Once trampled, they were skinned, skewered over fires, Groethe and clan with bellies probably bloated on drink, then feasted on cobra meat. Written in this Vatican book they even used cobra venom as a sort of…mixer for their wine. Female eggs, cracked open on skillets, scrambled or over-easy, all of it. Now you'd think drinking all that venom would have killed them. Apparently it didn't, hell, it only made them stronger, even more ferocious because the Romans were up next, but that's another story that needs to be corrected, Hollywood having gotten it all wrong with their *Gladiator* nonsense."

One Eye flicked away his cigarette, head bobbing. "Damn near ate the cobra population to its own extinction. What they didn't consume the winter got."

Dugula couldn't find his voice, mind racing, wondered about this insane story, if they were lying, but something in their eyes told him…

No, he thought, it couldn't be true. If it was, then how could this fantastic accounting of supposed history be kept from the world? Again the turbulence, and he would have sworn something was stirring beneath him. They caught the look, but there was never any doubt they would.

"Wondering if it's true, Duggie?"

"It is. And don't ask what the point is."

"It's this. You're the cobra, we're a couple of King Groethes."

Both lost the grins.

"Got the picture now?" Scar said.

"Are we clear on the point?"

"I'll take your silence and that constipated look as a yes. Now, we're going to have a talk to a few of the others before we land," Scar said. "Same drill, same option. We're going to point out, like the cobras of King Groethe's time, we are quite prepared to skin, skewer you over a fire. Only we won't eat you."

"We'll feed you to your militant pals."

Scar fired up another cigarette. "Or we can be your rapture, joy in Paradise or left behind to suffer Hell on Earth. See—" he paused, looked around the corner, lowered his voice "—in a very short while, telling you we're down to hours, you and the others are going to be freed."

Dugula felt his head spin. "What?"

"Freedom, Duggie, but only if you follow our explicit instructions."

One Eye was grinning, squeezing himself again. "Here's what's going to happen…."

THE COBRA MAJOR was embroiled in some intense conversation on his satlink, Bolan wishing he could eavesdrop. The difficulty on that matter, however, was twofold, and the whole display struck the soldier as scripted.

So what was new? he thought.

They were in the Gulfstream, somewhere over the Mediterranean, Collins in his com center. Bolan had claimed a seat facing the major, but Collins kept his back turned, which threw lip-reading out the porthole. Then there was Python, looking settled and relaxed in a seat next to his boss. Python was working on a beer, puffing up a storm in a chain-smoking routine that would have cleared out Yankee Stadium. The second problem was the rock music thundering from the boom box between Python's feet. Bolan could sense Python watching him from behind black sunglasses that rendered his eyes invisible. The guy was good—Bolan had to give him that much, acting as if the moment were simply Happy Hour, unwinding after a long, hard few days of lopping heads, tapping his foot to the music, working on beer and smoke, rocking his head. If the other commandos were annoyed by the ungodly racket, they were either too exhausted, too lost in thought or too grateful to simply be alive to give a damn.

Something, Bolan sensed, was in the works. And it

had nothing to do with what he'd been told by Collins, all that debriefing, interrogating-of-prisoners business.

Bolan needed to touch base with Brognola as soon as they landed at Camp Zero. The warrior had made sure that he kept his warbag close at hand during each stop, his own satlink buried beneath weapons and gear. Had it been opened when he was occupied in battle, a minidetector concealed in the bottom of the bag would have alerted him to curious hands. He kept a mini-monitor on his person at all times, and it would flash red if the bag was opened. So far, so good.

Bolan eased back in his seat, looked away as Collins shut down his satlink, stood.

"Turn that shit off," Collins growled at Python. "And that's your last beer. What's the matter with you? I don't need you guys breathing beer fumes all over the head shed when we land, bunch of fucking drunks can't even piss straight. We still have work to do."

Bolan was certain it was an act. He watched as Collins went to the small fridge and helped himself to a beer.

"Stone?"

Bolan faked an inviting smile. "I guess command gets certain perks?"

"Damn right. Want one?"

"I'll pass."

Bolan's gut warned him he needed to stay sharper than ever.

Moments later, Collins landed in a seat, faced Bolan.

"We've got a few hours to hash out the next step of the program."

"You've already told me. Tour the compound, debrief, days of interrogations…"

"More like weeks, maybe months. What you called the stooges have already learned we've got some real bad characters on our hands. Here, you're going to need this."

Bolan saw Collins hold out a patch of the American flag.

"Stick that on your left arm. It will allow you free roam of the compound, no Marine watchdogs barking to know what your business is."

Bolan had already seen this same free pass on the others. He took the Velcro emblem, fastened the straps. He watched Collins watching him.

"Been a helluva run, huh, Stone?"

Bolan felt the weariness settle in. "That it has been."

"This thing, this war on terrorism, well, I understand the head shed has another round on the drawing board. Something about Indonesia, the Philippines. Bagging a bunch of Abu Sayyaf beauties. You maybe interested?"

"Let's see how this one shakes out first."

The Executioner saw the dark hunger dart through the Cobra leader's eyes. An image of a lion stalking prey flashed to mind.

Collins nodded. "Yeah, let's do that."

CHAPTER NINETEEN

It was time.

Warlock had the first three marks in his sights, swiveling to his six, the five-man flight crew in black jumpsuits striding his way. Two were on the payroll, he knew, but three—navigator, flight engineer and radio-operator-loadmaster—were already gone; they just didn't know it yet.

"Hold up right there, gentlemen. I need a moment with you."

They parked it near the satellite-intercept-tracking station, Warlock then finding the last two Marines ready to head down the ramp, trail the prisoners being led to their cage by their fellow Marines. "You two soldiers, stand fast!"

"Sir?"

Warlock glanced at Cyclops, the initial play already hashed out between them. Sound suppressors screwed on to their Berettas, Cyclops had the Tranquilizer T-1 loaded with NARCON darts sheathed on his right hip.

"We need your help lugging some gear."

They hesitated, looked at each other, Warlock simmering inside, aware of their orders, Marines sticking to the book. But they were on the new clock set by Collins, and if it didn't go down by the numbers in a hurry they were all stuck and screwed.

"What is your major malfunction, soldier?" Cyclops barked.

"Sir, our orders are to remain with the prisoners until they are locked down and Raven One…"

Warlock gritted his teeth, but it was Cyclops who blew his lid, jabbing a finger at the American flag attached to his left arm with Velcro.

"You see this, son?"

"Yes, sir… I—"

"I see I need to refresh your memory, Marine. This means whoever wears one of these gives the orders around here. It means whoever has one of these tells you to do something, you step lively. Since I don't see either one of you wearing one…

"Shoulder those rifles and shag your asses!" Warlock snarled, and gave Cyclops the nod. "Now, Marines!"

When the Marines did as they were ordered, Warlock whirled in a one-eighty, Beretta in hand. They were in sync, but there was never any doubt in Warlock's mind. Countless times they had killed more than a few targets in a span of heartbeats before they even knew what hit them.

This time was no different.

Warlock ignored the shock and horror framed on the faces of the three Herc jockeys destined for termination. Three quick taps and they were falling, legs shooting out, skulls thwacking off floorboards. He wasn't quite sure what he heard behind him, but knew the sound shouldn't have matched his lethal plugs. Wheeling, he found Cyclops holding the Beretta, spotted neat red holes between the eyes of the Marines.

"Goddammit!" he snarled at Cyclops.

"What?"

"We were told they wanted ten live Marines. I thought we understood each other."

Cyclops shrugged. "Plenty more where they came from."

"Ten—you got that? Breathing."

"Sure. Relax."

Warlock kept his glare on Cyclops a moment, then turned the Beretta on Captains Benson and Marshall.

"Whoa, what the hell is this?" Marshall cried, throwing his hands up. "We had a deal!"

"Just wanted to see you two jump some. What that means is you two better be worth every penny of twenty million from here on. I want that transponder trashed and five minutes ago. Stay on-line to our frequency."

"Not a problem," Marshall said.

Really? Warlock wondered. So why wasn't Benson

quaking in his jumpsuit? What the hell was that in his eyes? Defiance?

"You got a problem, you want to say something, spit it out now, Captain Benson."

Benson shook his head. "No problem here."

"So why don't you look ready to shit yourself like your pilot? How come I think I see some agenda in your eyes?"

"No agenda. I figure you shoot us, who's going to fly this ship?"

"Trust me, cowboy, I spot cold feet and smell out some magic-show bailing act on your parts, I will shoot you down and I don't give a rat's ass if we're thirty thousand feet up. Know why? Because I can fly this ship my goddamn self."

"Hey, it's understood," Marshall said.

"Then drag these bodies into the cubicles. Leave the ramp down, one of you in the cockpit, one back here. Do not let anyone but us inside. I don't hear a 'yes, sir,' ladies!"

"We got it," Benson said.

Warlock holstered his weapon. The warbag draped over his shoulder next, he grabbed the handle on the footlocker. Cyclops took the other strap, lifted and they were moving.

Warlock shot his partner a grin. "Don't drop it."

He spotted the first sign of fear he could ever recall seeing in the man's eye as Cyclops looked down, checking to see if the lock was secure.

As Bolan deplaned behind Collins, warbag on his shoulder, M-16 held low beside his leg, he found a reception committee marching toward the runway. A tall man in black with a full head of gray hair led three other blacksuited men armed with HK MP-5s through the runway lights. Bolan pulled up beside Collins, the other Cobra commandos sweeping past. The soldier stole a few moments to take in Camp Zero.

The ballpark figure was something like two thousand Greek islands, he knew, most of which were in the Aegean Sea, the remainder scattered west in the Ionian. According to Collins, Camp Zero had claimed a piece of rock deep in the southeast Aegean in the Kritiko Pelagos, roughly 120 miles from the southwest shores of Turkey. They were far enough away from commuter ferries, with tourists on island-hopping holiday, cruise ships and such, that Collins claimed they might as well have been at the ends of the earth. It was, supposedly, a covert CIA waystation, Greek officials having long since given American intelligence agencies their blessing when the cold war was in full swing. Later, with all the tension and beating of wardrums between the various countries in the Balkans, it had been expanded to base American troops. It was monitored by cameras, motion sensors ringing the entire shoreline, likewise the hills alive with supertech detection. A little digging, if necessary, and Bolan knew the Farm could confirm the whole slice of information.

Bolan didn't think it would come down to that. At first surveillance, and he believed that maybe for once Collins told the truth.

The base was snugged in a valley, encompassed by walls of black jagged hills. South, Bolan spotted the squat block of Zero Main, the west end of the structure bristling with antennae, sat dishes, radio tower. The C-130, he found, was parked at the deep north end of Runway One, ramp down. The prisoners had been off-loaded, twenty-six Marines, said Collins, to guard the detainees. A sleek Bell JetRanger was sitting quietly on the large helipad near Main, Bolan finding no activity around the compound except for the newcomers pulling up before him.

"Major Collins. Good to see you, sir."

"Mr. Falconi," Collins said, "I'd like you to meet Colonel Stone. He'll be assisting in all processing and questioning of prisoners along with me."

Falconi held out his hand. "Colonel."

Bolan shook the proffered hand, nodded, then felt his gut tighten. He would have sworn he was looking at a carbon copy of Collins. "CIA?"

Falconi hesitated, Bolan catching Collins throwing him a look.

"From here on, Colonel," Collins answered, "the CIA will be a large part of what goes on here. Sitrep, Mr. Falconi."

"Raven One's ETA is sixty minutes, sir."

"The prisoners?"

"Caged and ready for processing, Major."

Bolan felt his mouth tighten. Caged? He felt a growing sense of urgency in the air, Falconi's stare narrowing, Bolan picturing the hungry lion again. Every fiber of his being warned him something was seriously wrong here.

Collins checked his watch. "Okay, Mr. Falconi, I want all the Marines but two in the courtroom for a quick brief before the head shed lands. I'll send two of my own to help watch the prisoners."

"Yes, sir."

Collins ran an eye over the three blacksuited men. "Where's the rest of Predator Five?"

There was a brisk breeze, tinged with the briny smell of Aegean Sea salt swaddling him, but despite the cool wind Bolan felt his blood suddenly run hot with adrenaline, instincts kicking into overdrive, combat radar blipping all over his mental screen.

"With the prisoners, Major."

"Okay, help get the Marines situated, ten minutes."

"Aye, aye, Major."

"Come on, Stone."

"What happened to the grand tour?"

"No time, Colonel," Collins said, striding toward the concrete facing of Zero Main, warbag slapping off his back. "The head shed will be hopped up when they touch down. The big shots will want to pick our brains the next twenty-four hours about the mission. No rest for the weary, Colonel, just keeping ourselves juiced on bad coffee and smokes. While we can, we need to get somewhat situated ourselves in our own quarters, dump off our bags. Now, whatever they ask, just tell them the truth about the mission."

Bolan watched as Collins glanced at his warbag. The truth?

"What about Gambler trying to put an eye in the back of my head?"

"We'll worry about that if and when it gets to that point. Now, I'm assuming, Colonel, you'd like a little downtime maybe? You've got a satlink in the bag you might want to make some calls with before we get started? You do, better do it now because you won't get another chance for a while, and I can't guarantee what that while is."

Bolan felt his heart thumping against his chest, the tension and heat radiating off Collins. Brognola needed an update anyway.

"Twenty minutes should do it."

"That'll work," Collins said.

Bolan looked at the oversize pistol hung in leather on the major's right hip.

"What's with the new addition?"

"What?" Collins snapped.

"I know a tranquilizer gun when I see it."

Collins chuckled. "I have to give you an answer for the obvious?"

"So far, Major, there's been very little about all this that's been obvious."

Collins frowned. "It's for the prisoners. One of them gets out of line...you have the picture?"

Bolan grunted, then turned as he felt a presence behind him. The soldier called Predator Five was trailing him.

"Would you like some help with your bag, sir?"

"I'll manage."

IT WAS ALL Collins could do to keep his nerves from showing, sparking out of his skin. The big bastard, as far as he was concerned, was the first problem that had to go. Stone didn't know it yet, but he wouldn't check out of the world, quick and painless. Stay cool, keep a poker face, he told himself, striding down Hallway A, Stone right beside him, the concrete walls shining a brilliant white beneath the stark glare of the overheads. He felt his face go flush from the heat of the moment, feared another minute of walking with the bastard in what was damn near a blinding light and he'd break out in a sweat, Stone—warrior instincts so keen the guy was almost psychic—smelling it out.

The clock was ticking. Everyone on the team knew their role. All they had to do was execute. The last-minute tinkering, Collins feared...

Screw it.

They were there, and it was on.

They were marching past bisecting Hallway B when Collins pulled up, decided to put on a show of checking on the two Marines standing watch over the cage.

The prisoners were housed in a steel mesh pen, capable of holding at least a hundred prisoners, mats already distributed, three open commodes. He saw a few hands gripping the mesh, bearded faces and angry eyes aimed at the Marines.

"Step back," one of the Marines ordered.

"Everything under control, gentlemen?"

Two affirmatives, and Collins began leading Stone down the hallway.

"You don't mind bunking with me, do you, Colonel?"

Was that a grin he saw dance over Stone's lips?

"You don't snore, do you?"

Was the silence meant to fray his nerves?

"Well," Collins said, as they moved past the iron-barred cell which, he knew, would become Stone's coffin, "it isn't the Hyatt, but we've got satellite TV, wet bar, our own bathroom and shower. Here we are."

Collins pulled up in the open doorway of their quarters, his companion hesitating.

"After you, Colonel."

He saw Stone looking over his shoulder, thinking about something, then turn away, easing into their quarters.

He had to have sensed it coming, but by the time Stone had gripped his Beretta, Collins had the T-1 out and chugging a dart. It impaled him, dead center in the American flag. Collins knew it would take a few seconds for the NARCON to fully kick in, the bastard clawing for his weapon, hanging on to fight back. Two more shots to the stomach, Collins gripped by fear as the big guy fought to stay on his feet, then he drilled his toe into Stone's groin for safekeeping.

He watched the man jackknife, then collapse.

CHAPTER TWENTY

The Executioner would never graduate from the school of "should have, could have, would have." That was reserved for the losing side, those Monday-morning quarterbacks and cable-news talking heads, all the second-guessing that didn't mean a damn thing.

But the soldier was only human, after all, flesh and blood, and he'd been dumped square on the losing side.

Right then he was enrolled in CSW 101, front row, final exam. How in the hell it had come down to this...

After all, his gut instinct screamed at rock-concert decibels that Collins and Cobra were a pack of cutthroat liars with a hidden agenda. After telling himself time and again to watch his six, after every clue, hint and vibe they dropped, alluded to, gave off, after knowing damn good and well something horrific was going to hit the fan, the warrior's instinct honed to a sixth sense and tuned to treachery on the table and ready to be thrown in his face...

After all that and here he was, sprawled on his face, the world fading away in a shimmering mist, stuck with tranquilizer needles, a human dartboard. He might have drawn the Beretta, moments ago, but it was the shot to his balls that sealed it, the white-hot, paralyzing agony floating away now to a distant horizon, telling him he was seconds away from going under.

Trussed up and finished.

From that horizon, shimmering further away by the second, Bolan heard Collins chuckle.

"That'll keep you for about an hour, Colonel. Just in case you wake up before we're done, I'll leave someone here to baby-sit."

He wanted to reach up and grab Collins by the throat, the nuts, anything he could get his hands on, but his limbs were swelling with numbness.

"I'll be back, Colonel. Then your buddies Larry and Curly want to have a little chat with you. Seems they're all bent out of shape you snuffed Gambler. I promised them your ass, and your ass they will have. I asked them to save me a piece, but, hey, we'll see what happens, no guarantees in life, you know. Sweet dreams, asshole—your heartbeats are on a one-hour clock."

Bolan saw the misty specter of Collins sweep out of the room, then the haze faded to black.

"DO NOT TALK."

Dugula saw the hope rise in the defiant looks, heard the excitement in the whispering of his fellow Muslims all around. They were wondering if the infidels were speaking the truth, when would it happen, what was happening and why when the two Marines snapped at them to shut up or they would all be separated to solitary confinement.

In Arabic, Dugula, and what he suspected were the leading voices of the group, told the others to obey. They fell silent as a group, the Marines glowering, standing back when Dugula saw the Scar and One Eye surge into view, pistols with attached sound suppressors up and aimed at the Marines. Shock and confusion hardened the faces of the Marines, assault rifles shimmying up in their hands, uncertain what to do.

"You're relieved of duty," he heard the one-eyed demon say, then two soft chugs sounded, the killshots echoing through the pen, the Marines toppling into the wall, crimson smears and grisly patches of brain matter following their slide to the floor.

Dugula was off his mat, the tide of prisoners rushing for the fence.

"Hold up!" Scar yelled.

"Fall back!" Cyclops ordered.

They quieted down, Dugula watching as both white men snapped up the fallen M-16s.

"Listen up, we're only going to say this once," Scar said. "You are going to be freed, as we promised. You will be taken straight for the same plane that brought you here. You will not be chained down. If any one of you attempts to fight back at any time, we will shoot down every one of you. We already have what we want. We really don't need you, but we made a promise to one of your leaders and we intend to keep it. Consider us the rapture and you the chosen."

"Now," Cyclops said, "if any of you have a problem with us sending your brothers on to Paradise and his nuts are itching for revenge, speak up now and you will forever hold your peace."

Dugula knew no matter what would happen they were all still seething these men had so cold-bloodedly killed two of their own before their eyes. Beyond that, all of them, he knew, had lost scores of fellow fighters during various strikes on their independent groups. Whatever this madness was all about, Dugula could stifle his own questions, willing to accept—even, God help him—trust in the enemy. What else could be done? He could only hope the others held their tongues, kept their hands to themselves.

"Move out in twos. I will lead the way. No talking," Cyclops said.

Three more infidels appeared by Scar's side, their subguns out and ready to cut loose at the first sign of mutiny.

"Dugula," Cyclops called out. "Front and center. Any of your people get froggy, you're the first to go. You understand, Dugula?"

Dugula saw Scar key the door open, the others parting to let him pass.

"Perfectly."

"Good boy."

COLLINS SLIPPED on his gas mask, HK MP-5 in hand.
He found Falconi, aka the Falcon, and two of his Predator commandos standing by the closed doors to the
courtroom. Mamba, Python and Diamondback on his
heels, Collins led the way down Hallway F, cocking
and locking, blood racing, victory in sight.

The double doors were closed, twenty-plus Marines
right now sitting in wooden chairs, backs turned to
them, Collins knew, facing the American flag and the
judge's bench. He felt no pity, no remorse over what
he was about to do, what had to be done. Ten were
promised for delivery to the ayatollah, and ten live
Marines he would get. Fuck America, he thought, this
was about him, his money, and this was his time to
shine. All that patriotic blubbering, the war-drumming
nationalistic "us and them" nonsense didn't wash, he
believed. There were two sides to every conflict, every
story, but he was only interested in one side.

His own.

After hearing about Cyclops's quick dispatch of the
two Marines aboard the Herc, he relayed the order
again in no uncertain terms he needed ten breathing
Marines. Another of Falconi's Predators was right then
en route to help lug unconscious and cuffed Marines
to the plane. There was only one way in and out of the
courtroom, and Collins had the key that would lock

them in, sucking on gas, figure fifteen, twenty seconds tops until they were out there in la-la land.

A check of his watch, and he found they had about thirty minutes to wrap it up until the big shots touched down. There was still the Stone matter in the wings, a not so little moment Collins was craving every bit as much as Warlock and Cyclops. A real treat was in store for the big bastard.

Closing on Falconi, he found the Marines had lined their weapons against the wall, as ordered. He was plucking a NARCON-D canister off his webbing when Falconi said, "Once we're in the air you and me need to have a talk."

"Really?"

"Really."

"So far, Mr. Falconi, everything is going along swimmingly."

"Here, maybe."

Collins didn't much care for the sound of that, wondering if there was some problem with the money.

"Just finish the job," he told Falconi, who took a canister, finger curled inside the ring.

"Mamba, pull one of these puppies."

Mamba stepped up, shouldering his HK, sleeping bomb in hand.

"I go nine, Mamba twelve, Falcon three. Diamondback take the door. Whenever you're ready, Mr. Diamondback."

Collins waited until Diamondback twisted the

knobs, shoved the doors ahead, then pulled the pin, counting off the four-second time delay, allowing for a full second to pass.

Three lobs, perfect tosses halfway around the clock, Collins finding the Marines sitting ramrod stiff, facing front—until the canisters thumped and rolled and clouds of gas erupted.

They were shouting now, leaping to their feet, but Collins slammed the doors shut and locked them in.

"God bless America." Collins laughed.

BOLAN THOUGHT he was coming around, but he couldn't be certain what was real, what was drug-induced coma. His skull felt swollen, limbs numb, reality coming at him, in and out, gooey blackness. There were voices, he thought, drifting from the ceiling, men shouting—one or two?

He rolled onto his side, vomit stirring in his guts, the voices growing louder, the sounds of men not in pain, but...

What? Panic? Terror? They were familiar voices, memory wanting to serve him...but...

He saw a specter looming over him, a ghoul grinning down.

"Just sit tight or I'll clock you back into dreamland."

His watchdog stepped back, weapon trained on him. Time, he thought, that was all he needed to get himself at least halfway together. Or would his time run out?

The sludge in his limbs grew heavier for some reason, the soldier figuring adrenaline was coursing the NARCON through his blood.

The haze wafted back, and whoever had been shouting in panic...

The voices carried, louder than ever, then there was only silence.

COLLINS, PAINFULLY AWARE of time, barked the orders for his commandos to slap cuffs on ten, start hauling them out, then swept into the dissipating cloud. A glance at Falconi, briefly wondering what the big talk was all about, and Collins thought the CIA man looked sick over the chore they had to perform. Whatever it was passed as Falconi began pumping one round each from his Beretta into the skulls of sleeping Marines. Collins shot three at point-blank range with his own pistol, looked over at Python, who flashed five fingers twice.

"Move, move! It's going to take two trips!"

"Aye, aye, Major!"

One more head shot, Collins taking stock of the body count, but Falconi moved up beside him, said, "I think we're finished here, Major."

"Walk through it once more," he ordered, checking the bodies, most of which were stacked near the doors where Marines had attempted to break out when the gas blew.

Out in the hall, Collins shed his mask, chucked it away. He rang up Warlock and Cyclops. "What's your situation?"

"They're loaded."

"Everything under control?"

"I think we've made believers out of them. Must've been the tale of King Groethe and his snake-eaters that got their bowels all twisted. The load is now nothing but meek lambs."

"Okay," Collins said, swift strides hauling him south down Hallway F, "meet me, and hustle up. You two have ten minutes and no more."

Collins cut off Warlock's chuckle, hastening his strides.

It was Stone's turn.

And it was going to be, Collins thought, unable to resist the chuckle, the sweetest thing next to payday.

LIFE WAS A CRAPSHOOT. Bad things happened to good people, and good things found a way to happen for bad people. Beyond that—perhaps nearly but not quite as mystifying—the mediocre prevailed, the world often falling at their feet, while the truly gifted, the worthy and the compassionate and the brave rarely shone, but were rather shunned, even cast aside, scoffed at, held in contempt. If there was justice in the world, it was the world's justice. If there was richness in the world, it was the world's riches.

It was a voice, floating somewhere in the darkness and jelly of Bolan's thoughts, swirling, calling to him. The voice told him all of this was obvious to a warrior who believed in the sanctity of life, that whatever good one did was simply for the sake of doing good, but that there was an answer as to why the unjust and the unworthy, the savage and the sick of soul were often rewarded with fame, fortune, the adulation of men, which, more often than not, was envy. They killed, raped and stole, and got away with it. They grabbed up obscene riches at the expense and misery of many, laughed and kept on living while others suffered and died and they turned a blind eye, indulging in all the world had to offer, and what man of conscience could possibly fathom why it was allowed to be so. The voice carried upward from the blackness, reminded him he was a warrior, stay strong, he was not alone. But it made no sense, the other voice—or so it sounded— went on to respond. Why did evil triumph so often over good? Why did the greedy and the proud and the willful and the murderous own glory in the world? Why did they appear to be rewarded?

"Their time is short. Eternity is a long time."

Two voices, or was it one?

Bolan couldn't be sure of anything, felt himself at once sucked down into some black hole, wanting to simply float away. Minutes passed. Or was it hours?

He thought he was coming back to reality, mired in the dark sludge, but clawing—breath by breath—his way out, sheer will, fear and adrenaline reserves reviving him, some strength returning, as he felt life in his arms.

Bolan was looking up, the mist evaporating, when the boot speared him in the gut.

CHAPTER TWENTY ONE

"This is for Gambler!"

Bolan suffered through a flurry of fists and feet, a hurricane of rights, uppercuts, straights, kicks to the ribs, legs, lower back. He felt each and every piledriving blow, whoofed and grunted as still more air was driven from already oxygen-starved lungs. They came at him, three snarling voices meshing as one, it sounded, the haze in his eyes bursting with stars. Each time he tried to stand, Bolan felt a fist pounding his jaw, eyes, skull, lights on the verge of winking out. The human body, especially one as finely tuned and superbly conditioned as Bolan's, was tough, could endure ferocious physical abuse. It was also fragile, and a blow to the head could kill with a bone fragment to the brain, a series of kicks to the stomach unleashing hemorrhage, a slow, bad and painful way to go, eventually choking on blood. Unlike Hollywood, where two fully grown men could bang away at each other for thirty minutes, nary a scratch, in reality one well-placed punch to the jaw or the side of the head and the legs turned to jelly, gave out, and when a man was down on the ground the other guy had all the advantage. The awful reality now was that Bolan knew he was meant to take the mother of all beatings before they killed him. Payback for Gambler, for starters, then there was the simple fact he was expendable, and now in the way of whatever their twisted plan. He was on the ground, at their mercy, and he was messed up, with more to come.

A veil of blackness began to descend, as he heard himself wheeze, sucking air, but the blows kept coming.

"He doesn't look so tough now, does he?"

"Bastard's going to pass out."

"Drag his ass over here!"

Collins, he heard, from the dark side of Pluto, barking orders. Instinctively, Bolan reached for his side arms, but found only empty holsters. He lifted his leg, then discovered they'd also taken his commando dagger.

Hands next, more like claws, dug into his shoulders, dragged him ahead. He tasted the bitter copper of his own blood, his face burning where deep gashes were already slashed open around his eyes and mouth.

If he was going to die, the soldier decided to die on his feet, fighting to the last bitter breath.

He craned his head, made out Collins standing by

the cell door, the bastard grinning at him through the mist, chucking something up and down in his hand. A combination of fear, adrenaline, superb conditioning and raw willfulness cleared Bolan's limbs of a good deal of sludge. They were laughing, cursing him still, when he galvanized to his feet.

"Jesus!"

Warlock was surprised as hell they hadn't beaten him unconscious, as the soldier whiplashed an elbow over his mouth. He followed up with a hammerfist, cracking Cyclops in his good eye, staggering the bastard. A two-foot charge and Bolan buried his toe in Collins's bread-basket, jackknifed the Cobra leader, nearly dropped him to his knees. The trouble was, Bolan knew he was too far gone, the world threatening to spin out from under him, double vision turning three attackers into six.

The punch to the back of his skull erupted another round of shooting stars, the fist to his kidney threatening to spew vomit as he felt the invisible knives tear clear to his sternum, back down to his toes. Hands dug into his shoulders, Collins cursing but sounding like some whiny kid as he sucked wind, and Bolan took the edge of the bars to the side of his face. It was a strange, sick feeling of disembodiment next, felt his legs moving in a sort of bike-pedal motion as he was run into the cell, then body-slammed through some heavy object with such force whatever they'd hammered him through splintered and collapsed. He was facedown, pressed against cold concrete.

"Let me at him!"

It was Collins, alive and raging, the air back in his lungs.

Bolan faded, in and out, barely felt the punches.

"Come on, Major!"

"Give us some room!"

"Fuck off!"

There was no air in his lungs, no life in his limbs. With the NARCON still cruising through his system, with men who were probably just as skilled with their fists as he was but who were amped up with murder in their hearts, Bolan knew it was beyond hope.

"Go get it. We're outta here."

Somehow he held on, the world spinning off its axis, just the same. He shuddered up on an elbow, sharp objects digging into his side. He shimmied up, back against the wall, saw two misty specters outside the bars, the door slamming shut with a snick as it latched.

This was it.

Bolan waited for the bullet to end it for good, but it never came.

As he sucked air back into burning lungs, deep intakes that told him that somehow, miracle of miracles, no ribs were broken—though every inch of his side and back and stomach ached and burned—his vision cleared enough to find Cyclops at the bars. There was something in his hand—a black satchel? Bolan wondered what was coming next.

"I still say you let me at least pump one in his gut, Major."

Collins shook his head. "Nah. He'll be dead soon enough, and this will be sweeter than just letting him bleed to death. What are you waiting for? Toss it."

Bolan would have sworn he saw the sack pulsing or thrashing with something inside fighting to get out, would have...

The soldier knew what was coming, and tensed. Cyclops unknotted the cord, grabbed the bottom of the sack. A flick of his wrist, and Cyclops sent the cobra airborne. They were laughing, as it coiled along on the floor, Bolan watching the serpent, but his vision was blurring from NARCON and the pummeling. He tried to stand, but there was no feeling in his legs, no strength anywhere. He watched the serpent as it wound a foot or so closer, then stopped, rising, as if thinking about something.

Satisfied he was a goner, they were laughing, then vanished without a word.

Bolan fought to stay awake, knew if he passed out now...

The cobra inched closer, tongue flicking, Bolan fighting with every fiber of willpower he could muster to keep from passing out as its hood fanned out, and the serpent rose higher.

"TALK ABOUT perfect timing, Major."

Collins resisted the temptation to rub his stomach.

The bastard had nearly speared the kick clear back to his spine, Collins wondering if he'd be pissing blood the next few days. Damn, but he gave Stone his due. He had taken a beating that no man should have walked away from, and Collins had the bruised and bloodied knuckles to show for more than a few wallops to the guy's face and head. Sure, like a cop who knew how to use just enough force to subdue a scumbag perp without inflicting obvious injuries, they had pulled back some on their punches. He wanted Stone to live just long enough for the cobra to get him. It was never really the act of dying itself that was so terrible, he thought. Not for him, and certainly not for a man of Stone's caliber, the guy nothing but balls and heart, all warrior.

It was the moments before, during which a man knew he was going to die, that could prove the worst, the waiting for the end to come, nothing he could do to stop it. In a way, he thought, it was a shame to kill a warrior as talented, as stand up and—what?—principled as Stone? Ten guys like the colonel, and he figured he could take down and control half the oil fields in the Middle East, nothing but money in the bank.

Screw him.

There was no way, what with his own moral code, that Stone would have ever been part of his team. What was this now? he wondered. Regret?

Forget it.

The thorn in his side had been removed.

Collins found Warlock looking pleased, but the bitter sheen in the eye of Cyclops told him the man wasn't too happy with the results.

"What?" Collins rasped, leading them toward the runway where the sleek VIP Gulfstream was taxiing to a stop.

"I don't like knowing the bastard might still be breathing."

"Give it up. That snake was going right for him. Cooped up in those sacks as long as they were and getting riled up the whole time, those things will sink their fangs into the first live flesh they see."

"I don't know."

"He's finished. That's the last I want to hear about it."

Collins picked up the pace, HK subgun off his shoulder, Python and Falconi turning their way. "You know what to do, gentlemen. Quick and clean, any crap from them, bust 'em over the head. I want them cuffed, stuffed and loaded up, two minutes."

Pulling up, Collins waited as the hatch opened, ramp unfolding. They deplaned, single file, briefcases in hand. Four of Washington's intelligence elite, he recognized a pudgy face or two from the talk shows which they were invited on, so-called experts who could shoot their mouths off but never said a damn thing worth remembering, always dancing around the critical questions, swaddling themselves in national security. This, Collins thought, as assistants leaked information to press hounds, and their bosses cajoled six- and seven-figure book deals over martinis with New York literary agents. Go figure. Fuck it, he was taking his slice now.

Oh, but they looked and smelled good, all perfumed and pink and polished, dark cashmere coats, the expressions chiseled with self-importance, the grim seriousness with the task at hand of drilling, indicting and judging terror mongers.

That wasn't going to happen. They didn't know it yet, but they were in a world of shit beyond their worst nightmare.

They were looking around, unsure, probably sensed something in the air, wondering why subguns were up and aimed their way. Collins waited until the bald bulldog was down and rolling up between his fellow elitists.

Python was up the steps, subgun out and ready.

"General Aberdeen," Collins said, then heard the cries and shouts of the flight crew as Python's stutter of subgun fire ripped through the fuselage, cabin portholes winking with muzzle-flashes.

"What is the meaning—?"

"The meaning, General," Collins said, stepping closer to the frozen four, "is that you four are under arrest."

"What?" The NSA guy bleated like a lamb.

"You're insane!"

"That could be, General, but one man's insanity is another man's vision of what has to be made right in the world. You are being arrested and detained for crimes and atrocities," Collins told them as Warlock, Cyclops and Falconi moved behind the group, "committed against all Islamic peoples. You are going to be tried and most likely executed for said crimes."

Collins heard the expected outrage, but Warlock and Cyclops were slamming their subguns off their skulls, driving them to their knees.

"What is this about?" Aberdeen roared.

"Hands behind your back," Warlock bellowed in Aberdeen's ear. "Do it now, or I will shoot you in the balls, I shit you not!"

Collins saw Cyclops grinning as he fastened the plastic cuffs on Aberdeen's hands. "Teachers."

"What?"

"You know, teachers. Those people you dump your kids off on while you and the little lady go play at being big and important. Teachers—those people who teach the next generation reading, writing and arithmetic, who are responsible for shaping and forming the character of your little darlings. Underpaid, underappreciated, barely get by while some assholes who can't read, write or add two and two playing kids' games get ten million dollars a year just for being assholes. It's about an upside-down system, where right is wrong and wrong is right—"

"Come on, come on," Collins urged. "You can give him the philosophical spiel on the decline and decay of America when they're loaded up."

"You're crazy, you'll never—"

"We've already gotten away with it, General," Collins said.

BOLAN KNEW he'd get only one shot to try to save himself. If he missed the first time, it was over. If it was a spitting adder—and right then he sure couldn't tell the difference even if he knew—he was finished. He would be blinded first, then bitten, some of the deadliest snake venom in the world coursing through his punished body, lungs collapsing, he believed, nervous system shut down in probably thirty seconds, rendered paralyzed, gasping for air, twitching out.

Slowly, staring into black orbs no larger than pinheads, Bolan reached behind, fingers curling around a thick piece of wood. The way the tip jabbed in his side he knew his fall against the cell's table had sheared off a strip as sharp as a spike. Would it be enough? Figure distance was a short lunge of three feet, but in his punished condition, eyes wanting to blur...

The black cobra appeared nearly kissing-close.

It rose, several inches higher, body coiling tighter. Now!

The creature struck, propelling itself forward, and Bolan felt his hand clamp flesh. He had it now, squeezing with his remaining strength just inches below the hood. It was hissing, fangs bared, dripping poison. Then Bolan had the snake on the floor, boot pinned on its fat serpentine body as he brought the sharpened stake down again and again, hammered its head, stabbing, slashing.

The world became a carousel next, instinct telling Bolan it was dead, the snake no longer thrashing.

Spent, the Executioner felt his legs melting.

Then he collapsed onto the wall, sinking on his haunches. He nearly slipped away into dark bliss, but clung to the real world, wondering how he was going to get out of the cage.

CHAPTER TWENTY TWO

"I'm telling you God's honest truth!"

Collins had the muzzle of his HK subgun jammed in Captain Marshall's belly. He looked at the bruise on the pilot's jaw, the man's arms above his head, eyes brimming with fear.

"Just clocked you and sashayed on out the door?"

"Coldcocked me. I never saw it coming."

"And you had no inkling your buddy was set to abandon ship?"

"Clueless."

"Guess now you maybe think you're going to get his cut?"

Marshall hesitated, Collins reading the wheels of greed spinning in the look.

"I'm happy with ten, but whatever you think is right, Major."

Collins looked at his troops. "How come this is the

first I'm hearing about Benson vanishing into the night? How come none of you bothered to tell me? Someone, anyone?"

"We didn't know until now," Diamondback called out.

"We assumed he was in the cockpit," Mamba said.

"We could do a quick sweep of the compound," Python suggested.

Collins gave that some consideration. The problem was the AWOL Herc jockey could be anywhere. The hills were pocked with caves, an ancient lattice of tunnels dug out by the Greeks dating back to the time of Alexander.

"No. Python, front and center!"

Collins drew back the subgun. "I take it the transponder's history?" he asked Marshall.

"All taken care of."

"Sir?"

"Want you to sit with Captain Marshall. Do not leave the cockpit for any reason. You have to take a leak or a dump, do it right there next to him."

"Aye, aye, Major."

"Python here," Collins told Marshall, "was a navigator on a Spectre during the Gulf War. You touch anything but the wheel and the stick for the landing gear, he'll know about it."

"Your boy back there," Marshall said, "already gave me fair warning."

"Move out and get us in the air."

Collins headed for the prisoners, hollered for someone to close the ramp.

SOMETHING GLITTERED.

Bolan, bracing himself against the wall, stood, searching the hall floor in front of the bars. With the slightest movement white-hot pain tore through every inch of his body, set fire to every nerve ending. No broken bones, but the blood was still flowing from deep gashes along his eyebrows that would need suturing, assuming he got out of the cell in the near future. Medical attention was actually the last of his concerns. Even still there wasn't one inch on his body that wasn't aching with raw fire, pulsing from the terrible breathing. The inside of his mouth and cheeks was a series of craters, the soldier hacking out thick, gummy blood as he shuddered ahead, forcing himself to focus at the object on the floor.

Most of his vision had returned, but the haze still danced in and out, pain throbbing right behind his eyes so hard it felt as if his eyeballs would pop out from the pressure. Hand on the wall, he shuffled three steps past the pulped cobra body, breathing steady, spitting blood. He shoved himself off the wall, amazed for a moment he could stand at all, but willing his legs to stay locked beneath him.

He was two feet from the bars—

And nearly laughed out loud.

Bending, he slipped an arm between the bars,

palmed the key. He drew it back, figured in all the excitement, Collins and company swept up in the brutal moment, that he had simply dropped the key. Then Bolan recalled the kick to the bastard's gut. That was when he had lost it most likely.

No matter. Bolan reached around, inserted the key and unlocked the door. Then he saw it, freezing in mid-stride, the last two feet of black tail sliding out of sight as the snake vanished down Hallway B. Beyond the serpent life, the Executioner sensed the utter stillness of death all over the building.

Not good, he thought, cobras on the loose, no telling where they'd crop up, but he was soon vacating the premises.

First he entered his quarters. Mistake two was the enemy leaving his warbag behind, M-16 still leaning against the wall. Oh, but they were laughing now, feeling good, but once he put in the call to Brognola he would make sure the man from Justice pulled out all the stops, called in every marker, the Farm using every bit of high-tech skill at its command and disposal to scour the earth. Make no mistake, the soldier would hunt them down.

Bolan faltered, weaving. Suddenly he felt sick, the world gyrating, wall shimmying. He dry heaved, fell to a knee. As busted up as he was, unconsciousness threatening him with every step, he knew he wasn't going to make it out the door anytime soon.

M-16 in hand, checking the load and finding a full

clip, it was all he could do to sweep the bathroom, the entire quarters for lurking cobras.

Clear.

He went and shut the door just as he heard a distant rumble and the hallway lights blinked out. They had blown the generator, he knew, gone for good. But to where? How many had they killed here? Why? What was the conspiracy about?

Stumbling around blind in the hall with serpents crawling all over the place wasn't an option. He palmed his lighter, flicked the lid, went and kicked his warbag a few times. They assumed the cobra would have done its deadly work for them by now, but he wouldn't put it past the bastards to stow a serpent in the bag. He was satisfied it was free of venomous creatures, about to zip it open and pull out his satlink when a wave of nausea washed over him, driving fiery needles deep into his brain.

Bolan fell backward and collapsed on a bunk.

COLLINS HEARD the expected threatening mantra from General Aberdeen, a few of the Marines jumping into the act—his ass was grass, he would pay, he was a traitor and so on and so forth. The Marines had to have known what was coming, as Cyclops thumbed all but two rounds out of a clip.

Collins took the Beretta, turned and told a terrorist, "You! Take this. Two shots, two Marines, two freebies. You pick 'em."

"Figure it's the least we owe you," Warlock said, training his subgun on the terrorist as he stood, uncertain, but took the weapon.

"No tricks," he told the terrorist. "Just don't do these four," he said, nodding at the head shed.

"Yeah, they're big TV stars back in America." Cyclops laughed.

Despite their hands cuffed behind their backs, legs manacled together, Collins saw them rising as a group, cursing, snarling. He put three down with tranquilizer darts, Predator Five, Warlock, Cyclops and Diamondback slamming subguns over their heads, driving them to their haunches.

"Go on," Collins urged the terrorist who strode up to the Marines.

"You'll pay for this Collins, I swear to—"

"I've already been paid, General. Any more squawking out of you and I might just decide you're not worth the trouble of keeping alive."

BOLAN STIFLED the groan, swinging his legs off the bunk. Assault rifle in hand, he watched as the door creaked open, flame wavering, the muzzle of a weapon poking into the darkness.

"Lose the weapon! Do it now!"

The Executioner sensed only one presence but was braced to cut loose on full-auto with the M-16.

The rifle was tossed to the floor, and a voice called out, "Easy. I'm not one of them."

"Are you alone?"

"Just me. Everyone else here is dead."

"Collins?"

"Gone with the prisoners—rather, their new prisoners, General Aberdeen and about ten Marines."

Bolan stood, grimaced. "Keep that flame on your face. What's your name?"

"Captain Benson."

"What are you?"

"United States Air Force. Retired. Fly for the Company now."

"Get in here and pull a chair. Shut the door behind you."

Bolan slid a wooden chair across the floor. The lean figure in a black jumpsuit stepped in, closed the door, then sat, the flame from the lighter showing Bolan a middle-aged graying flight jockey. Benson whistled as he scoured Bolan's punished features.

"Collins did that?"

"He had a little help from his friends Warlock and Cyclops, but, yeah, they danced a hell of a number on me. You come across any cobras on the way in?"

Benson nodded. "Six. I shot them. Collins even threw two of his own men into a cell with a few snakes."

"Who?"

"Tsunami and Brick I believe were their names."

"I was right about one thing, anyway."

"What was that?"

"The serpent handles, those were the ones in on

whatever this is about. They flew off in the Herc, Benson?"

"They did. I was their copilot."

"You picked some rotten company to fall into bed with."

"I woke up before it was too late."

"Telling me you grew a conscience?"

"That's what I'm telling you. I made a mistake."

"Seems to be a lot of that going around lately."

"Well, I may be a few bad things in life, but a traitor to my country isn't one of them. You must be Colonel Stone."

"That would be me. What's your story?"

"No story. They recruited me about six months ago. I was handpicked by the Pentagon's Cobra Command, which is actually run by Collins. Collins had some dirt on me, pictures of me and a woman other than my wife. The usual sins, extortion."

"That sounds his speed. What's this about?"

"It's about dumping off the head shed and ten Marines to one of the world's most notorious terrorists. Way I heard it there's going to be a sort of reverse military tribunal for the Americans. Confessions of crimes committed against all Islamic peoples, all of it video-taped, right down to their executions. You'll probably see it on Al-Jazeera soon enough."

"Let me guess, Collins and the rest are in it for the money."

"One billion dollars to be exact."

"Who?"

"Harin Salaan."

"I've heard the name. So you know where they're going?"

"I know exactly where they're going. Iran."

Bolan felt dizzy.

"Colonel, why don't you let me clean you up a little."

"When we get out of here. What's out front to fly?"

Bolan heard the list; Benson stating there was a first-aid kit on the Gulfstream.

"Just get us to Incirlik," Bolan said, then nearly pitched off his feet.

Benson jumped up, threw an arm around the soldier. "Colonel, I think you need to lay—"

"No time."

"Can you manage your bag, or would you like me to carry it?"

"You carry it. I'll watch for snakes on the way out. Let me be clear on something, Benson. I've had a bad night, and if I find out you're not playing it straight..."

"Understood, Colonel."

Bolan remembered he had been passed out before Benson appeared. "What time is it, Benson?"

"The sun just came up."

"Gives them about a four-hour head start. We get to the plane, I'll help you sweep it for snakes. You can stitch me up after that."

Bolan dredged up every bit of strength he could,

shuffled for the door, clacked open his lighter, M-16 poised to shoot the first serpent he came across. Soon, the Executioner knew, he would be hunting snakes of the human variety. And woe unto Collins and whatever was left of Cobra Force when he caught up to them. As far as Bolan was determined, payback was as close as tomorrow.

"Now, what is your major malfunction, Mr. Falconi?"

"Oh, just the little matter of a hundred million to collect and the fact our Russian pals seemed to have dropped off the face of the earth."

They were sitting alone in the com center, Collins puffing on a cigarette, Falconi looking edged-out.

"The Russians were your department. Part of us collecting the rest of our money was for delivery of those VX briefcases to the ayatollah of Rocknrolla."

"You changed the schedule by a full two days. Two days is when I am supposed to contact the Russians, no sooner."

"What are you saying?"

"I'm saying, Major, when we land in Iran, I don't think the ayatollah will just wire the rest of the money to our accounts and bid us a nice day."

"So we sit tight for two days. Sample the ayatollah's hospitality, help the head shed and the Marines get settled into their new home."

"While the entire might of the United States military and intelligence agencies are hunting for us.

You don't think this bird can be spotted and tracked?"

"That's why my men are right now creating ghost ships for any spy eyes. Another little marvel, courtesy of high-tech supercomputers. We go one way, any military installations tracking us find their screens showing us going the opposite direction." Collins blew a cloud of smoke into Falconi's face, the black op frowning. "Look, it will be at least two days before anybody discovers what happened at Camp Zero, since part of the plan was radio silence with Washington, which I arranged through my contacts at the Pentagon. By then, the Russians deliver the VX packages, we get our money, everyone goes their separate ways. Passports, new identities…"

"You hope it goes down that way."

Collins didn't like being second-guessed. "Mr. Falconi, we are in way too deep now to start fretting like a bunch of old hags over things that haven't happened yet."

"The Iranians are fanatics, Major. I'm amazed they even bought into this scheme."

"What are you saying?"

"I'm saying what's to stop them from either taking us prisoner like the others—or just killing us on the spot?"

Collins laughed around his smoke, patted his HK subgun. "Me, Mr. Falconi, that's what would stop them. You want out?"

"What?"

"You want out, I can go and open the door right now."

"You threatening me, Major? This is my deal, too."

"No threat. I merely asked a simple question."

Falconi bobbed his head, pondering something. "When I want out, I'll let you know. Two days, the Russians don't touch base, and I walk. We clear?"

Collins nodded. "Yeah, we're clear, all right."

ONE MORE SHOT cobra found twisting in the cabin, thirty-plus sutures later, a cleaned and sterilized but brutally punished face, and Bolan found himself in the air, putting Camp Zero behind, Benson at the helm of the Gulfstream. He settled the satlink on a table, sipped bottled water, fighting to keep it down. The soldier knew he would wear the war wounds on this one for some time to come, but it was far from over. The worst for somebody was waiting on the other end in Iran. And Bolan was hell-bent on winning the next round, or die trying.

Quickly he dialed up Brognola. Allowing for the time difference he tried the big Fed at his suburban Virginia home, roused Brognola from sleep.

Brognola came alive at the sound of his voice. "Striker? I was getting worried."

"Your worries have only just started."

Bolan fought to find his voice, bell still ringing.

"Striker, you all right? You don't sound so hot."

"I sound about the way I look."

"What gives?"

Bolan gave the bitter and the short of it to Brognola, finally told him he was on his way to the American air base at Incirlik. When he finished updating Brognola, he wasn't sure the big Fed was still there, then heard, "What a mess."

"Doesn't even begin to define it, Hal."

"Bastards."

"Doesn't even begin to define them, either. Now, this is what I want and this is how I want to play it. Get a pen. Here's the laundry list of what I need."

Bolan spelled out the hardware he would need, wanted Brognola to get the Farm on this ASAP, marshal up every resource he could to make it happen. He knew where they were headed, and Brognola knew all about Harin Salaan. A satellite would be parked over the region within the hour.

"Do you realize, Striker, if this comes to public light…"

"No time to stew over this one, Hal. Get the Man right away. Presidential directives for me across the board. I'm going in."

"Other than a flying armada, you're going in alone, Striker. We don't even know yet how many will be on the ground."

"I started this alone. I might as well finish it alone."

Brognola knew better than to try to change his mind. "Okay, I've got a lot of work to do and no time in which to do it. You get to Incirlik, call me."

Before he signed off, Bolan heard the grim and angry tone in Brognola's voice. "This guy Collins, he's the worst kind of rat bastard, Striker. How this all happened… Nail his ass."

"Count on it. I'm thinking, Hal, he had a lot of help in some circles your way or he couldn't have taken it this far."

"We're on the same page. Problem is, Striker, unless someone talks we may never shine the light on all responsible parties."

"I'm keeping the faith we do. I'll be in touch."

"Stay frosty, Striker."

Bolan rang off, slumped back in his seat, wincing against fresh waves of pain coursing through his body. He had some time on his hands before they landed, and he had no doubt Brognola would work his usual logistical sorcery.

The rest, Bolan knew, was up to him.

God have mercy on Collins and his pack of rat bastards, because the Executioner wouldn't.

CHAPTER TWENTY THREE

"They're here," one of Harin Salaan's top lieutenants announced.

"Bring them to me."

"They insist on keeping their weapons."

"But of course. Our prisoners?"

"Eight. A paltry number considering how many of our own were lost."

"Indeed. Take the prisoners to the quarters arranged. Have your own men stand guard. Do not unchain them. Do not feed or water them. We will treat them as the savages they are."

He opened his eyes, recognizing the voice of Pavi Khalq, his lieutenant's eyes angry dark orbs, the face hidden by the black hood. He could tell Khalq didn't like the idea of infidels roaming freely about the palace, armed to the teeth, Westerners who had slaughtered many Muslims before their plane touched down on the runway. There were many things, he knew, his men didn't understand these days, but they were paid to obey, serve his will since his will was merely a divine instrument of God. Lately he heard the rumors, whispered behind his back, how it was near blasphemy for faithful servants of Islam to be in league with Western devils, that it was borderline madness. And he caught the looks more frequently now whenever they entered the great hall, where he sat on top of the white marble table, legs folded, listening to American rock and roll, drinking Coca-Cola, occasionally slipping some American movie into the video machine, one that was usually rife with sex and violence. Recently, days after this glorious plan was initiated and he had opted to go ahead and hold hands with the devil to further jihad, he had gathered his flock of disciples, gently attempted to explain that to defeat the enemy they had to understand that enemy. Beyond that, as their ayatollah, he believed certain indulgences were owed him.

This was his palace, left to him by his father, who was one of the original oil magnates decades ago when the Anglo-Iranian Oil Company was created. These days he imported heroin from Afghanistan, the bowels of the palace refining drugs that were shipped to Lebanon, then to Europe and America. Let the infidels poison themselves; he didn't care. Their lust for drugs provided more cash than he could spend in five lifetimes, the sickness of the minds and souls of his enemies arming his troops, bringing the vision of acquiring weapons of mass destruction closer to reality by the day.

He shut his eyes, as six of his lieutenants settled into the white marble chairs, armed with AK-74s, black hoods concealing their faces. With the remote he cranked the stereo a few decibels louder, hit the replay button.

"Jeremiah was a bullfrog…"

He smiled, sipped his soda. If they thought him mad, so be it, since it was said madness and genius were kissing cousins.

His palace, his music, his world.

Soon, it would be his show of defiance to the Great Satan, interrogating the prisoners, filming for all the world to see their cowardice, evil and treachery as he put them under the knife, skinning them alive. Soon, when he had the requisite hardware delivered by the infidels as part of the deal, America would know horror from their sea to bloody sea. The entire Muslim world had been under the boot heel of the Great Satan for too long. Soon he would crush his enemies, but not before he tried and executed the Americans who were now his prisoners.

"They are going to want to know about their money."

Salaan smiled, knew his lieutenants were getting warmed up to fire away with all manner of questions and concerns.

"These jackals, I hear, murdered many of our brothers-in-arms."

"Somali, Sudanese, Lebanese, they were still of Islam."

"You intend to play host to these devils?"

Salaan opened his eyes. "I intend to perhaps give them just enough rope by which to hang themselves. The money is my concern, a mere grain of sand on the beach if it furthers our cause. Let us hear them out. They did as I had asked."

"How can you possibly trust men who so blithely betray their own?"

"Who said I trusted them?"

COLLINS COULDN'T BELIEVE what he was seeing, hearing. Leading his men into a massive conference room, the walls, domed ceiling and table gleaming white marble, he tried to keep his expression neutral. He had heard about the eccentricities of Harin Salaan, but what he found in the flesh wasn't what he expected. He balked at the sights and sounds, Python nearly walking up his back, Warlock throwing him a look, a sneer forming on his lips.

Ayatollah Salaan was a diminutive figure, five feet tops, white turban, white robe for starters, with a flowing white beard, a snowy complexion. Collins saw him sitting at the head of the table, legs crossed. The major found the black hoods a little unsettling, burning eyes aimed their way, sizing all of them up, assault rifles close at hand. The sooner he put Iran behind, the happier he'd be, but with the latest news about the Russians, well, two days, he feared, could feel like an eternity, might just become that if the Ivans didn't come through. He stole a look at stereo speakers that were ten feet tall if they were a foot, vibrating teak pounding out the classic rock. Whatever his views on the Western world, the ayatollah apparently liked his music.

It figured, he thought, made twisted sense. He had yet to meet a fanatic who didn't talk out of both sides of his mouth, espousing the virtues of Islam while doing just the opposite, the strict tenets of their religion meant for the other guy while those in charge partied like there was no tomorrow. Collins was grateful, if nothing else, the black hoods had allowed them to keep their weapons. That alone tended to tweak his nerves, sure they were sharpening the blade behind his back.

"Gentlemen, be seated."

"What?" Collins shouted over the music, pointing at his ear.

Slowly, a weird smile on his lips, Salaan lifted his remote and lowered the din.

"When you are in my humble home," Salaan said, "you are to walk only on carpet."

Collins looked down, the jeweled tile glittering, then, silently cursing the brazen little bastard, stepped only on Persian carpet, claimed a seat at the opposite end of the table.

"First, in keeping with our original deal, it is a mere courtesy on my part," Salaan said, "that you and your men are allowed to keep your weapons."

"We appreciate the big consideration," Warlock said, drawing a scowl from Salaan.

"Let's get down to business," Collins said, glancing at Falconi. "Mr. Falconi here says it will be two days before he can reach the Russians, arrange delivery of your merchandise."

"Really?"

Collins watched as the black hoods tossed looks between them.

"We had some minor problems. Just to name one, seems one of your people in the Bekaa," Collins said, "apparently knew a little more about the operation than he should have. I'm talking detailed records, naming names, threw our whole schedule off. That's why we landed earlier than I wanted to."

"That would not have been of my doing."

"Whatever, we're talking two days."

"Then it will be two days before you see the rest of your money," Salaan said.

"We sort of figured as much."

Collins heard his heart pounding in his ears, felt the first beads of sweat pop out on his brow in the lingering silence.

"The men that were left with you?" Falconi asked.

"You will be reunited with your CIA comrades in a few minutes when my men take you to your quarters. I will have food and water sent to you."

Collins glanced at the ten black hoods lined up,

flanking both sides of the doors. It sounded as if they were dismissed.

"I do hope the Russians do not let you down," Salaan said. "I would be gravely disappointed, since you have already been paid the bulk of your money."

"It'll happen," Collins said, but suddenly he wasn't so sure.

"See that it does. That will be all for now."

Collins rose, gripping his HK subgun, watched as the Salaan shut his eyes, smiling, and snapped back on the classic rock.

"House of the what?"

"Holy. House of the Holy."

Bolan chuckled, but it wasn't a pleasant sound. The Executioner was in some of the most terrible physical pain he could recall enduring in some time, but he was feeling as angry and amped up as ever. But he didn't have time to nurse wounds or dwell on the pain. The enemy had landed and he was busy crunching numbers, laying out the final attack strategy.

On a lightning presidential directive, Bolan had been granted full access to the American air base in Incirlik, no questions. Colonel Stone was in charge, and he would get whatever he needed to chase down Collins. The intelligence and black ops wheels were churning, every piece of hardware the soldier needed scrambled and dropped off by the time he landed and turned Benson over to the CIA for interrogation. The Executioner had claimed a private office adjacent to the special ops war room. Right then, an attack team—a combination CIA, NSA and Green Berets—was in the war room, nailing down the logistics to get Bolan launched. He was poring over every piece of pertinent intel, the skies over the Dashte-Lut desert region in southeastern Iran swarming with American reconnaissance aircraft. Along with recon photos, sat pics were flying across his table at lightning speed, at least four satellites parked over the region, leaving no piece of rock or stretch of sand unmonitored.

Bolan had a fighter squadron of F-15Es, Tomcats and a Spectre at his disposal, his own ride to the LZ a C-141 Starlifter. At first, Brognola told him, the President, so enraged over the treachery of American military and intelligence men entrusted to carry out the operation in the name of justice and the new war on terrorism, had balked at sending Bolan in alone. How Brognola convinced the Man to cut him loose, Bolan wasn't sure. It was happening. Figure one more deniable expendable, if it went to hell on the ground in Iran, and the political powers in Wonderland could simply wash their hands of the whole fiasco, cite a rogue operation they knew nothing about.

It happened, and all too often.

"The house that heroin money built," Brognola said.

"It will be the house of the damned by the time I'm through."

"Amen to that, Striker. According to the CIA and the

DEA, Salaan exports something in the neighborhood of ten to fifteen metric tons of Afghan heroin to the West every year."

"Ironic, don't you think?"

"You mean in a country like Iran, where if you get caught with a marijuana joint they'll march you out to the village square and lop your head off?"

"And all the mullahs just turn a blind eye to a major narcotics trafficker in their own backyard."

"I imagine they get their cut—or tribute—to see no evil. Besides, we know drug money finances terrorism. It's no different with Salaan."

Bolan checked his watch, needed to wrap it up with Brognola, engage his fighter pilots and Spectre crew in one last brief.

"Okay, Hal, I want constant sat imagery of the house of the damned shot to me as soon as you get it. The way it's shaping up from my first look, they've taken the head shed and the Marines to quarters at the far west edge of the compound. I'm seeing Collins and snakes traipsing the grounds, north, all of them armed, looks like they have their own quarters. The word I get here is that there are no servants, no women, no family members in the palace proper. Which means I can bring the roof down, wade in and blast away."

"So you hope—not that I doubt your ability—but you're talking eighty-plus targets between Collins's and Salaan's killers."

"That's why I'm bringing along the Spectre. And believe me, I've got one angry heart."

"The Man is giving you two hours on the ground, Striker, remember that. You don't nail it down by then..."

"You told me. They send in the Special Forces."

"For now, it's your show."

"Fear not, Hal."

"Bring back the head of this Collins snake, if you feel so inclined."

"I'm not planning on leaving him that much."

"If I was a betting man, sounds like I can make book on that."

"I'll be in touch when I'm in the air."

And the Executioner signed off, so close to the enemy now he thought he could damn near hear Collins chuckling, Cobra Force in the clear, money in the bank.

CHAPTER TWENTY FOUR

Pavi Khalq no longer bothered to concern himself over the sanity of the great leader. The ayatollah, as far he was concerned, was either truly insane or he was blessed by God with an extraordinary vision for the future of Islam, a savior of the Muslim world perhaps, gifted with insight into the deepest corners of the hearts and souls of all men, and devils in human skin. He could perhaps even see the future, a great victory for all Muslims. The ayatollah, he believed, was leading the global jihad to glory, their enemies trampled underfoot, snakes that they were.

He was merely a foot soldier in jihad, after all, and decided to leave the bigger questions of madness or genius to the will of God. Time, he knew, always sorted out the mystery, showed to the world at large what mortal men—and great men of vision—were really all about.

He had a job to do right then, barking out the orders for the demolition team to hurry and mine the length of the C-130, stem to stern. As he looked at the banks of computers and other high-tech wonder machines, he was stabbed by regret that such magnificent and ultra-sophisticated tracking and intelligence-gathering tools were destined to become scrap when the massive bird was blown apart. They could sorely use this equipment, he thought, and the infidels would teach them how to use it, before, of course, they were killed. Again he was in no position to question orders.

His men found two more bodies of dead Marines, stashed in the com center, which would make four total for the bonfire that would be filmed outside. But it was the two Muslims, executed and left on the floorboards where they had been slaughtered, that drew his ire. It galled him, just the same, that Ayatollah Salaan had chosen a path that cost the lives of so many fine Muslim warriors.

Revenge, though, was soon in coming.

Again he decided to not question the wisdom or the sanity of his ayatollah, as his men dragged the bodies down the ramp, into the lengthening shadows of dusk.

He was down the ramp, saw the main camera mounted on its tripod in the distance, the four corpses hauled, jouncing and bumping over broken ground, for several hundred yards, then dumped on the ground. He saw them next, the armed devils, climbing the rise of the hill near their quarters, looking his way, wondering. He hoped they enjoyed the show. In the distance to the north he made out the faint cracks of rifles as his snipers capped off more rounds. All of them were training nearly around the clock these days, a number of operations in the wings, only they were mired in limbo, waiting for the infidels to fulfill the rest of their bargain. When? He only hoped it was soon.

Back to the task at hand, he told himself.

Mentally he reviewed the message as he stepped up before the camera, the statement written by the ayatollah committed to memory.

"Is it on?"

"Yes, Pavi."

He waited until the bodies were settled behind him, an American flag draped over the corpses, then stared into the camera. He felt the smile harden his mouthline, aware how ominous he looked in his black hood, assault rifle canted across his chest.

"WHAT THE HELL?"

Collins topped the rise, wondering what was going on himself, following Bramble's stare toward the activity near and inside the Herc. The Cobra leader pulled up, his own men, Falconi and his Predator Five surrounding him.

The second CIA man, Mr. Cooper, cursed. "I really didn't want to have to see this. Those are American Marines, after all."

"So I'll find you a vomit bag," Collins snapped. "Toughen the fuck up. This is the home stretch."

"This isn't good, Collins," Falconi groused, jumping into the bitch session.

Collins glanced toward the firing range, took in the sniper activity, men in black hoods blasting away at dummies seated in parked SUVs or mounted on stakes. Looking around, he found they were clear of eavesdroppers, four hoods left with the prisoners, then watched the scene on the plateau floor. They had set up film school, a black hood in front of the main camera, other hoods dousing the American flag over the bodies with gasoline, then a pack of matches flared up and the fire was started. Two more fanatics toted video cams, one of them aimed toward the Herc.

"I guess Al-Jazeera," Collins said, "will be getting a special delivery from the ayatollah. Jihad on prime time, only I can't imagine they have any gals that look quite like what you see on CNN. I can't see their own version of Paula Zahn wrapped up in a chador."

"You think this is funny, Collins?" Falconi growled.

"Hardly. It will be damn painful if your Russian comrades don't come through."

"And if they don't?" Cooper said.

"Then we blast our way out of this shithole country."

"And do what?" Falconi said. "That's the rest of the demo team coming out of the Herc now."

"What?"

Collins peered harder, wondering what those packages were, and the cord…

"Shit!"

"Yeah, Collins," Falconi said. "They're getting ready to blow our ride clear across the border and dump it all over Iraq."

"We've been sitting in that stone hovel for a week now," Bramble said. "Shit in a hole, a few scraps of bread and a bowl of water every day. Maybe you noticed how your Muslim cargo was whisked away to the palace? Right now they're sipping tea and cooling their heels in a hot tub."

"What he's saying," Cooper snarled, "is I somehow don't think we were ever meant to leave Iran. We're going to end up having our nuts fed to us in front of a camera just like the head shed and those Marines you brought to the ayatollah."

Collins didn't want to believe that, but instinct warned him it was set to come unraveled. "Fuck 'em. If I have to, I'll kill them all my goddamn self and let Allah sort them out."

TOUCHDOWN FROM ten thousand feet up jarred Bolan to the bone. The Starlifter had sailed in from the northwest, jamming whatever radar and surveillance works the enemy had, using whatever available cloud cover near the DZ, three Tomcats riding the wings, but set to peel off and join in lowering the boom with the F-15E Strike Eagles. The weapons bin was off the ramp seconds ahead of Bolan, opening up from the static line, then he was on the ground, stripping off his chute pack.

The new Beretta 93-R with attached sound suppressor was out, scanning the ridgeline, but his infrared heat monitor coupled with the Starlifter's screens had already turned up no sign of life in the general vicinity. If the situation on the screens of his flight crew changed, or sat recon showed the prisoners had been moved to the palace, White Eagle One would patch through, as he fixed the com link around his head. The black cosmetics stung a little where his flesh had been stitched up, but this was no time to sweat out the pain.

He moved, silent and swift in a northwest vector, melting into the darkening shadows, GPS module in hand, the so-called House of the Holy 2.5 klicks beyond the rise and planted on the plateau. The transponder was painting him on the screens of his fighter jockeys, and he knew he was on their clock.

Thirty-eight minutes and counting to be exact, the soldier punched in the homing beacon for his weapons bin. Five hundred yards later he found it, keyed it open.

The Executioner hustled up as he loaded himself down for war.

It was game time, and the soldier put on his battle face. The enemy didn't know it yet, but the House of the Holy was about to go up in flames.

"WE ARE the holy warriors of the global jihad."

Pavi Khalq paused, his senses swarmed by the sickly sweet stench of cooking flesh. He listened to the flames, staring into the camera, allowed the silence to linger a few more moments. This was his moment to shine.

"Behind me are American Marines, evil instruments of the Great Satan who would further impose its will on all oppressed Muslim people the world over. The Great Satan and its Zionist pawns will soon be unable to continue to rape the earth of its natural resources, force their will on the Muslim world, carry on with their greed and their lust. They will know horror and great suffering and sorrow for their sins. In the name of God, who is all-powerful and all-wise we are issuing a global fatwa to our brother Muslim freedom fighters to kill infidels around the world. Wherever an infidel is found, the infidel must die. These Marines came to my humble country to murder Muslims and their fate is now the fires of Hell, as you see behind me. In the days to come the infidels will taste the terrible scourge of the wrath of Islam for all the atrocities they have committed against Muslims. America will perish soon in fire, and their Zionist boot lickers will be annihilated in the weeks to come. America and Israel and their demonic allies will soon cease to exist. Your judgment is at hand."

DUGULA FELT the air of rising anticipation mingled with anxiety as the ayatollah stepped into the large parlor room. They had just finished praying, lifting themselves off their mats now, facing the massive opening as one force where the small Iranian stood, barefoot and running a curious look over the group.

It was the Sudanese colonel, Ayeed something or other, who began firing off the questions. "This is what your emissaries promised us as the big event? Capture by American commandos, my compound razed, my soldiers massacred? Do you know how many of us have died in the interests of your big event? Are you aware they executed Muslims on the plane and before our eyes? That the Americans you appear to be in league with displayed hatred toward all of us, would murder any of us without blinking an eye?"

"Are we your guests or your prisoners?"

Dugula watched as an inscrutable smile framed the bearded face.

"Both. Neither. And I am aware of everything that has transpired. You have had an arduous journey, I grant you. You have kept the faith of Islam, and God will reward you your faithfulness. You will be fed well—you will be my guests here. I suggest you rest, for the times ahead will be perilous. There is much work to do, a jihad, a war to win. Should you wish to remain and join the ranks of global jihad, that is your choice. If not, I will return you to your country of origin."

Dugula wasn't sure he cared much for the sound of those last words. He was certain they were being issued an ultimatum. Over the years he had heard a lot about this ayatollah, a reclusive and mysterious figure who sold heroin to finance his empire. He had never once even seen a picture, even heard a description of the spiritual leader. Now he found himself somewhat amazed how the small Iranian—who looked more Western than Muslim—could wield such power, send out men who would so willingly go to their deaths for him.

Habir Dugula found himself craving to return to Somalia. Whatever madness went on under the roof, he wanted no part of it.

He wanted to go home.

He was wondering how he might broach the subject of return to Somalia, about to step up when a black hood materialized beside the ayatollah, whispering in his ear. The snow-white complexion seemed to darken with rage.

"I will return."

Dugula heard the murmuring of questions, sensed a volatile presence in the ayatollah ready to explode, but Salaan was already gone.

The Somali warlord suddenly feared the future, and even if he was among his own, it looked and felt dire.

"GODDAMMIT!"

Collins watched in horror as the C-130 belched apart in thunder and flames. Stem to stern, something like close to a billion dollars' worth of America's most highly advanced radar, tracking, sat interceptors, deception relay…

Gone. Blown all over the desert, vanishing in a cloud of fire.

"Is there any doubt now, Major, what the future holds for us?"

Falconi again, the worrywart. A terrible rage boiled up in Collins as he watched the contingent of black-hooded fanatics marching away from the holocaust, some bastard still filming the destruction for Al-Jazeera or whoever. Was that laughter he heard down below?

This was it, he told himself, but it was far from over. They still had nine hundred million, already electronically dispersed around the globe in various numbered accounts. The Russians were on their own.

Hell, everybody was on their own. He—his men—had come too far, killed too many, risked too much to stand on the sidelines, watch it all go up in fire and smoke like the Herc without getting some say—and some bullets—in with the ayatollah and his black-hooded thugs.

Collins took the HK subgun off his shoulder. "All of you with me. Time to go have a few choice words with the ayatollah. I'll be damned I sit here two days, sweat it out whether our lives are numbered in hours."

"Are you nuts, Collins?" Bramble asked. "We're outnumbered seven, eight or more to one, if you're thinking what I'm thinking…"

"Show some balls," Collins rasped. "You want to stay here, I'll make sure those of us who do the killing and maybe the bleeding walk out of here in one piece, help themselves to a slice of your pie."

He heard Python and Mamba chuckle, knew his guys would go the distance.

Collins wheeled, marching down the incline, the

domed mosque and series of minarets rising from the palace little more than blurs in the tunnel vision of red rage. It took a few moments, adrenaline pumping so hard he wasn't sure what he saw, then he spotted the contingent of black hoods rolling their way, another five or more fanatics stepping away from the walled courtyard. He slowed his pace, heard one of the hoods call out, "The great leader wants to speak with you. There is news. I am afraid it is not good."

"Yeah, well, I want to talk to his turbaned holiness."

Collins looked skyward, would have sworn he heard the distant but rapidly growing scream of fighter jets, then spotted the black shapes of warbirds streaking in, missiles already flaming.

The Cobra leader found the black hoods turning toward the first series of eruptions, briefly wondered what bad news they were bringing, then cut loose with his subgun. All bets were off, he heard his mind laugh, and what was another hundred million at that point anyway?

CHAPTER TWENTY FIVE

They were as brazen and willful an evil lot as the Executioner could recall coming across in either recent or distant memory.

And they had only just begun to pay the price.

Bolan was racing against the clock, under sixty ticks, knew Dragon Squad was en route and ready to cut loose the Sidewinders and Sparrows and begin to bring down the roof on the House of the Holy when the C-130 blew up across the plateau.

It signaled the beginning of the end for the damned on two fronts.

The soldier was moving out and down a rocky incline, guided by firelight and cutting a wide berth on the six of the hardforce in black hoods, when the fireball lit up the night with all the sudden swollen and blinding force of the sun exploding. Moments earlier he had spied the group of maybe twelve or thirteen on the distant northern rise, arms flapping, mouths working overtime, guys bent out of shape over the devil only knew what. Bolan had been tempted to take a peek through his infrared binocs, then the dazzling umbrella of firelight clearly illuminated the unmistakable angry face of Collins. Warlock, Cyclops, the snake-handled survivors of Cobra Force, the newcomers and Predator Five were embroiled in a serious discussion among themselves, then turned their anger on a contingent of black hoods marching their way.

Twenty-two pounds of firepower in his hands and leading his charge into the night—two hundred rounds of 5.56 mm full-metal jackets good to go in the Squad Automatic Weapon—and the Executioner was beelining a straight north vector for the prisoner quarters.

First the prisoners, freed and moving, Rescue One in the form of an oversize high-tech Gulfstream III built to NSA specs, five minutes and counting to touchdown to the west...

Then the gloves were off. At a time like this, outnumbered, outgunned and relying on the shock factor of saturation bombing, the Executioner fought back the 1001 "ifs" that could snafu the play, leave him broken and bloodied on the battlefield before the first Sidewinder was cutting wind. Two more box mags clipped to his webbing for the SAW, an M-16/M-203 combo hung from one shoulder and a multiround projectile launcher with twelve 40 mm frag bombs down the chutes—couple that with his standard side arms, another ring of 40 mm hellbombs in the instant-release ring clip, a dozen hand grenades in a bevy of flash-stun, incendiary and fragmentation...

If it wasn't enough he knew was in a world of hurt.

He sensed the first leg might go off without a hitch, hitting the south side of the prisoner quarters, the enemy none the wiser to his near invisible advance on their rear, then he heard the hollering and cursing to his far one o'clock. The black hoods who had blown the Herc were jogging up the blind side of Cobra Force when something snapped inside Collins and all hell broke loose in that direction. The savages on both sides went at it, point-blank autofire, howling and dying on their feet. If nothing else, Bolan figured they would shave the odds in his favor by flinging themselves into a mindless *Wild Bunch* routine.

The Executioner was carrying a heavy load of killing power, but figured the only way to lighten his burden was to start using up ammo. With plenty of targets to spare he figured that shouldn't be much of a problem.

THE AIR ASSAULT was so orchestrated, so lightning and outrageous, meant to vaporize, eviscerate and blow away so many of them on the ground and in the palace right out of the gate, that it struck Collins as a page torn right out of his own bloody manual. He was so pumped up on fury and adrenaline he almost laughed.

Their own side—stabbed in the back—had found them, now pulling that blade out from between their shoulders, hitting the palace with everything they had. Sparrows and Sidewinders were plowing into the front facade of the structure, a few other flaming steel arrows of doom arcing out of the sky, detonating on the roof, minarets likewise disappearing under the barrage. Not his problem, Collins figured. Let the Muslim bastards inside the palace burn or get buried beneath the roof. There would be fewer fanatics he'd have to kill on the way out.

And where there was grim will, he figured, there would be a way out. No way was he dying now when his own cut of that nine hundred mil was growing by the second. Just the same, Seychelles was on hold, the flashing thought he might never see his tropical paradise stoking the fires of his rage. He saw the huge dome of the mosque that rose from the palace lost in a cloud of white fire that dazzled his eyes. He looked away, aware if he was blind for even a split second he was finished.

Collins knew he might just be dead in the next few moments anyway.

The HK was chattering in his hands, anything in a black hood fair game, three toppling as he heard the subgun fire from his own men open up on the fanatics. He felt hot stickiness spatter his face, tasted the coppery taint spraying his mouth as he bared his teeth, sweeping the subgun left to right, mowing down five black hoods, snarling, cursing them as they died on their feet. Sweeping his subgun fire on, he glimpsed blood spurting from the shattered skulls of Falconi, Bramble and Cooper, the trio unable or unwilling to arm themselves, he figured, too slow on the draw to tackle this onslaught of bullets being flung their way.

Collins was pivoting, shouted for somebody, anybody who could hear over the din of weapons fire and the roar of missiles erupting throughout the palace, "Get the prisoners!"

BOLAN OPTED to go with the sound-suppressed Beretta 93-R, set down the SAW, then crouched at the edge of the stone hovel where the Marines and head shed were detained. Both warring factions were still grinding away with blazing weapons, shadows spinning and falling up the gently sloping incline. The yammering of the SAW might alert his adversaries to his presence, and he wasn't quite ready to announce himself.

Three black hoods came running out the front door, AK-74s up and aimed toward the pitched battle along and beyond the rise. Framed in dancing firelight, the Executioner tapped the trigger three times, coring head shots through their hoods, kicking them off their feet, lights out before they even slammed to earth. He grabbed the SAW by the handle, stole a glance at the warring savages, found them too swept up in their own murderous fury to be aware of the newcomer. Closing on the doorway, light spilling through the opening, he heard the voice shouting in broken English at the prisoners. The Marines were being threatened to stay put or they would be shot.

Bolan rolled into the doorway, took in the scene, two eye blinks, busy killing in the next heartbeat. One fanatic was clubbing a Marine to his knees with the butt of his rifle. Another militant was dancing around like an angry chicken, waving his weapon, shouting.

The Executioner sighted down, drilled the clubber first with one 9 mm Parabellum subsonic shocker through the temple. The chicken hood went next, wheeling toward the big invader in the doorway. He managed to cap off two wild rounds that slashed the jamb before Bolan pumped a third eye in his hood.

"Move out!" Bolan shouted at the prisoners.

He read the snarls and angry eyes for what they were—Marines who wanted to be uncuffed, unchained, armed and bulling into the fight.

"Move it out! Now!"

"Uncuff us!"

"I want a piece of these bastards!"

"Aberdeen," Bolan growled into the surging mass of prisoners shuffling in leg irons his way, finally picking out and pinning the Marine general whose face he had committed to memory from the intel package at Incirlik. "Get them under control! Out the door, to your three o'clock, down the back and to the airfield. Your ride is landing now! Go!"

HARIN SALAAN WAS simmering with grave doubts and gnawing fear. He led nine of his men into the great hall, waiting for Pavi Khalq to bring the infidels to him. He managed to keep up the calm and commanding appearance of the spiritual leader of global jihad, but the news he just received was coursing waves of anger and even panic through his body.

They had their own intelligence operatives inside Russia, namely Chechnya and Georgia. The word had just been radioed that General Gergus had been arrested by a joint FSK-American FBI team. And just as he was heading for his plane with his cache of VX briefcases. Was this the end of the dream of global jihad? Or was this merely a test of his faith, resolve and courage? Was God simply putting added pressure and stress on his faithful servant, making him work that much harder so the final rewards were that much sweeter?

Nonetheless, it was time to light a fire—figuratively and literally—under the feet of the infidels. They would be disarmed first, the standing order to shoot two of them if they resisted. With the numbers of fighters he sent to swarm them, the infidels both greedy and perhaps intimidated they were on foreign soil, no way out, no hope but to cooperate he believed—

He thought he heard the distant rattle of weapons fire first, balking at the sound, turning, his men freezing behind him. He was turning when the walls blew in, the dome overhead cleaved off by a blinding white fireball. He thought he heard himself scream as flying rubble pounded him onto the jeweled tiles with the force of a hurricane. He was sure of it next, the shriek driving nails of agony into his brain as he became aware he was on fire.

BOLAN WAITED until the last of the prisoners was around the corner, then unleashed the SAW. He chopped down a half-dozen along the rise off the starting block, bodies whirling this way and that, weapons flying from lifeless hands. Another five terrorists were ground up by the pounding 5.56 mm lead, gaping holes ripped up their spines, then the other combatants—maybe ten to twelve in all, staggered across the ridgeline—became aware they were being diced from the rear.

Holding back on the trigger, the Executioner moved out and up, sweeping the SAW back and forth, black-hooded fanatics flying away under the terrible driving force of the lead hellstorm.

WARLOCK WAS topping the rise, a fresh clip fed to his HK subgun. He cut loose, but he found the shattered remnants of fanatics being blown away right before his eyes, great patches of dark liquid looking oddly suspended in the air, then raining down over their toppling bodies. He figured a full-blown assault by at least a platoon of American Special Forces was under way. Which warned him, as he moved into the shimmering fire glow along the ridgeline, the prisoners were already freed. Still he had to try; he had to know for certain. The way it was shaping up none of them would leave

Iran alive, anyway. No way in hell would he just lay down his arms, snapped up by a bunch of pissed-off American commandos, dumped in a cell the rest of his life. Better to die a lion than live a sheep.

Maybe five fanatics were left, scattering, shooting wild and blind at the force below them. With Cyclops on his three o'clock, Warlock eased off the trigger, searching his flanks.

"No fucking way!"

What the hell, he thought, jolted, freezing for a heartbeat at the shout of rage mingled with confusion, even panic he heard from Cyclops.

Warlock was swiveling his head toward Cyclops, his comrade drawing target acquisition, but whatever he saw had stymied his reflexes. He recognized the awful yammering of the M-249 Squad Automatic Weapon next, Cyclops shouting something unintelligible as he was kicked off his feet, a few subgun rounds blazing skyward before he crunched on his back.

Warlock felt his heart lurch, bent on spraying and praying as he topped the rise. He expected to find a couple dozen commandos, hit the trigger where Cyclops had fired, but there was nothing dead ahead except a shimmying veil of firelight. It was nearly laughable, Cyclops gunned down by—what? A ghost?

"Looking for me, Warlock?"

Warlock felt his lips stretch in a taut grin even though he felt his heart leap into his mouth. He was turning toward the familiar voice of the ghost that had cut down Cyclops, but his gut warned him he was way too late.

He discovered he was right as the SAW flamed from the dark shadows, and he felt the first few rounds punch through his ribs.

"STRIKER TO White Eagle Leader!"

Bolan was up and over the rise, SAW leading the way as he spotted five armed shadows barreling for the wall that ran the length of a courtyard.

"White Eagle here, Striker. What do you have?"

The House of the Holy was engulfed in flames, but Bolan wanted to make sure nothing walked or crawled out of the fire and rubble. He didn't need to see the ayatollah go down for the count, figured if he was somewhere in what was now most certainly the house of the damned, he was cooked meat. The fighter jets had unloaded a few warheads packed with enough thermite to set a couple of city blocks on fire. Whatever they didn't get, the Spectre would make one last grinding strafe. Right then Bolan still had mop-up of his own to take care of.

And the Executioner had a good notion of who was on the run.

"Give me another hard run of the holy house. Raise Dragonship, but have my Spectre give me fifteen minutes to sweep the perimeter for stragglers."

"Aye, aye, Striker."

The Executioner gauged the range to his fleeing

snakes, unslung the multiround projectile launcher, settled down on a knee.

THE HEAT from the fire roaring from the ruins of the palace was so intense it wanted to suck the air from his lungs. Collins figured there was no choice but to tough it, sweat it out, head for the area reserved for terror training. A vehicle or two should still be intact there, and he believed he had heard Warlock inform him there was a helipad out back. With Python, Mamba, Diamondback and the lone survivor of Predator Five on his heels, Collins wanted to believe the worst was over, that they would make it out of Iran. They were being chased—that much he knew, having seen Cyclops and Warlock shot down near the top of the ridgeline. Whatever cropped up in their path—Muslim or American commando—it was history.

He hugged the wall, moving swiftly ahead, the bitter stench of toasted flesh inside the ruins swelling his senses with nausea. He was almost afraid to look back, discover just how many commandos were gunning for them, but chanced it, waving his men ahead. He turned toward the slaughterground up the hill, spied the lone shadow crouched in a kneeling position, puzzled.

One commando? Impossible, he told himself, then heard the next wave of missiles screaming more fireballs through the ruins, making sure any live ones still writhing around in that mess were nailed for good. Hell, he would have done the same, but he didn't much care for being on the receiving end of this shellacking from above.

Collins figured out next what the lone figure was wielding in his hands. He was up, grabbing the top of the wall to throw himself over and to cover, then realized he was too late as the blast ripped through the night. The shock wave hurled him into the wall, pinning him there like some bug under a microscope.

Collins saw the world shimmy, heard his groan lost somewhere in the thundering racket of the air assault. He toppled over, nearly succumbed to darkness, but sensed the lone shadow on the move, and knew he needed to find his weapon.

BOLAN SLOWED his pace as he advanced on the sprawled bodies. He held back until the last of the fighter jets had streaked on, then waded into the carnage. The 40 mm warhead had impacted near the head of the pack, sent them flying in all directions. He spotted movement in three bodies, recognized Python and Mamba. The SAW swinging up, Bolan nailed them to the ground with a long raking burst that left no doubt.

For whatever reason, Collins had lagged behind, but he was coming around.

"It's me, Major," Bolan said as Collins peered at him.

"Stone?"

He spoke his name like a dirty word.

"It's over, Collins."

"Look, Stone, there's a lot of money…ten million, you let me walk away…"

Bolan wasn't up for a tough-guy eulogy, but felt

compelled to tell Collins, "Look around, Major. This is what happens when men love only money and themselves."

Collins scrabbled ahead, teeth bared, hands clawing for his subgun. "Love? What's love got to do with it? There's only money, Stone. There's only the world, you foolish asshole! There is only me—there is only you. What am I supposed to love anyway? Other people? God? Wake up and smell your own—"

Bolan remained silent as he hammered Collins with a long burst of SAW fire. Men like the major just didn't get it.

THE SWEEP TOOK all of six minutes. Bolan found nothing but shell-shocked terrorists running toward a motor pool. The Executioner made quick work of the rabbits, reducing vehicles and savages alike to shredded ruins, expending the multiround projectile launcher, dumping a few more rounds into the fiery mess to make sure. When no lives turned up on his screen...

There was no way, he knew, anything could walk out of the inferno he was now putting behind.

He patched through to Rescue One, found the situation under control, he was on the way. It was all Bolan could do to retrace his path, stay on his feet. He didn't give Collins or the others a glance as he moved past them.

He was putting distance to the house of the damned when the Spectre dropped from the sky to mop up.

EPILOGUE

"Colonel Stone? Sir?"

She looked real enough to reach out and touch, but his subconscious told him it was only a dream. Or was it? The sun sure seemed bright enough, waking up in his chaise longue after a lengthy dozing off, arms and chest bubbled up with the first signs of sun poisoning. It was time to get off the beach, as he saw himself sit up, ready to go...

Whoa! She was all of twenty, twenty-five tops, with long legs and buttocks framed with nothing more than a string bikini, the whole beautiful package aimed his way, for his viewing pleasure—he was sure of it. He didn't want to be caught staring, feeling like a dirty old lecher, slipped on the sunglasses, turned away. His mind told him he was conscious of his age, the young woman making him feel the miles and the years, but stirring a fire of youth inside.

Time to get off the beach.

He was on his feet, gathering up his towel, when he heard the voice call out. He didn't have to look to know it was her. He turned slowly, found her leaning on an elbow, looking at him.

"Do you have the time, sir?"

He held down the chuckle, managed a straight face, looked at his watch...

"Exactly when did I become a sir?"

He pried open his eyes, focused on the blacksuited pilot standing over him.

"Colonel Stone? Are you okay?"

Bolan clawed his way back to reality, a part of him wishing he could stay right where he'd been. Gradually it came back, the mission, from A to ugly Z. He reckoned they had landed at Reagan National, but for some reason he wasn't sure of his surroundings, owed the fog to exhaustion, dehydration, the pulsing inside his skull. He recalled he had gotten a pass, thanks to Brognola, for any lengthy debrief at Incirlik. Beyond that everything was a blur, except for the long-legged young lass.

"You're home, Colonel."

"Home," he said quietly, then groaned, every inch of his body bruised and battered.

"You need some help, Colonel?"

"I'll manage."

Bolan wasn't sure if that was compassion or curiosity on the pilot's face as he stepped past him, squinting at the harsh sunlight stabbing through the Gulf-stream's hatch. One slow step at a time, he moved down the ladder-ramp, spotted his longtime friend waiting at the bottom. He faced Brognola, too damn tired and hurting to speak, too drained to the core of his soul over the evil he had seen, and survived.

"You eat anything lately, Striker?"

"I can't remember."

He was grateful Brognola didn't make a point of scouring his battered face.

"But right now I feel like a couple of cold beers, then take me to the Farm. I feel like I could sleep for days."

"Understood," Brognola said. "Feel like some company when you get settled in? Watch a little cable, wake up the chef?"

"I don't know, Hal," Bolan told the man from Justice, a tired smile tugging at his lips. "For right now I'd rather be alone. This one was tough. I wasn't sure I was going to make it. I had doubts."

"You're only human, Striker, and I often worry about that myself. But I'm always glad when you come home."

DEATH LANDS®

Shaking Earth

*Available December 2004
at your favorite retail outlet.*

In a land steeped in ancient legend, power and destruction, the crumbling ruins of what was once Mexico City are now under siege by a bloodthirsty tribe of aboriginal muties. Emerging from a gateway into the partially submerged ruins of this once great city, Ryan and his group ally themselves with a fair and just baron caught in a treacherous power struggle with a dangerous rival. An internecine war foreshadows ultimate destruction of the valley at a time when unity of command and purpose offers the only hope against a terrible fate....

James Axler
Outlanders

ULURU DESTINY

Ominous rumblings in the South Pacific lead Kane and his compatriots into the heart of a secret barony ruled by a ruthless god-king planning an invasion of the sacred territory at Uluru and its aboriginals who are seemingly possessed of a power beyond all earthly origin. With total victory of hybrid over human hanging in the balance, slim hope lies with the people known as the Crew, preparing to reclaim a power so vast that in the wrong hands it could plunge humanity into an abyss of evil with no hope of redemption.

Available November 2004 at your favorite retail outlet.